THE RING OF TRUTH

Martin Nathanael began to appreciate the world's philosophies as a young adult. A direct mystical awakening led him to work as a priest. More recently, he has been teaching meditation, or leading courses and workshops on various aspects of inner transformation. His varied career took him into secondary education, where he served as Head of Religious Studies in two London schools, teaching world religions to A Level. Between 2004 and 2008, he assisted in training interfaith ministers as a tutor at The Interfaith Seminary UK.

He now focuses on writing and working as an independent teacher, encouraging engagement with the challenges of the spiritual life.

The Ring of Truth is his first novel.

Martin lives in York with his wife Kathleen.

THE RING OF TRUTH

A Philosophical Journey

Martin Nathanael

DIVINITY BOOKS

Published in the UK by Divinity Books in 2025

A CIP catalogue record for this book is available from the British Library.

ISBN 978-1-0684904-0-8

Typeset by Clare Brayshaw

Cover image ID 20486761 © Vasyl Duda | Dreamstime.com

Manufacturer: York Publishing Services Ltd
64 Hallfield Road, Layerthorpe, York YO31 7ZQ
Tel: 01904 431213 | Email: enquiries@yps-publishing.co.uk
Website: www.yps-publishing.co.uk

Represented by: Authorised Rep Compliance Ltd.
Ground Floor, 71 Lower Baggot Street, Dublin D02 P593, Ireland
www.arccompliance.com

To my wife Kathleen,
whose love and support are priceless

This is a strange repose, to be asleep,
With eyes wide open; standing, speaking, moving,
And yet so fast asleep.

(William Shakespeare, The Tempest, Act 2, Scene 1)

Awake, O sleeper, and rise up from the dead ...

(St. Paul, Ephesians, Chapter 5, Verse 14)

Chapter 1

It was one of my usual Sunday mornings, or so I thought. Sunday was a great day for unwinding before the working week began its regular attempt to devour all my energies. I genuinely love my job, teaching English up to A Level at a local school in North London; however, it becomes an all-absorbing occupation during term time.

Back to this Sunday. I had dropped into my favourite local café, with newspaper in hand, and settled down comfortably to relax, read and sip my Americano. Whatever the rest of the day held in store for me would just have to wait – until *after* this peaceful start to my Sunday.

As a regular, I was known to the staff, and my stay was never disturbed, however long I chose to remain there.

Then, out of the blue, this particular Sunday developed in a way I could never have imagined, turning into the day of *The Meeting!* Well, that's how I chose to remember it, and how I referred back to it.

It began with the words, "May I join you?"

There was a pause, as it gradually dawned on me that I was the one being spoken to.

Looking up from the paragraph I was reading, I found a well-dressed gentleman standing across from me, a cup of something hot in his hand. By now, the place was pretty crowded, but there was a spare seat next to mine.

"Of course," I replied, "be my guest." *Well, what else could I say?*

He thanked me and sat down.

"You're a regular," he said, in a way that could have been interpreted as a statement or a question.

I nodded, whilst wondering how he knew. Was it a guess? Or had he noticed me on previous Sundays? Maybe *he* was a regular.

As if reading my mind, he said, "I've seen you here on a few previous occasions."

I looked up, smiled, and half-jokingly said, "Great minds think alike!" Having said this, I noticed that we both seemed at ease with each other; there was a natural rapport, despite the two of us barely being acquainted.

He then somewhat surprised me with what he said next:

"As you say, 'great minds' – and great hearts and souls! You and I are one in consciousness, one in being."

Upon hearing this unexpected weighty declaration, I found myself looking at him with renewed interest.

He continued: "If this realisation of oneness was more widespread, there would be less conflict in the world, more respect, more co-operation, more sharing of resources, more of everything that does justice to the status of being human."

Christ! This fellow doesn't do small talk – that was almost a speech. And yet his words were delivered without any sign of frustration or any other form of negativity. He spoke in a way that was simply matter of fact. And nothing was patronising about his manner. I was beginning to warm to him.

Now, I sat up, and put down my newspaper so that I could engage with him more fully. I noticed that I had not taken his unexpected appearance as an intrusion. Why was that? I was intrigued, without really knowing why!

After what seemed like ages, but I'm sure was no more than a short pause, my new "friend" continued:

"You're probably quite surprised to find someone speaking to you so directly; someone you know nothing about. But what I observe in front of me is a young man who's not at all put out by this turn of events; instead, you are rather intrigued, are you not, and wondering where this is all heading; am I right?"

I laughed because he was so spot on.

"You know," I replied, "it's quite refreshing to meet someone without having to engage in small talk about trivia ... you know, the weather, various political scandals, the latest films, whatever ... Although it would be good to know your name!"

"Fitzwilliam Sebastian Temple, but Fitz will do perfectly well."

"OK. I'm Zachary Marshal, call me Zac."

We shook hands.

"What you began saying," I then said, "well, I have often considered such ideas. Just recently ..." I was searching my memory now. "Yes, now I remember; not so long ago, I did read something that touched on the matter of oneness at the heart of everything; I found it interesting ... no, more than that, it was an attractive concept, perhaps even something which touched me deeply. But I never followed it up ... I suppose that initial intention just got swallowed up in the daily grind!"

"It's very common for this to happen," he said in a quiet tone, as if musing to himself. "People read something that inspires them, or receive a deep intuition, or even have a mystical experience. That very moment in time is truly beautiful, but soon the monkey mind steps in, the conditioned mind that feeds on limitation and doubt, and then that precious gift is lost. The mind questions the very reality of what was previously uplifting, revelatory, and authoritative."

He was quiet for a moment before adding, "There is an ancient proverb, '*Where there is no vision, the people perish*'. For change to happen, a certain sustained intention is required. One must come off the fence, and truly work on oneself, to allow the inner intelligence of the conscious Self to override the slothfulness of the ego-mind, afraid as it is to step out of the run-of-the-mill cocoon it has created for itself."

I took it that Fitz was making a general statement; nevertheless, on the receiving end, such as I was, it felt like he was getting at me personally. But as I looked up to meet his eyes, which were alight with nothing but a constant kindness, I felt the habitual eruption of a defensive response dissolve; instead, I was able to summon a truthful reply.

"I don't know if you meant this," I said, "but your words have really put me on the spot ... I *have* allowed opportunities to slip by in the way you've described. I *have* had moments when I've seen things from a deeper perspective, or had '*intimations of immortality*', to coin a phrase – I think from a Wordsworth poem – yes, and ..." I stopped speaking at that point, because it suddenly felt unnecessary to continue; I could see that my companion knew all this anyway, and I felt some relief as we both fell into a few moments of silence.

It was Fitz who finally spoke.

"It is not necessary to dwell on the past, other than as a spur to live in the sacred present. Most people find it hard to sustain the necessary intention to keep watering the precious seeds of a spiritual awakening. It becomes easier when the way is shared with others of like mind."

"Well, I don't happen to know anyone who might share this outlook with any enthusiasm; my closest friends usually have family or career, or even sport, at the top of their daily priorities."

"Well," replied Fitz, "are we not sharing this interest of yours right now?"

He let the question drop into the silence, knowing full well that I would welcome the implied offer of friendship. I sensed that Fitz was not only befriending me, but he was hinting at being prepared to continue giving me the benefit of his wisdom.

What was it about him that made me immediately like and trust him? I could not put my finger on it but, somewhere within me, I knew that this meeting was like a divine appointment, and that I needed to let it play out, wherever it might lead.

"Yes, we are," I said, and knowing that it was incumbent on me to take this further; knowing also that this man had made me an offer without any pressure attached to it, I continued: "If we could meet again, it would mean a lot to me ... of course, if that's OK with you."

"Same time, here, next Sunday. Bring with you any book that has inspired you."

He smiled, got up from his seat, and left without another word.

Chapter 2

Over the following few days, I found myself reviewing what had happened the previous Sunday. I noticed a definite lift in my spirit, and I even made some time, not only to look for a suitable book for the next meeting with Fitz, as he had suggested, but also to revisit a basic meditation exercise which I had picked up a year or two before at a local Yoga class ... or was it from a Buddhist centre that I had visited a couple of times?

It involved sitting quietly, focusing on my breathing, and treating all thoughts as of no importance, whilst letting go of any tension; and enjoying whatever peace might come.

On the other hand, I still wanted to berate myself with the accompanying, all-too-familiar, "*did this really happen?*" attitude. The meeting in the café had proceeded so smoothly, a part of me was questioning whether I was being hoodwinked or *taken for a ride*, as some might put it. What right did this man have to impose himself on me so completely?

But thank God, I did make time for the odd period of meditation – even if a little half-heartedly. It was during those few moments of quiet that I knew I hadn't been imposed upon at all. Had I not willingly assented to his invitation to meet again? And I knew that something in me resonated with his direct and philosophical way of speaking.

Looking back now, I can see that even the perfunctory allowance of stillness that I gave myself was shedding light on my habitual sabotaging of things that mattered to me, whether it related to relationships, work, or in this particular case, matters of the inner life and deeper purpose. I was able to admit to myself that I *needed help to become more centred, more focused, and more committed to things that mattered.*

So, I began to get myself ready for the next meeting with Fitz.

Bring with you any book that has inspired you.

Looking through my books, I was pleased to find that I still had two books containing the works of Plato. I was reminded of the deep impression one or two of his Dialogues had made upon me when I was in my late teens. I can remember thinking, "Why weren't we taught this at school?"

One of those books, *The Last Days of Socrates,* contained four Dialogues, the last one, the *Phaedo*, dealing with the immortality of the soul, and the fearless way Socrates, Plato's teacher, faced the death penalty for various "crimes", which included corrupting the youth of Athens – by helping them to think for themselves! At that time, Socrates rose to the top of my unofficial list of heroes!

The other book was an anthology of passages from most of his writings, each chapter containing selections dealing with different aspects of his philosophy.

I decided to take both books along with me.

The following Sunday, I arrived at the café to find that Fitz was already there. He was sitting in the corner we had shared previously, with a cup of something in front of him. He stood up to greet me, and ushered me into the vacant seat next to his.

"I'll get you a coffee," he offered. "Same as last time?"

As I began to reply, he was already making his way to the counter. He returned with my Americano, obviously knowing exactly the way I preferred it!

Fitz wasted no time in getting down to business, and I was beginning to see that this was a way entirely natural to him, and for me, quite refreshing.

"How has it been since our meeting last Sunday?" he asked.

It was very easy to be honest with him, in a way I'd not previously found possible with anyone else. I was able to lay before him a basic rundown on both my good feelings concerning our fledgling association, and also the doubts that had reared up in me when faced with something my mind was telling me was "too good to be true".

I also shared how going back to a meditation exercise had helped me to see the latter as a habitual and stale attitude, that I often used to my disadvantage, and how I'd seen through it – which was why I was sitting across from him now.

When I had finished, he simply said, "Great! What book did you bring?"

I rummaged in my shoulder bag and brought out the two books of Plato's writings, which I placed on the table between us.

Fitz seemed delighted with my choice; he picked up both books and spent a short while skimming through them. While he did so, I described how these books had inspired me, especially the account of Socrates' heroic approach to his imminent death, coupled with his teaching about the immortality of the soul.

"How real did the teaching of Socrates seem to *you*?" Fitz asked. "A teaching is only real when you make it your own; it is then no longer separate from you, no longer just words in a book. Also, what do *you* understand about death? Do you have ideas about it, any concepts, or is it a knowledge that is indelibly written in your heart?"

These words certainly felt like a challenge, and Fitz could see that I was about to go fishing in my head for an answer, so he added, "Take your time ... answer me from your heart. This is not an examination. Just speak truly, friend to friend; whatever you choose to share will be perfect."

Again, his kindness touched me deeply, and as a result, a memory was liberated, an unexpected flashback; suddenly, I saw the connection between a powerful childhood event and the inspirational words of Socrates, as relayed by Plato in his writings.

"Fitz, before I get into how reading Plato affected me, I've just remembered something which happened years ago, and I don't know why, but I feel I'd like to share it with you. What if it was a kind of preparation for what I later read in these books? Do you mind if I tell you about this first?"

"Of course not, go ahead."

"Well, when I was at my primary school, I must have been seven or eight years old, there was a swimming lesson with my class at the local pool. We were accompanied by teachers and a few parents. This particular lesson was due to begin at the shallow end, but as we trooped out from the changing rooms, which meant walking past the deep end, I slipped on a discarded inflatable arm-band and fell into the water.

Strangely, even though I had not yet learned to swim, there was no panic or fear. Then, all of a sudden, I became aware of being separate from my body; I was completely free of it, seeing it in the same way I would see someone else's! Yet everything felt so normal; I was very curious about what was happening, and making no effort to save myself. In retrospect, though it might sound odd, I would even say I was enjoying myself!

One of the reasons for that ... I was aware of being enveloped by a wonderful Presence in which I experienced utter peace; it was so joyful; you couldn't compare this in any way to a 'normal' experience of pleasure or happiness. I cannot remember anything so thrilling; and this is the thing – there was a certainty of complete invulnerability – I knew: *nothing, absolutely nothing*, could as much as scratch what I am ... *ever*!

It seems almost impossible to describe the sheer wonder of what I was going through. In this Presence was the greatest love I have ever known."

I paused for a moment to allow the events immediately following to be clear before carrying on. Fitz had been giving me his full attention, and he just waited, without any fuss, for me to continue when I was ready.

I continued:

"At no time, while I was under the water, did I feel the slightest discomfort. I was still outside my body, when a couple of adults pulled me – I mean *my body* – out, and laid it at the side of the pool. I was watching all this from above as various desperate resuscitation measures were being applied to it. One of the adults was saying, 'Hurry up, hurry up – he could still drown!' And then, suddenly – *whoosh* – I was back in my body, looking up at the faces of the worried adults.

There've been times since then when I've had that same sense of complete invulnerability ... usually during moments of actual or possible danger."

Fitz was beaming, "That was a very important initiation for you," he said. "We will come to its significance in due course. But first, how is this related to what you discovered in Plato's Dialogues?"

"That's just it!" I exclaimed. "While I was reading the section in Plato on the immortality of the soul, something in me shouted, *'I know this! I really know this!'* It was a definite *eureka* moment. It seemed that what I was reading confirmed my intuitive understanding about death and the soul. That, in a sense, there is no death, only a movement into, I don't exactly know what ... but into some other kind of existence. I didn't then connect this sense of invulnerability with my near-drowning episode. Now I do.

And another thing, I was just so inspired by Socrates' fearlessness. That too, I knew, deep down, was how we could all be if we *knew*, in the way that he did, about what we would be facing when our time comes to let go of our physical existence. I can see now that I was without fear whilst under the water, totally trusting in the love which held me ... so timelessly, if that makes sense.

This must have been working away in me, but unseen at a conscious level, whilst I was reading Plato."

For a few moments, neither of us spoke,

Then Fitz broke the silence.

"Now that you've made the connection between that early initiation and the Socratic dialogues you read in later years, we can explore together what all this means; it can act as a platform from which to proceed further into even greater understanding.

But not right now. You shared these experiences – the near-drowning and the reading of Plato – with a greater clarity than you realise. I suggest our next meeting will be to draw out the implications of what you know, and to be clear about the measure of your inner life going forward.

But not here. Instead, come to my place, same time, next Sunday. Let's exchange contact details."

Having exchanged phone numbers and addresses, we said goodbye to each other, this time with a hearty embrace.

I stayed for a while longer in the café, gifting myself some time to absorb as fully as possible what this second meeting meant to me, whilst realising, both happily and somewhat apprehensively, that this developing rapport I had with Fitz would undoubtedly turn out to be life-changing.

Chapter 3

The next day, I was aware that the week ahead felt like an eternity; with all that nervous energy bubbling away inside me, I decided to find some excuse to ring Fitz before visiting him next Sunday. *What could I ask him?* It didn't matter, I thought. I knew that all it would take was a brief exchange with him, and it would settle me down. I would be able to visit him with a little more confidence.

It was Tuesday morning when an idea came to me, and I picked up the phone, quickly dialling before I thought too much about it, and backed out.

After three rings, he answered, "Fitz Temple."

"Fitz, it's Zac. I hope you don't mind me ringing you," I said. "To be honest, I would welcome any suggestion from you about what I could read in preparation for our next meeting."

"Better still," he replied, "whatever time you are giving to the meditation practice you referred to, *double it.* It is important to see that the key elements of the path of spiritual awakening are *stillness* and *non-attachment.* I'll share more about this when we meet; enough to say for now, there needs to be a balance between *knowledge* and *being.*" After a short pause, he asked: "Are you free on Thursday evening?"

"Yes, I am."

"My place, 7.30 pm," he said, and ended the call after giving me the directions to his house. Just another example of Fitz's directness.

I was relieved, delighted and excited by the outcome of the phone call. I thought carefully about what he'd said and considered how much time I was giving to meditation. Truthfully, not much. On some days none at all; on others, about 5 or 10 minutes at most. I decided that for the next three days, I would meditate for at least 15 minutes. I'd use what I'd been taught at the Yoga class, as much as I remembered it; I was sure that at some point, Fitz would help me to advance in my "practice".

I kept to this resolution, and on the Thursday morning, it being such a sunny day, I walked to the local park and sat quietly on a bench, which was set back between some trees. I felt at peace with the world, and counted myself very lucky, although I was sure Fitz wouldn't see it that way. *How would he see it?* No doubt I would soon find out.

That evening, I walked to the address Fitz had given me; it was only a few blocks from where I lived, and I soon found his place, a semi-detached house, set back in a quiet close. I noticed a car in the drive; nothing fancy, a basic four-door saloon. I checked my watch; I was at his front door at 7.20 pm. I didn't think he'd mind me being early, so I rang the bell.

"I hope I'm not too early," I said as Fitz opened the door.

He ignored my remark, ushered me in, shut the door and led me into his sitting room. We sat down on some comfortable seats next to a coffee table on which stood two glasses of water.

"Before anything else, we'll meditate," said Fitz. "After that, we'll see what requires our attention."

Without further ado, he closed his eyes. That was clearly a sign for me to do likewise. As I closed my eyes, I noticed he hadn't said how long the meditation would last. But again, I realised that that was itself simply a distracting thought, so I turned my attention to my breathing, as taught in the Yoga class, and endeavoured to keep it centred there until such time as Fitz asked me to stop.

I don't know how long we had sat together before Fitz spoke again, this time quite softly:

"I'll shortly ask you to open your eyes ... When you do, stay centred ... do not move ... carry on the meditation with your eyes open."

Then a few more moments passed before Fitz said: "Now ... when you are ready, open your eyes."

Once my eyes were open, he said: "Let your eyes be soft ... colours, shapes, whatever's in your field of vision ... let it all come to you ... be free of any effort."

After a short while, he added: "Good. Meditation over. Let's talk after some refreshments."

He left the room and returned a few minutes later with a tray of drinks and biscuits.

"I've made some herbal tea; I hope you like it," he said, handing me a cup. I took a sip, and was pleasantly surprised; it seemed quite refreshing, although I didn't recognise the ingredients.

"Now, I'm sure you have some questions relating to our previous conversation," he said.

I'd come prepared. "You referred to my near-drowning experience as an *initiation*; can you say what you meant by that?"

"Ah! Probably used that term a little prematurely ... but since you ask, let me say something about the ancient Egyptian and Greek Mysteries which were, in part, designed as an initiation for those adults who were considered ready. Candidates were led to an underground area where they then participated in a ritual that simulated the process of death. The purpose was for the initiates to come away with a good grasp of their inherent immortality.

The symbol at the core of this rite was a grain of wheat which was cut silently, and the why of this is very well illustrated by the words of Jesus recorded in John's Gospel: 'Unless a grain of wheat falls to the ground and dies, it remains just a seed: but if it dies, it bears much fruit'.

This connects the Gospel teaching with the Mysteries. Our 'friend' Plato was himself initiated into the Egyptian Mysteries during his travels, following the death of Socrates. Plato was later criticised because in his writings he dared to publicly reveal many of the secret philosophic principles that were taught to the initiates of the Mysteries.

Now to your experience in the swimming pool. Did you not come away with a very real grasp of your inherent immortality? No ritual was required in your instance. No, Life Itself was your initiator! Life Itself deemed you ready. You slipped and fell into the water – that was no accident.

In time, you will see that all the key episodes in your life occurred according to the esoteric principle, '*When the student is ready, the Master appears!*' The *appearance* may refer to someone you meet, a book that speaks to you at just the right moment, a word or two that you happen to overhear, an accident, a challenge, an opportunity that presents itself, and so forth. *Life Itself is a Mystery School!*

Reflect on what has occurred for you since that childhood event ... It was no accident."

This way of seeing things was so new to me, I was at first tongue-tied. I eventually said, "Thank you. That's a perspective I've not come across before. But it sounds so right."

"The importance of this is whether it rings true for *you*," he replied, with a questioning look on his face, somehow combined with a playful smile. He continued, "While we have this opportunity, let us see what it is that you know without any question, through your own experiences and spiritual reading to date."

He brought forward a flip chart stand that had been lurking in the corner and placed it closer to our seats.

"We can list here what you definitely know."

First of all, he wrote:

I have a body – I am not this body – I inhabit this body

"You can't take issue with what I've written, right?"

"That's right."

"Because you know this from direct experience. Yet, most people act as if they *are* their bodies; it's even ingrained in the way we speak. For example, we might say *John died yesterday*, not *John's body died*! We say, *I feel cold*, not *my body is cold*! *I am tired*, not *my body is tired*, and so on. Our everyday language demonstrates just how identified we are with our physical vehicles.

Although you may fall into the conventional manner when speaking about your body, or any body, *you* know the real truth, Zac, and this leads to the next thing you know."

He turned again to the flip chart and wrote underneath his first statement:

My sense of personal identity is not dependent on the body

"That follows from the first statement. Agree?"

I nodded. "I was outside my body, but I was still me," I said.

"Exactly!" Once more, he turned and wrote:

I have subtle senses which are independent of the brain and the physical sense organs

"You know this because you *saw* your body from a vantage point that wasn't available to you before then. You were not looking with your physical eyes, were you? They were very much in the body you were looking *at,* which was a short distance away! Just as your brain was '*over there*', so to speak.

The knowledge concerning our subtle senses is very ancient, and probably best set out in the Yoga and Vedanta traditions of India."

Fitz came and sat down with me. He said:

"You, in fact, know a lot more than what I've written down here."

I looked back at the flip chart.

I have a body – I am not this body – I inhabit this body

My sense of personal identity is not dependent on the body

I have subtle senses which are independent of the brain and the physical sense organs

Fitz continued as I endeavoured to absorb what he had written:

"It's important for you to acknowledge what you truly know, making sure you inwardly digest it well; this will ensure that your words and actions properly reflect the level of consciousness to which your understanding belongs.

That's enough for now. Come back here on Sunday morning as previously arranged, and we'll take this a step further.

In the meantime, reflect on these few statements, take them to heart, and ascertain that it *is* what *you* know. Even this basic understanding is already changing your life."

I copied down the words Fitz had written before thanking him and leaving.

Chapter 4

Before Sunday arrived, I bought myself a folder and wrote down all that had happened since that first meeting, and what I had learned. After I'd finished, I read it all through and filled in any gaps with whatever had resurfaced later in my mind. I intended to keep it up to date, adding new teaching and insights *as and when.*

Fitz was right. Apart from the historical background which he had presented me with, such as the ancient Mysteries, it was *all that I already knew*. But I could also see that it is one thing to *know* it, quite another to *live* it. And I saw clearly that I needed to question what Fitz had said during our phone call, about the "balance between *knowledge* and *being.*" How does this work?

As before, we sat together in meditation before Fitz stood up and commandeered the flip chart. Beneath the three statements that he'd left there since Thursday, he wrote the following:

> *My essential nature is inseparable from a pure and all-loving Presence in which I am indestructible, invulnerable, immortal*

Once he had written this, he turned to me and said, "No wonder you were so inspired when reading Plato's account. You were being reminded by Socrates' fearlessness of your *own* lack of fear as you fell under the water. You were reminded of your own innate invincibility. And was there not also a timeless quality to that experience?"

"Yes, there was."

"You are more than one with a divine Presence; you *are* that Divinity! The great Sufi poet Rumi put it this way: *You are not a drop in the ocean. You are the entire ocean in a drop!*

Occasionally, as I believe you mentioned, that Presence has come to the fore in your life, especially when you've had to face a difficult situation or a challenge of some kind.

The Work that my friends and I are engaged in is to ensure that these fleeting openings into the deeper levels of being become *less* fleeting. I'm not sure if I'm making this clear. Put it this way: What if this pure sense of your true, immortal nature was to flow more fully through your thoughts, words and actions? How would that be for you?"

"Amazing," I replied. "It would mean being more able to respond to what life brings ... Perhaps I'd be more aware of why I'm here; I'd have a greater sense of purpose ... and less of an ego ... perhaps ..."

Fitz laughed. "Don't look so down. The old ego is likely to be around for quite a while. But it's onward and upward from here, I'm sure. One step at a time."

He appeared thoughtful for a moment, and then said, "Here, just hold on a minute, I've got something for you."

Fitz left the room and came back a moment or two later, holding a book.

"This is the *Bhagavad Gita*. The words of the title are *Sanskrit* for 'Song of the Lord.' Just read Chapter Two for now. Instead of ancient Greece, you have here a classical Indian text. The teacher is Krishna, regarded as an *avatar*, a divine incarnation; the pupil, Arjuna, a great warrior. Focus on the verses about the nature of the *Self*. Test them in your own experience.

Continue to meditate regularly. Adapt your practice as you see what works best for you. Trust your own perfectly capable intelligence."

"And report back when we next meet?" I suggested hopefully.

Fitz smiled: "I was going to come to that. When I mentioned my friends, I was referring to a group of us that meets regularly to pursue these universal teachings. You'd be most welcome to join us. Our next meeting is 2.00 pm on Saturday; we usually finish at about 4.30 pm."

"Thanks. Count me in," I said. "What do you call yourselves? Does your group have a name?"

"Well, a name is useful so that you know who or what you are referring to. We simply call ourselves *The Group*. We meet somewhere else. Geoff, one of the members, has a much bigger living room; it would be a bit of a squeeze here. Let me give you his address."

Once he'd written down and passed me the information, we parted. Fitz saw me to the front gate and waved me off, almost like someone seeing off a family member who was going away for a while.

I found this rather pleasing and, at the same time, very touching.

Chapter 5

As the week progressed, I found less resistance to making time for meditation, although I did not always sit for a full 15 minutes.

I found Chapter Two of the *Bhagavad Gita* an eye-opener. My reading up to this point had focused mainly on Western writers, some ancient, others contemporary. I had read an engaging book by a modern Sufi, although even then, he was an English convert.

I loved the directness of Krishna's advice to Arjuna. As Fitz had suggested, I gave specific attention to the passages about the *Self*, and I found it helpful to write a summary of them in my notebook.

Here is what I wrote:

The Self is not born, does not die (imperishable)
The Self is eternal (timeless), changeless, limitless
The Self cannot be harmed
The Self is all-pervading ... which means there is only one Self

As well as the qualities I had experienced during my childhood "initiation", there were two others to which I'd given less attention: *eternal* and *all-pervading*.

The first was that the Self is *eternal*. I'd put the word "*timeless*" in brackets beside that word; it was Fitz who'd discerned that I must have experienced a degree of timelessness. When he'd questioned me about that, I'd affirmed it immediately – I recognised that the quality was there. The common phrase "all the time in the world" jumped into my mind, and triggered the realisation that I'd also had this experience more recently.

Back to school days again, but this time as a teenager. It's School Sports Day, and I'm running for my House in the year group 400 metres. I've been allotted the outside lane; it's not the best because you have no visible opponents to chase; the inside lanes are shorter, so they start further back.

With the sound of the starter gun, I just run. And then it's as if the running is happening by itself, while I savour the whole scene, immersed in an effortless, timeless sense of freedom. My awareness embraces everyone (pupils, teachers and parents alike) and everything contained in the situation.

I reach the finishing line well ahead of everyone else, and I'm later told it is a new School Record for my age group. But there is no exhaustion; it feels as if I've just *witnessed* the whole race.

Once that change of perspective had occurred, right at the beginning of the race, I no longer felt like a competitor. It felt more like I was simply an enjoyer of the moment, with the race seeming to be of secondary importance.

I remember sharing this experience with an uncle who was an ardent outdoor runner in his spare time. He told me that he too had had similar experiences; when "time stood still", his words, when the running was most enjoyable and effortless.

I also realised that a measure of this quality of timelessness was sometimes present during meditation; that you only needed to let go, and simply *be*!

The second quality I gave some extra thought to was: *The Self is all-pervading*. Regarding the verses about the nature of the *Self*, Fitz had said, "Test them in your own experience". The *all-pervading Self*? Whereas I had no problem acknowledging a familiarity with the other key attributes of the *Self*, here it was a matter of taking the idea on trust, being open to the *possibility* of knowing it in truth. It certainly felt true. That one *Self* is the *Self* of all and everyone; the "entire ocean in a drop", as Fitz had said, quoting Rumi.

I could now see the wisdom behind Fitz steering me towards this wonderful text. It awoke in me a strong sense of inner direction. The powerful teachings of Plato and the *Gita* were playing within me like a harmonious duet, a divine melody, strengthening the love of truth in me, which I knew I could no longer ignore.

Chapter 6

I kept Saturday morning clear to prepare myself inwardly for this first visit to Fitz's group. Geoff's house was a bus ride away, in a leafy suburb, with plenty of room off-road for parking. I rang the bell a few minutes before the group's start time of 2.00 pm.

The door was opened by a young woman. "Do come in," she said with an easy manner. "You must be Zac; by the way, I'm Hina."

Hina, whose swarthy looks suggested an Asian background, led me into the house and through to a large, finely carpeted sitting-room where about fifteen chairs were set out in a semi-circle facing a single chair, no doubt placed there for whoever was going to teach. A flip chart was parked conveniently beside it, as was a small square table sporting a glass of water, some Tibetan bells and a couple of books. In the centre of the room was a small, low circular wooden table, with a squat unlit candle resting upon it.

A number of the seats were already occupied by people sitting quietly with their eyes closed. Fitz entered the room and greeted me warmly, but without speaking. To my surprise, he made his way to one of the spare seats beside me, and sat quietly. I'd assumed he would occupy the seat at the front; I was wrong.

After a few more minutes, a petite woman, who appeared to be of Far Eastern heritage, entered the room and sat facing us. She began to look around at everyone, smiling as she did so, her eyes seeming to shine with delight. Fitz stepped forward and lit the central candle before returning to his seat.

"Before we start today's meeting, a warm welcome to those of you here for the first time." She singled out a young woman sitting a few seats away from me: "Welcome, Jenny," she said; then, looking my way, "Welcome, Zac." She spoke with a genuine warmth, and I wondered if I detected a touch of mischief in her manner. "My name is Susan Leung," she quickly added. "Everyone just calls me Susan ... no Ma'ams, Miss, or the like, thank you."

She continued: "Our practice is to begin each session with a moment or two of silence, to become centred, to allow everything that has happened up to this moment to fall away. So that you are here *now*, fully engaged in the present ...

Right ... join me now, eyes closed."

We sat in silence for a short while until Susan broke the silence using the Tibetan bells that were beside her.

"Good," she began. "As there are two new people here, please allow me to repeat a word or two about certain ground-rules, or principles, which are probably universal for a group like ours. I've written down four principles that govern the way we work together."

She turned over one of the flip chart pages to reveal a list which had been written in advance:

PRINCIPLES OF GROUP WORK

1.	*Confidentiality*	*2.*	*Verification*
3.	*No Judgement*	*4.*	*Working Together*

"I'll go through these briefly with you and Jenny and Zac, if you have any questions about any of this, talk to one of our experienced group members during the refreshments break.

First of all, *Confidentiality.* You must all feel free to speak, and if necessary, share very personal matters, without wondering if your words might be broadcast to others outside the group, or in any public setting. Nor should the identity of any member be disclosed. If anyone chooses to let others know that he or she is a member of this group, that is another matter.

Secondly, *Verification.* You are asked neither to *accept* nor *reject* any teaching presented to you. Whatever you hear – test it in your own experience, discover the truth for yourself. This is not a cult. You are all here freely, and each one of you is responsible for your own inner life, your own level of understanding and self-realisation.

Thirdly, *No Judgement.* No member of this group is to be judged or criticised, either outwardly or inwardly. You know the saying, '*There but for the grace of God, go I.*' That's it in a nutshell!

Finally, *Working Together.* Yes, you are each primarily here to free yourself inwardly. But this is a group. You are engaged in what we call 'The Work.' Working with and for others lifts consciousness for everyone, so your individual self is included. You help yourself by helping others. That's how it works."

Susan stopped for a moment, took a couple of sips of water, looked around the room at the group members, and then continued.

"You know, any teacher who sits in front of you is a kind of mirror, reflecting back to you. For all knowledge comes from the Spirit within you, your essential Self, which is your *Inner Teacher.* When you resonate with what you hear, is it not because you already possess the knowledge?

Maybe the teacher was simply the catalyst to awaken what was currently dormant.

Where did the teacher get the knowledge? From within. If not from within, it will carry no force, it will not inspire.

The genuine teacher, through meditation, through their spiritual practice, receives knowledge directly from the Divine Source.

So, my friends, whenever I speak to you, whatever I say, do not believe a word. Does it ring true, does it set you alight? If so, you are receiving your own knowledge; it was always yours.

If you don't get it, that's also OK. All I ask is that you don't immediately reject the teaching. Hold it for now, store it away. In time, it may come to life when you are ready for it."

I must admit that, at this point, I was somewhat mesmerised by the power of the teaching emanating from the diminutive figure sitting in the chair opposite. Her words were like *manna* to my soul! I realised that I was in the presence of a very special individual, and that I owed it to her to seriously engage with her teaching, and to make my life mean something as a result. As if she could read my mind, it seemed that her next words were especially spoken for my benefit, although my rational mind knew they applied to everyone present.

"Now, following from this," she continued, "I strongly recommend that you make the practice of meditation an integral part of your daily life. *Why meditate?* Right meditation makes you inwardly receptive to the *Inner Teacher*, your divine Self. It is a process of Self-enquiry, answering to the question, 'Who am I?'

An ancient Indian scripture points out that the senses are turned outwards, not inwards; then it goes on to say:

Now and then, a daring soul, desiring immortality, has looked back and found himself.

You are invited to be 'daring souls' – using meditation as a tool for inner freedom and self-understanding, which includes the experiential knowledge of all layers of your being!

As you '*look back*', as this text puts it, you begin to see everything you are not. You are not the body, you are not thoughts, you are not emotions – *nothing* which you perceive can be you. You are the Witness. As you go beyond the layers of conditioning, whatever you see loses its hold over you; you are gradually becoming the master of your own destiny.

As you free yourself from the ever-circling maelstrom of thoughts, ideas, memories, and the like, your mind becomes more spacious and therefore more receptive to the deeper intelligence of your spiritual nature – the divine consciousness *that you are*.

Meditate. Don't put it off. You are the only one who can free yourself!

We'll meditate together now for about 20 minutes."

I found it very helpful to be meditating together with others. The sense of time vanished, and I felt more inwardly spacious than usual. When Susan brought the period of meditation to an end, I had no idea how long I'd been sitting with my eyes closed.

"Let's take a break," Susan said. "Fitz, will you look after our newcomers, Jenny and Zac? Pair each of them up with someone who can support their meditation practice. Thanks."

She quietly left the room.

Chapter 7

Everyone proceeded to an adjourning room where a large table was laid out with plates containing various fruits and bowls of nuts. Flasks of hot water stood by an array of jars of herbal tea. We were invited to help ourselves by a man who introduced himself as Geoff, our host and the resident owner of the property.

Fitz, as instructed by Susan, sought me out, took my arm, and led me over to where Hina was standing. She smiled as we approached.

"Zac, let me introduce you to Hina Jaiswal; she's been part of our group for four years ..."

"Six," Hina interjected.

"... for six years. We usually pair a newcomer with one of our long-standing members. I've already asked Hina to be your unofficial group mentor if that's OK with you, Zac. You can ask her anything about how the group works, about meditation, and anything else you think is important. You'll soon see that not everything hinges on the teacher; supporting one another is part of our philosophy.

Right, I'll leave you to it; I need to set Jenny up in the same way."

That said, Fitz went off to find Jenny.

"Let's get some drinks," Hina suggested, "and then we can see what you want to find out."

We took our drinks out into the garden. I had a question for Hina that I'd been saving up since the start of the session. Once we'd sat on a wooden bench, Hina inclined her head, as if to say, *go for it!* So, adopting Fitz's direct manner, I posed the question:

"I thought when I came here today that Fitz would be the teacher, and was surprised when he sat down next to me, and then Susan came in. By the way, I thought she was great. Does Fitz do any teaching for the group?"

Hina laughed. "When I started, Fitz *was* the teacher; Susan was already a member. It was soon clear to me that Susan was quite an advanced soul from the way she spoke in our meetings. She'd already been on this path for a while in Hong Kong before emigrating to the UK.

One evening, Fitz unexpectedly said to Susan: 'You are the teacher', stepped down, and handed over to her. Just like that! We were all stunned. So was Susan, who at first queried his decision.

But Fitz said to her, 'No. You are more than ready. It would not be right to hold you back.' All this in front of us all. Susan then suggested that she would start from the next meeting, and Fitz happily conceded to that.

Fitz occasionally takes to the chair if Susan is away. He's amazing; I'm not sure if he's ever had an ego!"

We both laughed.

"Yes," I agreed. "It's because of Fitz that I'm here. I've never met anyone before whom I've felt so at ease with ..."

Just then, Fitz called us back to the meeting room for the start of the next session.

"Oh!" I blurted out. "I had some questions for you about the earlier teaching ... about group rules, meditation, and probably other things as well."

"There's plenty of time," Hina assured me, as we made our way back to our seats; this time, she took a seat next to me. She discreetly leaned over and whispered, "We'll talk later."

Everyone got settled while Fitz relit the central candle. Then Susan returned to the room, and a short period of silence followed before she resumed her teaching.

"Let me say a bit more about The Work," she began. "Why do we call it *The Work?*" – *That was one of the questions I'd meant for Hina* – "There are all kinds of work, but *The* Work is summed up in two words which were inscribed above the entrance to the ancient Temple of Apollo in Delphi: *Know Yourself!* All the great mystical or philosophical teachings emphasise this. In the Gospel of Thomas, Jesus is recorded to have said that unless you know your Self, 'you are in poverty, and you *are* poverty.' A billionaire who lacks knowledge of his Self is a pauper! It couldn't be any clearer.

When you know your Self, then you will know that there is but one Self, the Self of all. Know this, and everything else falls into place.

This is the purpose of meditation. This is the purpose of Self-enquiry. And it goes beyond just the formal periods of sitting in meditation, important as these are. It includes maintaining watchfulness throughout the waking day. During activity, you do not lose your centre; you allow a still intelligence to pervade your work, your leisure, your relationships.

One of the most beautiful descriptions of this way of Self-enquiry occurs in the writings of Plotinus, who lived in the third century."

Susan turned to a book that was on the small table beside her, and looked for the page she wanted. She turned back to the group:

"Listen to these beautiful words of Plotinus:

> Withdraw into yourself and look; and if you do not yet behold yourself beautiful, do as does the maker of a statue which is to be beautiful; for he cuts away, shaves down, smooths and cleans it, until he has made manifest in the statue the beauty of the face which he portrays.
> So with yourself. Cut away that which is superfluous, straighten that which is crooked, purify that which is obscure: labour to make all bright, and never cease to fashion your statue until there shall shine out upon you the godlike splendour of virtue …

Plotinus invites you to work – to enquire – in this manner, to 'cut away all that is superfluous' until 'nothing more can prevent you from becoming one', and you reach the 'unbounded' and the 'immeasurable', when 'your whole Self is light and light alone'.

There is a short Sufi saying which sums this teaching up: In order to become *what you are*, first step out of *what you are not*.

Some of you have heard me speak in this way before. There is no harm in being reminded of the core reason why we meet. Those of you new to the group, take this to your hearts: *Who am I?* is the most important question for you. It is the essence of the Grail Quest, the true work of Alchemy, of Yoga, of the Christian Mystic, and all authentic paths that are expressions of this understanding.

Those of you who have been assigned mentors, meet with them soon, so that the love of truth within you may 'shine out in godlike splendour'.

I look forward to seeing you all again at our next meeting."

Chapter 8

I found Hina waiting for me as we left the house. The group had finished bang on time, at 4.30 pm.

"We could go for a bite," she ventured, "and we'll be able to catch up on the things we didn't get round to during the break."

"Sounds like a plan," I agreed. "Where are we going? This isn't an area I'm familiar with."

"I know just the place; it's a short walk from here. I've been there many times."

"Lead on," I said, catching up with her as she had already started to briskly walk off.

We arrived at a quaint independent place called *The Urban Lounge,* where several empty tables awaited us. Hina chose a place at the back, giving us a modicum of privacy. We ordered our food, and then Hina immediately retrieved a notebook and pen from her handbag.

"Before we get into any discussion," she said, "I act as secretary for the group, and send out communications as and when required. Could you give me your contact details – your address, email, and phone number?"

I did so, and she wrote them down.

"The only other information we record, Zac, is a person's occupation. So ..."

"I work as a teacher at a State School, teaching English up to A Level. Just out of interest, what do you do?"

"Currently, I work in a book shop, but I'm hoping to move on eventually. I'm in the third year of a part-time course in counselling; that's closer to what I want to do eventually." Hina then put on a serious face:

"Zac, let me clear up something before we begin looking at any questions you might have. I'm only your mentor while you 'bed in' to the group, as it were. In time, you won't need a mentor, and who knows – in the future, you might also be invited to mentor someone who's just joined, assuming you're still with us. Fitz may not have made it clear, but it's a two-way matter – you don't *have* to have a mentor, but it does help in the beginning."

"Look, Hina, I trust Fitz, and you're already making things clearer for me."

The food arrived and we both tucked in, our conversation about The Work put on hold. Instead, we chose to share a little about each other's backgrounds. Hina's grandparents came from India, but she, like her parents, was born in the UK and was schooled locally. Her brother, Mahendra, was married to a Scottish woman and lived in Edinburgh.

"Well," I said, once we'd had our fill, "we haven't got very far with our conversation about the group, apart from what mentoring means."

"I know," Hina acknowledged, looking at her watch. "Look, it's only just turned six. If you're up for it, we could make our way to Harmony Park and make some more progress there; let's be really *decisive*, *strong-minded*, *resolute*!" With each of her last few words, she giggled as she punched the air, causing a few of the other diners to turn in their chairs.

I was enjoying her company, and loved the way she could be serious and fun-loving at the same time. It was a no-brainer; we walked to the park.

Hina led me into a beautiful, geometrically organised park which seemed like a big garden. We sat by a small pond which was frequented by a variety of happy sounding birds.

After a few moments of simply enjoying this scene, I turned to Hina:

"OK. There is something I want to ask you."

"I'm listening."

"How do people come to join the group? Do you advertise? Do you vet people? Or is the way I joined the norm?"

"We've never advertised. Members can introduce or recommend somebody. It's quite organic and has evolved like that from the start. It means that there is a natural closeness between everyone. Our organisation is kept to a minimum. We don't charge, and everyone who contributes to The Work, including the teacher, does so voluntarily.

You are there because you want to be. You teach because you choose to. Mentoring likewise. People are *asked* to do things; no one is *told* to. We are a group, and we are like family."

"What about costs, say, the refreshments at Geoff's house?"

"Geoff is quite well off; he's always refused to accept any financial help hosting the meetings."

Just then, as Hina was speaking to me, I noticed a couple of young men walking purposely in our direction. They looked a little worse for wear and were walking unevenly, maybe because they'd been drinking too much. I noticed myself becoming quite alert, sensing trouble.

Now Hina saw them and she gasped, "Oh no!"

"What's up?" I asked her.

Before she could say anything else, the taller of the two sauntered forward and leered at her.

"Well, well. If it isn't Hina itself, our little flirt, digging her claws into some new victim." He then turned to me: "Watch out mate, best to scarper before it's too late."

I stood up and looked directly into his eyes. The familiar and wonderful Presence that I'd known before seemed to fill my entire being, and there was no anger or fear in me when I spoke to him.

"No need for this. You are interrupting our meeting. Just go, and all is forgiven."

There was a slight look of astonishment on his face, momentarily frozen, before he almost collapsed with laughter, his companion smirking next to him.

"Listen to him. What a great gentleman ... my arse ... move aside mate, so that we can check the goods, see if she's still hot ..."

He lurched towards Hina, but before he could reach her, I caught his arm, swung him round and kicked him in the shin. He went down bawling.

"I don't like violence," I said calmly, "but I can't stand anyone who mistreats a lady. So once again, get going!"

While I was speaking to the one on the ground, his companion screamed some profanity, and in my peripheral vision I saw him lunging at me with something shiny in his hand.

It was all over in a split second! He joined his mate on the ground, face down, my knee on his neck. The shiny thing, now seen to be an open switch-blade, was a few yards away on the path.

After remaining in that position for a few moments, I rose to my feet, picked up the knife, and threw it into a large bush. Instinctively, I reached for Hina's hand and led her back to the park's entrance. We walked along together for a while without speaking; I could sense that Hina was very shaken by what had just happened.

I was in a different space altogether. All time appeared to have vanished. What I did back in the park had felt effortless – as if someone else had acted, and I had just been looking on!

It was Hina who broke the silence.

"Zac. Oh hell. I don't know what to say ... I'm so sorry you got caught up in this. What they said about me ..."

"Hina, you don't have to explain anything. Let it go; the past is dead. I know what you are ..."

"No, please listen. It will help me to share this with you."

"Alright, but I'm seeing you to your home, just to be sure, although I don't think those two are in any fit state to bother anyone for a while."

Hina didn't live too far away; we eventually came to a hairdressing salon where a door at the side led to some steps. We walked up to a first-floor apartment.

Once we were inside, and Hina had closed the door, she burst into tears and collapsed onto a settee. I sat with her and put my arms around her. She eventually quietened, took a handkerchief out of her bag, then blew her nose quite noisily. She giggled; I laughed. She then seemed somewhat relieved and ready to share.

"At my school, I was elected Head of Year when I was fifteen. Ben, the one who threatened me in the park, was in my class then. So was Liam, who was with him; he was like Ben's yes-man. Ben asked me out, probably for the kudos of going out with the then Head of Year, but I didn't like him. He was a bully. No way would I want to spend time with him. From then on, he would intimidate me whenever he got the chance. I think his pride was badly wounded, and he somehow had to get his revenge.

It gets worse. I had a good relationship with a certain male teacher, and it's true, I suppose I fancied him, nothing that wasn't normal for girls of that age. Occasionally, I'd bump into him in town, and once, just once, we went into a café and chatted over a drink or two. Ben saw us. And he used this to put it around the school that I was having an affair with him, a married teacher. Of course, the school authorities found out, and the teacher was suspended while he was being investigated. It all blew over once they realised the accusation was completely groundless.

And then, to cap it all, when I went to university, Ben turned up there, though thankfully for a different subject. Even so, he would make his presence known, in a not very nice way, whenever he got the opportunity.

Zac, whatever he said about me ... it was his twisted mind ..."

I stopped her, took both her hands, and looked into her lovely eyes.

"Look at me, Hina," I said, "I wasn't interested in a single word that man – Ben – said. In the few hours I've known you, you've made such a deep impression on me. What a gift – your wisdom, your support as my mentor. I've never said anything like this to anyone before, but I'm saying it to you now: you just shine with that 'godlike splendour' that Susan quoted from Plato ..."

"... from Plotinus."

"Yes, Pilatus."

"Plotinus."

"Yes. him too!"

We both folded up with laughter, and spontaneously reached for each other, embracing and kissing, stopping in between just to take each other in.

It was Hina who eventually drew gently away and said, "Let's have a drink. What would you like?"

Not having a clue at that moment, I said, "Anything."

"OK," she said, "You've asked for it. I'll just make it, and you can tell me what it is."

Hina sounded much more buoyant and skipped into the kitchen to prepare our drinks.

While she did that, I checked my watch. It was 7.50 pm. I'd met Hina earlier that afternoon when she opened the door at Geoff's house. That was barely six hours ago. *Six hours!* That's all that I'd known Hina for. And yet, it felt like we'd already connected deeply at a soul level.

Hina came back with a tray of drinks and cookies.

As I began to drink from my cup, Hina asked, "So what is it?"

"It tastes like a mild sort of coffee."

"Close. It's made from Dandelion root; it's called Dandelion coffee."

"It might take getting used to, Hina."

When the drink and a few cookies had been consumed, I stood up, turned towards her front door, and said,

"Thanks, Hina, I'll get going now ..."

"Don't go. Please ... Stay ... I'd like you to stay."

"Are you sure, Hina, we've only just met?"

"Zac, are you measuring the time? Think about what you said to me earlier ... the deep impression I'd made, the way I shine ... Where is that deep impression, Zac? What in you sees that light? Could it be the same light in you, like recognising like? What has time got to do with it?"

"Hina, you'd make a great teacher; you've convinced me. So, I'll be straight with you. Of course, I'd like to stay with you. I wouldn't want to be anywhere else."

We stood looking at each other for a while. Then Hina gently approached me, took me back to the settee, and said, "Let's talk for a while; it's too early to retire for the night."

Chapter 9

Our subject was Love.

It followed on from a question that Hina put to me:

"Zac, where did you learn to fight like that?"

"Honestly, it wasn't much of a fight. I used to attend a martial arts class at the first school I taught at. Some of the training has obviously worked, because that's the first time I've had to draw on it outside of a class. Look, those guys were semi-drunk, and unsteady – honestly, they didn't stand a chance."

"I noticed you never lost your cool. You stood up to them and spoke directly; you showed no fear."

"Well, maybe it's some of Fitz's characteristics rubbing off on me."

"No, Zac, don't sidestep this. It's the other way round. I think Fitz saw a potential in you. He saw *you*! It's why he went to talk to you. Be still for a bit; just reflect on what was going on within you during that run-in with those two." *Hina, the mentor, stepping in!*

We sat quietly while I reflected on the episode in the park.

"Well," I eventually said, "you are right to make me look at this, and I feel I can share this with you. It's the kind of thing I would normally keep to myself ... I felt no hostility towards those two. Strangely, I even felt somewhat caring, if you can believe it; it was a kind of compassion for the state they were in ..."

"I'm pushing you on this for a reason," Hina said firmly. "There's more. Just tell me. Don't water it down."

I was beginning to feel tearful, in a good way. I took Hina's hand. I understood why she was doing this.

"I felt love for them. It sounds ridiculous but ..."

"*Own it*," Hina insisted.

"I did the minimum to defend you from Ben, and then myself from Liam. Their bruises will heal quickly. I only hurt them because I had to, to stop them. I acted without any thought or emotion. There was no fear; I felt totally safe. Just like a few other times in my life, I was aware of Something looking after me, of being held in a great Presence in which I knew, *really* knew, that in essence, I can never be harmed!"

"What did this show you about love?"

After a short reflection: "It was completely impersonal. It didn't matter who was on the receiving end. Friend, foe, stranger, anyone."

Hina flung her arms around me. "It's what Susan once said. Love *is* impersonal! You *demonstrated* it, Zac. Even in the middle of a fight, OK, a non-fight! I'm sure that at some level, those two will have picked it up; it could change their lives.

There are people in our lives who are difficult to love, aren't there? We find their behaviour so irritating. What if we were awake enough to see beyond their annoying effect on us? We'd be in touch with their essential nature, the divine Self, in which we are all one. We are all, to different degrees, trapped in separateness. Those of us who've been drawn to The Work are so blessed, aren't we? We've been given a chance to throw off all the old baggage so that we might discover the true measure of love."

"What can I say, Hina. You speak with such authority. Usually, when I'm with a friend, our conversation would be more limited. To be with someone, sharing the deepest reasons for being human, is what I've always wanted."

"Zac, I'm just sharing what I've learned from attending the group, although it's what I truly endeavour to live by. There is so much more to learn about love. I'll ask Susan to speak about it at our next meeting."

"Can you do that?"

"Of course. Even though you might look up to someone like Susan or Fitz, we are all friends. Susan and I are close; we play tennis sometimes or go out for a drink. It doesn't affect the respect I feel towards her when she's up front teaching."

"Can anyone request a one-to-one with her?"

"You won't need to do that. As someone new, she will ask to see you. Soon, you'll see."

"I'll look forward to that, and to the next meeting. Actually, when is it?"

"We meet every first and third Saturday, same time. We are also encouraged to meet up with each other at other times. Some members have taken the initiative to form smaller study groups. There's a group studying the Christian mystics; another meets to practice *Tai Chi.*"

"Are you in any smaller group?"

"No. But I am close friends with Susan, Fitz and Tamara, whom you haven't met yet. We all get to see each other outside the group. Tamara and I are doing the counselling course together …

Zac, do you have any plans for tomorrow?"

"Apart from preparation for my lessons at the school on Monday, no."

"OK. Why don't you go back to your place after we've had breakfast here, and prepare your lessons? Fitz has arranged to meet me for lunch tomorrow. I'm sure he won't mind if you join us. I hope you will."

"I'd love that. Am I still …"

"Shhh!"

Hina took me into her bathroom and offered me a toothbrush and a towel.

"Do what you have to do in here, and then, please ... I'll be in the bedroom next door."

After I'd cleaned my teeth and had a quick wash, I went into Hina's bedroom. She was already in bed, wearing what looked like a cotton nightie. There was nothing to say, except get undressed and join her. I stripped down to my briefs and joined her under the covers.

Hina pulled me to her.

"Zac. I'm so pleased you stayed – no, even more, I'm thrilled. For tonight, though, I just want to be held. I hope that's OK."

"Hina, you are so lovely. May I have the privilege of holding you tonight?"

Hina sighed, and nestled into me. I felt really content, feeling her body so close, hearing her breathing slowing down; I simply allowed myself to savour these sensations for a while. Shortly, I noticed that the ceiling light in the bedroom was still on. I turned my head slightly to suggest turning it off and found Hina was already fast asleep. Not wanting to disturb her, I let the matter drop and eventually fell asleep beside her.

Chapter 10

I awoke the next morning to find the ceiling light had been switched off, and an empty space where Hina had been sleeping. After using the bathroom and dressing, I went to find Hina. She was seated in the kitchen, drinking a cup of something.

"Lazy you," she said, good-humouredly. "I've been waiting for you for ages. I've washed and meditated, and nearly started breakfast without you."

"You wouldn't do that, would you?"

By way of answering, she got up and greeted me with a hug and kisses.

"I'm so pleased you stayed with me last night ... it was so right; it completed such a special day. Zac, thank you, thank you."

Before I could respond, she skilfully untangled herself from our embrace and began raiding the fridge and kitchen cupboards. In a few ticks, the kitchen table was covered in breads, jams, milk, cereals, and other breakfast goodies. Hina had waited for me, after all.

After we'd finished breakfast, we arranged to meet back at Hina's flat, and she would take me to the restaurant, where we would join Fitz. As it was a Sunday, and the buses were less frequent, I ordered a taxi to save time. All I needed was an hour or so to get up to date with a couple of lesson plans, get my shoulder bag ready for the next day, and put on a change of clothes. *I added a few toiletries and changes of clothes just in case ...*

I was back at Hina's place just after midday.

When she opened the door, I had to check myself from gasping out loud at the vision that appeared before me. Hina was wearing a traditional golden coloured Indian sari that sparkled from the multiple sequins sewn into its silk cloth. She looked like an Indian goddess, or what I imagined an Indian goddess would look like.

"Do you like it?" she asked with a hint of shyness, knowing full well the impact that she was making.

"*Like* it! You look fabulous!"

"Occasionally, I like to honour my Indian heritage, even though dressing like this is not always practical. Come in, then."

We went into her flat, and Hina wasted no time pulling me into an embrace before we sat down.

"Fitz will be here shortly; he rang after you left and offered to take us in his car to an Indian restaurant at the edge of town. He has booked a table. Can I get you a drink while we wait? You don't have to have the Dandelion coffee; I've got an assortment of herbal teas, if you're interested."

"Do you have a ginger tea like the one I had yesterday at the group?"

"Coming up!"

While we were waiting for Fitz, Hina told me that he was the one who'd introduced her to the group about six years ago. At that time, he was the teacher.

"How did you meet?" I asked.

"Not in a café!" she confirmed. No doubt Fitz had filled her in about our first meeting. "My dad and Fitz crossed paths through their work in the diplomatic world. I can't tell you more, for neither of them will give you a straight answer about what they actually do.

Sometimes Fitz would visit our home when I still lived with my parents. He told my dad about the group, and although he was interested – my dad has strong spiritual leanings, but keeps to his Hindu upbringing – he declined. Then my lovely dad thought of me. He knew that I was someone who sought answers to important questions, and suggested Fitz have a word with me. The rest is history. Fitz thought I was 'ripe', his word, and he invited me to the next meeting."

Fitz rang the doorbell, and since parking in Hina's street could be difficult, we wasted no time going out to meet him. We jumped into his car, Hina in the front passenger seat, while I stretched out behind them.

On the way to the restaurant, we talked about the events of the previous day. Hina admitted that she had given Fitz an abbreviated account when he'd phoned her earlier that morning.

"It was important," Fitz commented, as usual getting straight to the point, "that you didn't get emotional with those fellows, that you didn't express any hatred or disgust, or any other negative attitude. That is the mark of a true *kshatriya*, or warrior. A warrior defends, never attacks. He carries no hatred towards anyone. He is full of love, but he is no softie! He will do the minimum required to protect his loved ones.

Even though he may inflict some necessary pain upon an attacker, he bears no ill will. From the way Hina described it to me this morning, this was another important initiatory step for you, one which you seem to have come through flawlessly".

"It was as if I didn't do anything, Fitz; like I was just looking on, and everything looked after itself. And I was aware of that same boundless Presence that I've told you about before, and well, it's as if Something is looking after me all the time."

"At some time, we'll talk about non-attached action,

which is the essence of Yoga," Fitz replied.

"Zac, when Fitz talked about the qualities of the warrior," Hina volunteered, "you might have heard him use the term *kshatriya*. It's the *Sanskrit* word applied to the third level of the Caste system in India. Caste has been greatly misunderstood and abused in our culture. It often angered me when I came across those of a so-called 'lower caste' being discriminated against, or worse, being treated as outcasts. It has even emigrated to the UK along with some Hindu families.

This concern prompted me to have a good look at how this system first appeared in India.

Originally, there was no hereditary status connected with caste. It was simply a classification based on human innate capacities. In reality, the four-grade Caste system represents the stages of spiritual evolution for any of us. It is described like this in some ancient *Sanskrit* texts.

The *Sudra*, the first level, indicates those mainly interested in meeting their bodily needs and desires, and generally, they are seen to gravitate to manual work.

Then the *Vaisya*, as well as satisfying the senses, they want something more creative. They like to organise, usually for worldly gain. Their abilities often lead them into business or farming, for example. They need an outlet for their mental abilities.

The *Kshatriya*, which Fitz has already spoken about, is next. Each stage includes the previous. So, the *kshatriyas,* while possessing the previous levels, go further: now they seek for the meaning of life; they endeavour to root out all that ego-based baggage, and to live by their spiritual nature, becoming increasingly aware. Therefore, they are capable of self-discipline. They are born leaders; they possess a natural authority. That's what *kshatriya* means: holder of *kshatra*, or authority.

Finally, the *Brahmana*. They are no longer at the mercy of the ego because of their natural affinity with the divine reality. They live and breathe by the light of consciousness, even in the midst of everyday affairs, which they certainly do not shun, as some might believe. They are God-knowing and God-loving, which means they also have a boundless love for humanity. They are therefore the greatest teachers, and best placed to guide anyone who seeks true Self-Realisation."

I was drinking all this in, with the questions in me piling up, when Fitz said, "We are here."

As we got out of the car, Fitz turned to Hina and said, "That was an excellent summary of the Caste system. Of course, Zac, there is so much more to it and you'll find in time that there are Western versions of these grades. It comes from a universal knowledge of the stages of inner realisation.

But now, it is time to eat!"

Chapter 11

We were in the parking area next to what looked like a converted barn. From the parked cars, we walked through a leafy courtyard to reach the entrance to the restaurant.

Once inside, we were shown to the reserved table which Fitz had booked.

During the meal, Fitz asked how the mentoring arrangement was working. Hina and I looked at each other, and I left it to her to answer the question.

"We've spent time mostly talking about how the group works, including the part played by mentoring, but our main aim now must be to focus on meditation. We'll find some time over the next week, I'm sure, to practice together and explore its subtleties."

"Sounds good to me," Fitz said approvingly. Then he changed tack: "I admit to a hidden agenda for inviting Hina out for lunch today, and since you're now here as well, Zac, thanks to Hina, I've thought carefully, and I sense something synchronistic is behind this turn of events. I try to pay attention to these unexpected occurrences and be guided by and trust intuition. So ... I'm going to share this with *both* of you. Let's be open to where this might lead us."

I could see that Hina was both mystified and wide-eyed with anticipation about where this was going, and I was probably feeling much the same.

"As you know, as well as our regular gathering – and I am aware, Zac, that you've only been once – members are free to form their own study groups, or associate as friends for a shared interest, or just meet to enjoy each other's company ..."

"I've filled Zac in on that," Hina interjected,

"Great. Well, I have a proposal to make. I've shared this with Susan, and she's given the project her blessing. It will be a way of reaching out to people who would not otherwise come in contact with the teachings we enjoy in the group. It involves the creation of a School of Spiritual Philosophy. Of course, such an entity, if it comes about, may be given a different title. Members of the group would be welcome to support it, but its responsibility would remain solely in the hands of those who run it.

The way our group works, its spontaneity, its minimalist structure – this doesn't work for everyone, which is why we are careful about who we introduce. Those who come to the group do so because they are seen to be ready. But others who may be just opening to the *possibility* of a spiritual path might need more nurturing; they may need some gentle direction, a safe structure, and a more graduated approach, perhaps organised like a course. This is perfectly in tune with how the ancients worked. The Pythagoreans distinguished between 'meat for the perfect', the *teleios* in Greek, someone with a sufficient degree of discernment, and 'milk for babes', those not yet ready for the deeper truths of the Spirit. This distinction crept into the New Testament letters of St. Paul, and in the early days of Christianity, the *catechumenate* was the vehicle by which enquirers would be offered a graded preparation for the rite of initiation, quite different from the formalised, often automatic, baptism we find in the churches today.

Ramakrishna used the analogy of a mother who feeds her older children with solid foods, but her infant with milk. She loves them all equally, but their powers of digestion vary! There is, therefore, no discrimination involved in this process, as some might object. Even Jesus shared 'the mysteries of the kingdom' only with his closest disciples, but spoke in more homely terms, often couched in parables, to those outside his inner circle.

So far, apart from us, only Susan and Elizabeth know about this."

"Elizabeth is Fitz's daughter and also one of our members," Hina explained.

"It was Elizabeth's idea. It came to her following a conversation with one of her clients. Elizabeth and her husband Daniel run a Natural Health Centre which offers alternative therapies. One of Elizabeth's regular clients said during that conversation, 'I'd love to learn more about the spiritual side of life, but there are so many books, it's so confusing.' Elizabeth did not get the sense that this woman would benefit from the group, so it got her thinking. Later that day, she sat still with the question, *What would serve a person like her?* Elizabeth told me that the idea of the School came to her in the form of a seed. In her mind's eye, the seed opened, and the plan for it, she told me, just unfolded by itself. She took this to be a divine calling.

Initially, Elizabeth will be the main teacher in the School; I am happy to act in an advisory capacity. She'd like one or two others to be involved in the teaching as the School expands. She particularly would like Hina to join her team, and is open to suggestions regarding anyone else."

I could see Hina's eyes widening again as she took all this in.

"Am I dreaming this?" Hina exclaimed. "Working with Elizabeth ... it would be so wonderful!"

"Hina," Fitz said quietly, "you have a great way of sharing your understanding that is always so beautiful; you'd be a real asset to this venture."

I couldn't wait to chip in. "Fitz, I've learnt so much from Hina in such a short time," I said. "She's a natural. Is there any way I can support this?"

"Ah. I have a slightly different suggestion for you, Zac. But it must be something you *choose* to do, not because I'm asking you. Are there after-hours clubs at the school where you teach?"

"Yes," I replied. "There's a chess club, a dance class, tennis, and other activities."

"Could you start a meditation class? If you did, I would help you set it up."

I looked at Hina; she nodded as she took my hand.

"I'm waiting for Hina to give me some direction in meditation," I said, receiving a playful nudge in the shoulder from Hina as I was speaking. "Right now, since meeting you, and then Hina, I believe anything is possible. The summer term ends in a few weeks. It's something that will have to wait until next term, which starts early in September. I'll do it; I think I know a couple of A Level students who would be interested."

"Excellent," said Fitz, beaming. "This will be a good preparatory experience for you. I can see you eventually contributing to the School; you have a fine mind, you express yourself very well, and what is even more important, you are open to the promptings of the spiritual world.

Now. Time to go home."

With that decision, made in his usual resolute manner, Fitz stood, summoned a waiter, paid the bill, and ushered us outside to his car.

Chapter 12

We headed back to Hina's place, and Fitz said goodbye to us outside the hairdressing salon before driving away.

I have to admit that, despite all that I had learned since meeting Fitz, my mind was in something of a whirl. Without question, I was very attracted to Hina, and not just physically. But she was my mentor! Furthermore, was it just the fracas in the park that had brought us closer? Was her invitation to stay over last night just a short-term need on her part? Was I reading too much into what was happening between us? I did not wish to sabotage our friendship if that's all it was.

As we sat together on her settee, it was as if she could read my mind. I was aware of her smiling, quizzical look.

"Zac, why be so glum? Don't we have a lot to feel thankful for? What if we're both going through the same inner questioning right now? We've just been catapulted into each other's lives."

"Look, Hina, I want everything to be right between us. Already, you mean so much to me. I know we only met yesterday, but I'm trying to accept that sometimes two people can be drawn into a powerful bond in no time at all. Who knows, maybe what happened yesterday was *meant* to bring us closer."

Hina, her eyes tearful and shining at the same time, spoke to me gently and lovingly:

"Zac, I've never met anyone like you before. In some ways you are very strong, in others a little vulnerable, even uncertain. I'm warming to both sides of you. We should absolutely stick together ... I want that, but a little space at the moment seems to be in order. To help us see clearly.

We both work during the week, and I'm sure you, like me, have other responsibilities. How about we skip a few days, say until midweek. We can always meet as friends, however that might develop, and when we meet for group work, which will be meditation practice in the first instance, we'll hold to that."

Agreeing with Hina wasn't too difficult. Inwardly relieved, I knew that this was the right way to nurture our fledgling friendship. We swapped phone numbers and agreed to meet on Wednesday evening at *The Urban Lounge*, my treat. The time after that would be for meditation practice, which we'd fix while at the restaurant.

As I began to leave, Hina pulled me close. I could feel the strong emotion running through her.

"Zac, I *am* very fond of you. Really. Our next time together ... so grateful it's so soon ... Don't you say a word! Just go, and whatever you have to do, *do it beautifully*."

As I left, I thought to myself just how much Hina understood me, and how she always seemed to know what to say to lift my spirit.

During the days that followed, I seemed to give more of myself to my work, remembering the "*do everything beautifully*" encouragement from Hina. I thought of Fitz's hint about *non-attached action*, and that I'd remind him to spell it out for me soon. I was sure those two qualities – *beautiful* and *non-attached* – were connected.

After my English A Level class, I asked two of my best students, Shona and Grant, to stay behind. I floated the idea of a regular meditation class and asked whether they'd be interested. They looked at each other; it was Shona who spoke first:

"My dad's a yoga teacher, but I've always avoided going to his class of geriatrics." The three of us laughed.

"I'd come," Grant said. "I've tried it a bit, but couldn't stick with it. A fresh approach might help."

"Then, count me in too," Shona added.

I told them we'd start next term. And that was that; my new commitment was now a reality.

Chapter 13

Wednesday soon came around. I'd booked a table at *The Urban Lounge* the day before to make sure that Hina and I weren't disappointed.

I arrived early and was happy with the table we'd been allotted. A different Hina soon turned up; no sari this time – instead, t-shirt, jeans and trainers, and hair tied up into a ponytail. As I stood to greet her, I was immediately rewarded with a wholesome embrace.

"I'm glad our break wasn't any longer," she said affectionately. "I think I might have pined away without you, Mr. Marshal!"

"Ditto, Miss Jaiswal!"

"Seriously though, seeing you has made my day already. Right, flattery over, what now?"

"We eat, drink and get to know more about each other."

Once food and drink had been ordered, Hina began to tell me more about her background. She had family in the UK, as well as in India and Mauritius. Her grandparents on her father's side came to the UK from Mumbai in India; on her mother's side, they were from Bangalore in South India. Both her parents were born in England and met at King's College in London, which is not far from the Indian Embassy.

"I mention the Embassy," Hina stressed, "because dad soon got a job there. My mum has always been very artistic; she designs clothes for several fashion houses. My brother and I grew up in a traditional Hindu home, but my parents were always very liberal, and my mum even joined the local interfaith society.

After I finished my A Levels, I felt the urge to travel. With two others, both girls from my school, we travelled to India, and came back to England via Italy and France.

In India, we visited several *ashrams* – they're spiritual centres – and at one of them I met a wonderful female *guru* called Radha Devi. I was so inspired by her inner beauty, serenity and wisdom that I stayed at the *ashram* for several months, while my friends went off to do other things, before we met up again for the journey back to England.

That wonderful woman touched my soul deeply, Zac. She opened my heart and mind to the deep philosophies of Yoga and Vedanta. I knew my life would never be the same when I returned to England. And as I mentioned, I was soon invited to join the group by Fitz, in whom I saw the same light that shone so brightly in Radha."

Whilst she was speaking about Radha Devi, her eyes were moist and shining. *The same inner light is also shining from you, Hina.*

"Now you," Hina said quietly, after a few moments of sitting with me in the shared silence.

"Nothing as exotic as your ancestry. As far back as I know, my family has been English. I grew up in Dorset, with no brothers or sisters, but moved to London after my university days. My dad is in finance, my mum is a teacher like me, but she teaches History. We're quite close really, although we don't get together all that often. We keep in touch, though, by phone and WhatsApp.

I've always been big on reading, especially science fiction, so I did well at school in English, and not knowing what to do when I went to university, I drifted towards a degree in English Literature. As it happens, I thoroughly enjoyed it. Then I trained as a teacher, same subject. I moved here to my second school because I was given more choice about the curriculum."

"Not because of a salary increase?"

"No, although there was the basic incremental increase, which would have come anyway. In the first school, I was treated as a novice, and had to put up with how things were done there, and wasn't given any say. Now, I get on well with my head of department; she allows me to choose the syllabus for my GCSE and A Level Groups.

It works so much better when you love what you're teaching the students."

"That's lovely, Zac," Hina said. "With students catching your love for what you teach them, I'm sure there'll be an interest in your proposed meditation class."

"Hope so ... but if I am to run such a class, I have to 'walk the talk', as the saying goes, so I must book a session with my mentor!"

"Not this evening though; let's keep this evening just for Hina and Zac, friends united, please."

I was happy with that, and after the meal, we made our way to Hina's place, where we behaved like 'normal' people and watched the latest *Star Trek* film. We decided before I left for home to meet over the weekend to work on my meditation practice. We'd decide where to meet a day or two before.

Hina couldn't let me disappear before we'd shared a long and sweet embrace by her flat's open doorway; it was as if we both knew, without the need to voice it openly, that our relationship was secure, even if neither of us was certain where it was headed.

Chapter 14

It was back to focusing on my teaching for the next two days, with the following week being the last before the school broke up for the summer holiday.

Early on Friday evening, Hina telephoned to tell me that Fitz had offered his home for Saturday afternoon. He had made one of his rooms into a meditation space, and since he would be out all day, we would not be disturbed. We agreed to meet there at 1.00 pm.

The next day, I'd been outside Fitz's house for a few minutes before Hina arrived; she was looking good in a blue sleeveless denim dress. We greeted each other with an easy affection before Hina produced a key and opened the front door.

"Fitz suggested I keep this key some time ago when I used his address for a small planning meeting," she explained. "Secretarial duties!"

Once we'd settled down in Fitz's living room, Hina suggested that she go over the basics of meditation practice with me before we moved to the meditation room.

"I'll get us some water for now; let's save having a hot drink for later."

Hina went to the kitchen, returning with two glasses of water, which she placed on a side table.

"OK, Zac. First of all, it may sound weird, but in meditation, you must eventually find your own way. What I am offering for now is my own experience, suggesting steps for you to follow. In other words, what works for me. If, as you gain more experience in the practice, you find greater inner freedom without these steps, great; don't use them. Treat them as guidelines to fall back on, if needed.

I've written it all down for you."

Hina produced an A4 sheet of paper from her bag and set it down between us.

"I'll take you through it first, then we'll meditate together. You can keep these printed directions as a reminder for when you meditate on your own."

We sat down together while Hina took me through the printed steps:

In the beginning, meditate for at least 15 minutes.

It is best to meditate whilst sitting. Sit upright. Look straight ahead, but with eyes closed.

Feet on ground, hands on lap.

Find the balance between relaxation & alertness.

Let go of any tensions in the body. You can do a slow sweep from the top of your head down to your toes. Do not concentrate, but note any place of tension or tightness, and let go as required, releasing any tension wherever you find it.

Keeping your eyes closed, now open your awareness to include everything that is going on – in the body, the sounds around you, and in the mind with its parade of thoughts. Allow everything to be as it is, by simply witnessing without interfering.

Now let go into the awareness itself; this awareness is your own presence ... there should be no effort ... it's more like just allowing it to happen ... opening into the boundless presence in which everything exists,

and therefore in which all sensations, thoughts, and feelings appear and subside ... appear and subside ...

You'll notice that everything that arises in awareness comes and goes, while awareness, or presence, does not ...

The main purpose of meditation ... to be master of your inner life, so that you are completely open to the wisdom and intelligence of your own being, your core Self.

There are secondary benefits – these come naturally, but they are not the aim.

Hina then turned over the sheet of instructions and drew a diagram:

person/ego level
> witness
> awareness
> pure being
(the Self, the Inner Teacher)

"This diagram shows the basic stages you can go through as you meditate.

The *person/ego* level is where the majority of people spend most of their waking days. You begin by shifting from this level of personal identity with its egoic tendencies, the level of non-stop thought processes, into the *witness* phase, watching without getting involved.

Once you are established as the *witness*, you can then allow the *witness* itself to relax into its source, from which it originates, which is the *pure awareness*. This is all you can do.

The final stage, when the awareness comes to rest in *pure being*, your true Self, is not in your hands. It will happen when it happens, at exactly the right moment. Let's say, by Grace.

Shall we sit in meditation?"

I nodded. We then went into Fitz's specially adapted room, which boasted a quality wooden floor, with a geometrically designed rug in the centre. Around the room were placed a few straight-backed chairs. The room was well lit by a large window which looked out into the back garden.

Hina pulled two chairs into the middle of the room and placed them facing each other.

"We'll meditate for about fifteen minutes," she said. "I'm not going to do any more speaking. Zac. Just trust what you know." And with that, she shut her eyes and sat still with a lovely straight back.

I closed my eyes and followed suit.

Chapter 15

As I began to let go into this meditation practice, I was aware that my mind was awash with a host of conflicting thoughts. About Hina, of course: how are things evolving with her? About whether I could get to grips with meditation based on my past half-hearted efforts. Concerns about the quality of my teaching at school. Old stuff! I inwardly shook myself, and as instructed, endeavoured to rise into the witness level, above it all. It seemed as if this was a hopeless task, as other thoughts began jostling for attention.

Then, in the midst of this inner tumult, as I was trying to extricate myself, it was Susan's words that unexpectedly came to me, as if she was speaking to me personally: "Be a daring soul!" It was her voice I heard piercing the mental noise. My heart just opened, and something in me surrendered. As if on cue, all those whirling thoughts simply vanished, and with them all sense of a personal identity had been completely dispelled. It is almost impossible to describe what was now present. Let me try: a point of nothingness, which seemed to be both nowhere and everywhere at the same time.

This nothingness gradually became filled with a pure blazing light. And I was that! I was both the nothingness *and* the light. In this light was the purest love, and a boundless joy that could never be erased. I *was* the love; I *was* the joy.

In this nothingness so full of light, love, and joy, all the personal concerns of Zac Marshal had dissolved, as if they had never been. This was the pure being of Hina's diagram, the Inner Teacher, which I now knew to be ever at hand, whether known at the personal level or not.

This was no longer a practice, but the fullness of the natural state. Being fully present and centred in what I am, I allowed my eyes to open.

Before me was a young woman sitting very still, and breathing evenly. I beheld new depths to her beauty. The same pure light that had emerged from the point of nothingness in me was shining from her, surrounding her, and filling the room. It was as if I was seeing her for the first time, in her wholeness – body, soul and spirit all at once.

I stayed like that without a care for what might follow, simply enjoying the "sacred present" that Fitz had referred to during our first meeting.

Eventually, Hina opened her eyes and looked at me. Our eyes met.

She knew.

We *were* that light, and were held as one within it.

"You are on fire," Hina said at last. "You look as though you know who you are, and have never not known who you are. You won't need the meditation guidelines I've given you anymore."

"I'll keep them. I'm not taking anything for granted. But right now, I feel immense gratitude that, not only did you take me in hand, but now I'm seeing you, the real you. You are what I am. Everything is so much clearer. To *be* this light, and allow it to guide everything. It includes whatever is to be between me and you. I am happy to watch how it unfolds; there's no need to push anything."

"That's right," Hina agreed, reaching for my hands. "And here we are. Together. Understanding one another at a deeper level. We can allow this to be what it is."

We didn't stay at Fitz's place for any refreshments. Instead, we agreed to separate for the rest of the afternoon. I told Hina that I'd like a few hours to be by myself in nature somewhere. I'd phone her later and we'd meet early evening for a bite. Hina, feeling much the same, happily agreed.

I returned home briefly to wash and change before setting off for the nearby woods. After passing through an avenue of trees, I came to one of my favourite spots, an unspoilt clearing with a small pond that attracted a variety of water birds. Choosing one of the old wooden benches that circled the pond, I sat for a while drinking in the scene.

What I had experienced in Fitz's meditation room was still with me. I somehow knew that its intensity would undoubtedly fade with time, and that this was necessary in order to get on with the requirements of everyday living. I also took heart that what I now knew would always be with me. In the stillness near the pond, I felt that every molecule of my being was suffused with love, and there was an overwhelming desire to always be true to myself in my engagement with others.

Before leaving to return home, I quietly reminded myself: "I am the Light of Presence; I am the Light that pre-exists and is deeper than any thoughts or emotions that make up the personal identity of Zac Marshal. What does this mean day to day? I can play the role of Zac Marshal, though without the usual self-indulgence of the ego."

I smiled as I recalled Hina's words from a week ago: *whatever you do, do it beautifully*. These words had now taken on a greater depth.

Chapter 16

This time Hina came across to my part of town. We met at my favourite café. Only three weeks earlier – *three weeks, or a lifetime?* – was when I'd first met Fitz. I smiled inwardly: *The Meeting!*

We decided on a simple snack rather than a full evening meal. I chose a toastie and my usual Americano; Hina went for a sandwich and some exotic smoothie.

Hina told me that I needn't explain to her what I had experienced during the meditation that afternoon. She just knew. She knew, and she was delighted. She felt that her mentoring days with me were numbered, but I told her that I highly valued her experience, and that I was sure that we could relate to one another in different ways, as long as we were aware of what we were doing. Hina concurred. Since we were discussing our relationship, I took the opportunity to voice what felt true for me about the nature of our closeness, irrespective of our short time together:

"Hina, we met a week ago today. It's crazy, but it seems like I've already known you for a lifetime. I want to name what I feel right now, without any pretence. So ... I would like you to be my girlfriend. You are more than a girl, obviously, but don't know what other word to use."

Before I could finish, Hina had taken my hands in hers.

"Can I now call you *darling*, then?" She somehow managed to speak through a big grin.

"You can, *beautiful one*!" *I still couldn't find the right word!*

The joy we shared was so evident to both of us that no further discussion was necessary. We'd moved beyond being just friends, *and* Hina was still my mentor in matters concerning the group.

Later, Hina came back to my place and stayed over. There was an unspoken agreement that we would not make love just yet. Somehow, I knew that the first time would be recognised by both of us, without any prior agenda; it would be spontaneous, and a sharing at every level – body, mind, and spirit.

The next day, after breakfast, we meditated together. Unlike the day before, nothing special appeared to happen, although the experience was pleasant enough. After the meditation had come to an end, Hina shared some thoughts about this.

"There's no such thing as a good or bad meditation. One day, there could be a great revelation; on another day, it's a struggle just to stay awake. The important thing is the discipline of regular practice. You accept the way it is ... each time.

It's important to understand this, Zac: the mind can never reach what lies beyond it, because the mind is always looking for an object, however subtle; but there is no object in meditation, because you, the subject, are already the pure Self. When this is genuinely known, there is a spontaneous letting go of any attempt to experience what is truly *beyond* all experience. Then one is home, as the divine Self, the one Self.

The fruits of a regular meditation practice show up in our outer life. It is most likely that others will see important changes happening within us before we notice them ourselves. I've heard a metaphor about this, I can't remember where: with each practice, the mirror of the mind is being polished, and the stains that obscure the inner light are gradually wiped away."

"That's a helpful analogy," I said. "As you say: *accepting the way it is*. Sounds to me like a definition of *non-attachment*; Fitz said he'd talk to me about it soon."

"You should share yesterday's meditation experience with Susan when you see her. I've given her your phone number – she'll contact you soon. Talking of Susan reminds me; I've arranged to play tennis this afternoon with her, as well as with Tamara and Geoff. You can come along if you want."

"No, Hina. Thanks for asking. I'd love to join you another time. But I'd like to get myself ready for the final week of term; a lot is happening, and I also want to give my parents a ring. I'll catch up with you tomorrow evening, if you like."

"Tomorrow evening, I'm meeting with some of my counselling co-students to celebrate getting through our course in one piece."

"OK, Tuesday then," I suggested.

"Great. Can you come round to me on Tuesday?"

"Can't think of anything I'd rather do."

"Well then, *boyfriend*, before I go, I *demand* a proper kiss!"

"*Demand?* That's not very non-attached!"

But Hina was already wrapping herself around me, arching her head, with lips searching for mine. Being helpless, I had no alternative but to surrender.

Chapter 17

I was glad of no distractions for the next two days. At the school, we were wrapping up the term, making arrangements for the new academic year to begin in September, and, amongst other things, saying goodbye to colleagues who were leaving or retiring.

On Tuesday, the last day of term, most teachers were required to take on various roles to ensure the smooth running of Sports Day, with fretful expectations of chaos usually proving to be unfounded.

I went home once all duties had been completed. After a wash and changing into less formal clothes, I made my way to Hina's place.

We spent a little while taking each other in and enjoying our reunion before anything else came up. Hina then told me that during Sunday afternoon's tennis, she had filled Susan in about our burgeoning relationship. Susan had conveyed that she was delighted for us both.

"She also asked me to tell you she'd welcome a one-to-one session with you after next Saturday's group meeting. Just stay behind when the meeting is over."

"Next Saturday!" I exclaimed. "Goodness ... when I'll have known you for an extraordinary two weeks!"

"Well, we've had a week and three days to live the unexpected together," Hina replied, while dancing around the room, and around me. "Whatever is to come – bring it on!" *I loved the way Hina celebrated life without any inhibitions.*

"I feel like going out somewhere, Zac, to celebrate the ten days we've known each other. What do you suggest?"

At that precise moment, my mind was a blank, and I shrugged, at the same time taking in a framed photo that stood on a side table. It featured two young women, one of them Hina, arms around each other, with a sunny beach behind them. I pointed at the photo.

"Who's that with you by the beach?"

"That's my friend Tamara ... That's it! Let's go right now and see her. She's been itching to meet you, anyway. I'll give her a ring. She might be with her partner, David. But that shouldn't matter."

Hina and Tamara shared a short phone conversation, after which Hina said to me: "She's at home with David, and just trying out a new recipe of stuffed mushrooms and roasted cauliflower. She says she could easily cater for the four of us. I know you weren't expecting this, but please, will you come with me?"

And with that, our evening took care of itself. We took a short walk to a sweet little bungalow and were cheerfully greeted by Tamara and David. While on our way, Hina told me that Tamara and David were both members of the group, and that they had been together for about two years before joining.

We were ushered into a spacious living room, and my eyes were immediately drawn to a seven-branched candlestick which occupied pride of place on the mantlepiece. Beside it was a picture of a young teenager wearing a prayer shawl around his shoulders, his hair covered by a skullcap.

David explained: "Tamara and I have both come from a Jewish background, although neither of us are much observant these days. However, those things you are looking at make our parents feel at home whenever they visit. The candlestick is called a *menorah* and is lit during the festival of *Chanukah*. It's also a very attractive ornament. The boy in the photo is Tamara's younger brother, Josh, showing him aged thirteen on his *Barmitzvah* day. That was seven years ago."

"Come and join us in the kitchen," Tamara called out, so we followed David through to what I would call a kitchen-diner. We sat around a square table, and David and Tamara served up. The food was delicious. After the meal, we returned to the living room carrying drinks.

"I saw you at the group," Tamara said to me, "but we didn't get a chance to speak; you were getting *mentored up* with Hina. And then, bang, bang, bang, it's been a rollercoaster, I believe. Anyway, David and I are so pleased to meet you, and glad that Hina has at last found someone to keep her in order."

"Well, I think that might be an impossible undertaking," I replied with a smile, as Hina somehow kneed me under the table before turning the tables on Tamara.

"Why don't you tell Zac how you two met? If ours was a rollercoaster, yours was more of an express train!"

Tamara and David laughed as they looked at each other.

"David, you do it," Tamara said.

"Well, we were quite young," said David. "We both came from fairly orthodox Jewish families, and attended the same private Jewish school, although I was two years ahead. Tamara's dad was – still is – a rabbi.

Anyway, about a week or two before we really got together, Tamara had a bust-up with her dad. She'd met a Turkish lad whilst on an outing with friends to a bowling alley. They seemed to hit it off, and they exchanged contact details. Not much happened, really; they texted each other a few times, and were arranging to meet up at the same bowling alley, but on the very day they were due to meet, her dad told Tamara he wanted to take her to meet a family from his synagogue who had a *nice* teenage son. Tamara didn't want to go, but her dad insisted. In the end, Tamara, due to her truthful nature, told him the real reason – she'd arranged to meet Hamza, and she'd been looking forward to it. Her dad was furious ..."

By this time, Tamara was a bit tearful, but she took over from David.

"He shouted at me and slapped me. I was stunned. And then the real crunch – if I dated a non-Jew, he said, I would no longer be his daughter. I was so shaken that I almost became a nervous wreck. I stormed into my bedroom and stayed there for hours. My parents eventually went out without me. My mum would have been terribly upset, but she never went against my dad, although she often disagreed with his decisions.

A few days later, I'd pulled myself together and decided to run away from home. I packed a bag and crept out of the house very early. At first, I didn't know where to go. I wandered into the town centre and waited at a bus stop for the cafés to open. When they did, I went into the nearest one. I went to get myself a cappuccino, and guess who served me? It was David; he was working there part-time until he started college. He remembered me from our school days. Seeing the state I was in, he asked the manager for some time out to 'help a friend'. He was so caring! We've been together ever since."

David continued: "Tamara absolutely was never returning home, no way! One of my aunts had rebelled against the same strict upbringing herself, and she willingly and unofficially adopted Tamara, who thrived in her more open household. My aunt, Jasmine Todd, is one of the founders of the group; you'll meet her soon. It's through her that we eventually joined ourselves."

"Zac, as Hina knows, we have no regrets," said Tamara. "We count our blessings, as the saying goes. My traumatic conflict at home led me to David, who is my beloved, my dearest friend, and soulmate. And it's through David that some sort of reconciliation has happened between me and my dad. David called on him without warning one day and delivered some strong home truths, which got through his defensive shell. He and mum have been here a few times now."

"No doubt Fitz would call this journey of yours an initiation," I said to nods and laughter.

"The more we engage in this Work, the more we start to see the interconnectedness of everything," Tamara added. "It's so good to have you as part of our family, Zac; I know there is so much that you'll bring to us. We all learn from each other."

David suggested we meditate for a short while before Hina and I left for home. He lit a candle, and we sat down in a circle. Following this shared practice, I came away with a sense of deep contentment.

Back at her flat, Hina insisted that as it was late, I should stay over. That saved any discussion about the matter. She had to be up early to work at the bookshop, so we wasted little time before settling down for the night.

Chapter 18

With Hina out all day at the bookshop, and it being the first day of my summer break, I was at first unsure what to do with myself. However, a little voice inside me said, *Why don't you begin the day with a short meditation?*

It was evident that I was listening to myself! The meditation proved very helpful. I considered it must be one of the side-benefits that either Fitz or Hina had mentioned. Whereas I could see that the main focus of meditation was Self-enquiry, the nature of the practice itself brings a certain clarity to the mind. On this occasion, I knew exactly what to do: a series of practical things – tidy my home, do some shopping, and, why not, buy a first present for Hina.

Bearing in mind that it's the thought that counts, I decided to buy for Hina the first item that seemed right for her, and not to get into an internal debate about it, a persistent tendency which I recognised through the increase in inner stillness that was now available to me.

After taking care of the other intended business, I bought a collection of the poems of Kabir, a celebrated Indian mystic of the fifteenth century. I'd opened the book casually and read the poem that was presented to me, which sold it to me instantly:

Are you looking for me?

Are you looking for me? I am in the next seat.
My shoulder is against yours.

> You will not find me in the stupas,
> not in Indian shrine rooms,
> nor in synagogues, nor in cathedrals:
> not in masses, nor kirtans, not in legs winding
> around your own neck, nor in eating nothing but
> vegetables.
>
> When you really look for me, you will see me instantly – you will find me in the tiniest house of time.
>
> Kabir says: Student, tell me, what is God?
> He is the Breath inside the breath.

At just after 5.00 pm, I gave Hina a call, knowing that her day's work at the bookshop should have finished. As it was a fine sunny evening, Hina suggested we meet in town near where she worked, at a café with outside seating. Our time together had a different feel to it this time; very low-key, relaxed, with comfortable periods of silence.

Reflecting on this later, I realised that first and foremost, we enjoyed *being* together, and that sustained conversation was not always necessary.

After a simple snack, I gave Hina the book. She loved her present, and we read a few of the poems to each other. She then suggested we turn up to the group on Saturday as a couple, since that's what we were.

"And it would be lovely if you could come to me on Friday," she added. "I'll cook an Indian dish for us, and Zac, please stay over. I'm meeting with Fitz, Susan and Elizabeth tomorrow. We'll be looking at the proposal for the School of Spiritual Philosophy. It will be a day of meditation, reflection, and discussion. Then it's over to

Elizabeth's home; there is something she wishes to talk over with me."

"I'll be there on Friday," I said, and after sweet kisses and a gentle embrace, we left the café and went back to our homes.

Chapter 19

I arrived at Hina's place around 7.00 pm on Friday, and we wasted no time before enjoying a carefree embrace with gentle caresses thrown in for good measure. I could hear music coming from somewhere in her flat; not the kind I'm used to, but no doubt of Indian origin. Hina looked lovely in what looked like a kind of dark green long kaftan, worn over loose trousers that narrowed just above the ankles. It wasn't a kaftan as she soon made clear.

"We are having an Indian evening," she announced, "and what you see me wearing is called a *salwar kameez*, which, like the *sari*, is also very common in India. The scarf that goes with it is a *dupatta*. Tonight, you are going to enjoy Indian food, Indian music, Indian incense ..."

"... and a beautiful Indian woman," I couldn't help adding, which got no verbal response, just a lovely smile.

Hina had set up a dining table and two chairs in the middle of the living room, everything prepared apart from the food we would be eating.

"The food is ready," Hina proclaimed, taking me into the kitchen. "You can help me carry it all to the table."

All the food was in separate serving dishes, which I helped Hina transport to the dining table. I was already aware of the custom in Indian homes and restaurants for diners to help themselves from an array of dishes. The wonderful aromatic spread was made up of vegetable curry, chickpea dhal, rice, and raita (yoghurt with cucumber and mint). There was also a plate containing flatbreads, naan and chapati. Already on the table were some pickles, including my favourite, mango chutney.

"Hina, you've excelled yourself," I marvelled. "What other hidden talents do you possess?"

"Just be patient," she cajoled, "and in time all will be revealed!"

The food not only smelled good, it was delicious, and not a scrap was left when we'd finished.

"The music you're hearing is classical Indian, which contains a lot of improvisation; the main instrument is the *sitar,* and the drums are called *tabla*. I'll turn the sound down a little while we drink our *chai*, that's proper Indian tea, by the way, with added spices ... and then it would be good to catch up with each other."

Once we'd settled on the settee to enjoy our spicy tea, Hina brought me up to date with the meetings she'd had the day before.

"Fitz, Elizabeth and I had a great day together, and our aim to start the School of Spiritual Philosophy has taken a few steps forward. When Geoff was told about our intention, he was so strongly taken with it, he generously offered the use of his house as its base in the first instance. If, as we hope, the School expands over time, a bigger place will need to be found. For now, there are two sizeable rooms available. Geoff says it wouldn't affect his lifestyle because there's more than enough room in the rest of his house.

Elizabeth will teach the first crop of students, and I will sit in with her. If we get unexpectedly high numbers that we need to divide into two groups, then I will take one of them. We will limit the size of each group to 20 people. Fitz suggested that there should be a second ancillary teacher to support each group. We have two people in mind. Angelo and Jill from our group have agreed they will be available if called upon.

We began drawing up the subjects for the first few sessions, with titles such as 'Who am I?', 'Levels of Consciousness', 'The Sacred Present', for example. But we will be flexible, and all this could change before we come to start the first session. Fitz and Elizabeth are meeting again to finalise the introductory programme consisting of ten sessions, and agree on a starting date. Also, what do we call the programme itself? I suggested: 'Uncovering Your Deeper Self'. Fitz threw in 'The Perennial Philosophy' for good measure. But we may come up with something better, or more accurate.

We also have to decide the extent to which we advertise. So far, we've just agreed to place an advert in the local paper, and put posters and leaflets into any libraries, cafés and shops that are willing to accept them."

"It's wonderful," I said. "And so needed in our rather aimless society. Look at me, I wasn't going anywhere, until Fitz gave me his extra-special version of a shove!"

Hina laughed. "You weren't as aimless as you make out, otherwise you would never have responded the way you did."

She continued: "There's something else – now that I've completed my counselling course, Elizabeth has offered me two slots at her Natural Health Centre. It will be two half-days; I could see three clients on each of them. We've yet to agree on the exact days, and I will need to fit it around my work at the bookshop. I can't give that up yet until my client base has grown enough to do so.

Zac, I'm so excited. It kick-starts my work as a professional counsellor. As I said when we first met, this is closer to what I'm meant to be doing. I'm calling it 'spiritual counselling' because, as well as the mostly psycho-therapeutic work I've been trained in, I will acknowledge each client's spiritual nature for their healing to be more complete."

"I'm so pleased for you, Hina. I know you deserve both of these new opportunities. Let me know how – in any way – I can be a support for you."

Hina was shedding tears of joy. "Darling, you will be my support just by being by my side, being in my life, and because of who you are! Honestly, I'm so happy."

I took her in my arms and gently held her. After a while, as I was still holding her, she began slowly unbuttoning my shirt, whilst saying, "Come with me!"

Nothing more needed to be said.

Chapter 20

That evening turned out to include an advanced course in "making love"; not from a book, not from someone's wise words or experience, but directly from the woman I now knew without doubt that I loved.

What we shared was completely free of any expectations. In reality, there was no love to "make" because the love was already present. It was more a "*celebration* of love" – an expression of the bond that was maturing between us. We helped each other stay as present to each other as was possible; both of us gentle, caring, and generous in our giving.

We learnt from each other, what I consider now to be the "art of loving"; body to body and, simultaneously, soul to soul.

In the morning, we happily took our time before venturing out of the bedroom. We showered together before getting dressed, and this too felt like a continuation of our celebration. Throughout, we hardly spoke a word.

Our first duty of the day was to clear up and wash up after yesterday's meal. That done, we decided to treat ourselves to a late breakfast at *The Urban Lounge,* the first place where we'd eaten out together. We didn't speak about the events of the previous evening, but they did spur me to ask Hina a question:

"Did you speak to Susan about the possibility of talking about love at today's meeting?"

"Yes, I did. She said she may well do so, but you never know – something else could come up and demand her attention. Let's see, shall we?"

I was content with that. By the time we'd left the café, it was already the afternoon. Hina suggested we amble slowly towards Geoff's house, and get there nice and early. It was Fitz who opened the door for us. He looked first at Hina, then at me. "I see," he said, and broke out into a broad grin. He hugged us both before ushering us inside.

I'm sure you couldn't hide a thing from this man!

Hina wanted to introduce me to some of the other members I'd not previously interacted with. Geoff was the first. It was good to meet our host, a man built like a boxer, and casually dressed. Looking around, there seemed to be no dress code; everyone being free to turn up as they saw fit. Every time I'd seen Fitz, he was immaculately dressed in suit, tie, waistcoat, and shiny leather shoes.

"There's still time for drinks; let me get them for you both," Geoff said, and when Hina and I thanked him, he set off to get ginger teas for us, so that I could continue to be introduced to other members.

Next, Hina took me to meet Jasmine. She was dressed in a long floral dress. She was standing with David, her nephew, whom I'd met earlier that week.

"David enjoyed meeting you recently," she said. "You must come and visit me with Hina sometime; we all know how you helped her recently, and she's a precious friend of ours."

"Well, I'm glad too," I replied, taking Hina's hand. "I feel it was meant to be."

Geoff turned up with our drinks and joined the conversation.

"This is where the group meets," he said, "but it's my home too, so I hope you'll pop round to me some time for drinks and a chat."

It was time to go into the large room for the meeting, to sit quietly until Susan arrived. While we waited, Fitz stepped forward to light the central candle.

As before, as soon as Susan had sat down, she began looking around and smiling at everyone individually. She then guided us into a short period of quiet preparation before she began the afternoon's teaching.

Chapter 21

"I've been asked to speak about love," she began. "First of all, let us be clear what love is *not*. Love is *not* an emotion.

Emotions are rather fickle things; they come and go depending on circumstances. So, *fear* may be present, but disappear when the object of fear is removed or if some protection shows up. Likewise, most would say that *happiness* is a positive emotion, but happiness can easily be dashed if some precious gift is stolen or someone you adore steps out of your life.

But states of being, unlike emotions, do *not* come and go – they are attributes of our essential nature. Such states of being – joy, peace, love, and the like – need no reason for their existence. This is the difference between *true* happiness, for example, which pervades the individual irrespective of the circumstances, and *false* happiness which is based on identification with some outward fortune, person or object, and so is unreliable, since it is vulnerable to any changes in the relationship with that situation, person or object.

Love is a quality or state of being, of *your* being.

You *are* love. And when nothing clouds the love that you are, you can't help but see that love everywhere; for everything is love.

When you say 'I love him' or 'I love that flower,' you have objectified the love. Then you may identify with him or the flower. When that happens, love is lost, replaced by attachment.

Love is impersonal, as I'm sure some of you have heard me say on previous occasions.

When love is fully present, there is no thought. If thought comes in, there is a disconnect from your own being, which is love. When the mind gets in the way of love, that's when all the trouble starts. For example, you may hear the cry: '*I can't bear to let her go*!' True love is free of any relationship; it doesn't try to limit freedom; if someone goes, there is no fuss, because in truth, love cannot be lost.

Love cannot be abandoned, because it is complete in itself. All need is in the mind. That is why the great sage, *Shankara,* said, 'Bondage and liberation are of the mind alone.'

Therefore, the ego, which exists at the level of the mind, must be prepared to die, be extinguished, for the sake of love. All its pain derives from refusing to let go.

To love *anyone* requires that you love *everyone*. To love your child is the love of every child. 'I love you, but I hate him' is ignorance. How love reveals itself depends on the moment. No thought comes into it.

Any questions?"

"Then are relationships a waste of time?" Looking around, I saw that the question came from Jenny, who, like me, was relatively new to the group.

"Of course not. A relationship can be the catalyst for uncovering the love that you are. Or it may stifle love because of possessiveness or neediness.

If you are in a relationship, let it be a means for truthfulness, honesty, being straightforward, humility … for love is the bearer of all those qualities.

In love, you are not afraid to tell things how they are. In a healthy relationship, you feel free to express a difficult home truth or be on the receiving end of one. Let your partner hear what doesn't sit right with you. If you can give it, and if you can take it, then your relationship is transformative, as the old ego gets squeezed out of the equation, and more room is made for genuine love.

There are a multitude of dangers that can creep up unseen within a relationship. One of them is *familiarity*. You start to see the other through the prism of the past. You are seeing the mental image of that person; that image may incorporate past negative experiences that you have failed to let go of. You are not responding to the one who is actually in front of you. Is that not a form of mistreatment? That is why, as I have said before, meet everyone as if for the first time, especially those close to you.

Start right now. Whether you've met them recently, or known them for thirty years, or more. Whoever it is, meet that person in *the sacred present*; let what you see be new, fresh. Then love is possible.

The other side of this is the image you have of yourself. Suppose you get hurt, poor thing! Your partner has called you an idiot. But you have an image of yourself that is so much better than that, haven't you? As that image of yourself is a characteristic of the ego, it gets hurt! But if you have no image of yourself, that is, if the real you is present, then there is no resistance to your partner's accusation, so there is nothing to get hurt.

So, a relationship, like any other aspect of your daily life, calls on you to live every moment free of all images, whether of others or yourself. Check this out: everything you think about yourself, or anyone else, is not true. What *is* true is what you are in this moment, or what he or she is in this moment. That is why the curse of gossip, and all idle chatter, is strongly discouraged, because you unjustly dishonour those who are the object of your intolerance.

You've asked about relationships. But in fact, the same challenges apply to every situation. Life as a whole is a

Great Mystery School – each moment, you are either fully present and as such an illumined soul, or you notice that the '*old you*', the ego, has been in charge, and you choose to give him the sack … without any prior notice, I might add.

Yes, time to give the ego the sack! I've never thought of it that way before, but it seems an apt expression.

That's enough for now about love. Since your essential nature is love, am I not speaking to the converted?

Let's take a break."

Chapter 22

After the break, Susan invited us to meditate for a short while before continuing with the afternoon teaching.

This time, I could see the value of meditating with others; there was a kind of group consciousness providing an anchor for the practice. There was a sustained sense of presence in the room in which the individual self wasn't lost but appeared to be stretched out towards a more universal identity.

Susan brought the meditation to a close and then called Elizabeth to the front of the group to share with everyone the proposed creation of a School of Spiritual Philosophy. Elizabeth finished her presentation by asking for suggestions: what to call the School, and what title to give to the course, for example.

Once Elizabeth had returned to her seat, Susan looked thoughtful for a few moments before she addressed the group.

"Our next subject seems to have chosen itself," she ventured with a smile. "On teaching and being a teacher.

Everyone in this group is a potential teacher. For now, with the oversight of Fitz, Elizabeth and Hina will take on this role in the upcoming School. They will be strengthened by being part of this group. When the time is right, some of you may be called upon for the same purpose.

One of the keys to teaching is to see every student as *your* teacher. The one in front of you is *your* teacher. In fact, *everything* is your teacher. There is a lovely poetic reference to this in one of Shakespeare's plays, *As You Like It*. He has one of his characters saying that he

> Finds tongues in trees, books in the running brooks,
> Sermons in stones, and good in everything.

The true teacher is therefore a perpetual student. When in front of a group, the teacher tunes in to its energy, listens, and follows any guidance that reveals itself. This is happening right now, with the teaching on teaching appearing as if from nowhere!

The true teacher is free of any personal agenda other than to follow obediently the dictates of the Spirit within. The teacher serves!

When Jesus sent his disciples out into the villages, they asked him, 'How will we know what to say?' Jesus reassured them that they need not do any preparation, for the Spirit of Truth would be with them, implying that they would voice whatever needed to be said in the *sacred present*.

One will not always need a teacher. In the early days, yes. But when someone reaches a certain level of integration, and the *inner* teacher is strongly present, the good *outer* teacher will recognise this, and will not be surprised at all if that individual moves on. They may, of course, remain friends, but the teacher-student relationship is over.

A teacher does not usually decide to be a teacher; Life decides. The teacher never claims anything for himself; he knows that he is just one link in the chain of teacher-disciple-teacher that has existed since the very beginning.

The teacher must 'walk the talk', must teach by example as well as by words. There is a story about Gandhi which illustrates this:

A woman came with her young son to Mahatma Gandhi's *ashram,* complaining about her child's addiction to sugar.

'My son won't stop eating sugar,' she told him. 'Please, could *you* tell him to stop? He might if you speak to him.'

Gandhi listened to her and then asked her to come back in two weeks.

Two weeks later, the woman and her child returned to Gandhi. He looked at the boy and said firmly, 'You must stop eating sugar.'

The mother was mystified and asked him later, 'Why couldn't you have told him this two weeks ago?'

To which Gandhi replied, 'I couldn't, Madam, because two weeks ago I was still eating sugar myself.'"

Laughter broke out among us all, while Hina and I smiled at one another.

"Gandhi spoke to the boy from a place of integrity. At an energetic level, his words also carried the force that comes when one is living what one speaks.

Now, as I hope I'm being an obedient teacher, I sense that we've had enough teaching about teaching.

May every blessing go with you all.

And '*may all beings know their wholeness.*'"

With that, Susan stood up and began circulating among us.

Chapter 23

Because I was due to have my arranged meeting with Susan, Hina took her leave, and we agreed to meet at her place later in the day.

Once everyone else had gone, Susan approached me and took me into a smaller room, where she invited me to sit with her. She reassured me that our conversation should flow informally and that whatever we said would remain confidential, unless I wanted to share it with anyone.

She began by repeating the welcome she'd offered me and Jenny at the previous meeting. There was a great warmth behind her words, and I felt very relaxed in her presence.

"Everyone brings their own particular energy and intelligence when they join us. Certainly, in terms of days, you are new to us, but your life journey, right up to this moment, has refined you, and brought you to this stage, which could have been lifetimes in the making. You belong, as an equal, rest assured! You possess a nobility and strength of character that go with your open heart and mind. We'll all benefit from you being with us."

"You are kind, saying that," I replied. "First, Fitz came into my life, and I've gained a lot from his wisdom. And now, more recently, Hina ... she's such an amazing woman, and suddenly we seem inseparable! I count myself truly lucky."

"Luck doesn't come into it," Susan countered. "Don't let Fitz hear you speak like that!"

I laughed. "Yes. He'd say we were destined to meet, and that my relationship with Hina represents an important initiation!"

"Now hear *yourself* say that! Remember, this is also a great step for Hina. She was also ready; you came into *her* life at precisely the right moment. If it's *your* destiny, it's hers also. And, at the same time, *her* initiation.

Hina will mature into a fine teacher, and with you beside her, it will happen sooner rather than later. Your inner strength, so natural to you, is your gift to her ... plus, of course, your love."

I was very moved by her faith in me, and for a while I sat quietly processing her words. I noticed that Susan was content to do likewise; it was as if, without words, she held me in a silent, yet very real, spiritual embrace.

"You may wonder why I asked to see you," she eventually said. "I do this with every newcomer. I like to reflect back to them something of their true nature, for that is what I see, beyond any conditioned view they may have of themselves. That's all I've been doing so far with you ... that you may see for yourself what I see.

Is there anything you wish to ask me?"

"There is. As you know, I'm getting great help with meditation from Hina. Are there any other practices I should adopt to support my spiritual growth?"

"There's no need for a whole range of practices, Zac. Keep up the meditation; that is paramount. As far as your day-to-day life is concerned, the key is to remain vigilant. Keep coming back to the present moment – the *sacred present* we like to call it – when you notice you've been lost in thought. Life is always *now*.

Punctuate the day with moments of stillness; don't rush from one activity to another. In other words, be watchful, as life unfolds before you. Live from your awareness, not from your mind!

From this raised level of awareness, you will begin to see that whatever comes your way unsought has its origin in the divine ground – call it God if you like. Meet it with the fullness of your awareness, love, and intelligence. Endeavouring to respond out of your conditioned ego-sense is what causes all the trouble.

Your question concerned 'spiritual growth', did it not? That's something of a misleading concept, Zac; I'd drop that idea. You cannot *grow* something that is already complete in itself! Because *you* are already complete; you *are* love, you *are* the eternal Self ...

You pull a curtain aside to let the sunlight into a room – the light from the sun was already there; you just removed the obstruction. That's all you are doing when you come into the present, manifesting what is already the truth of you.

The more you allow your natural awareness into your moment-to-moment experiences, you'll begin to notice that while the course of events hasn't changed, your attitude has, and this is what matters. You are less of a victim of circumstances. You stand tall.

In the Bhagavad Gita – Fitz has given you a copy, hasn't he? – Arjuna is given the description of the wise man. Such a man remains steadfast in the midst of success and failure; he is never thrown by the unexpected; being free of attachment, his composure never wavers. Of course, the wise man is awake in the fullest sense. In him, there is no ego-based sense that 'I-am-the-doer'.

So, Zac, what I have just spoken about, make it your intention for your daily life. Don't worry whenever you forget, that is inevitable. As many times as you *notice* that you are locked in thought, just as many times you can return to the present. You just keep starting again with no concern about so-called previous failures. In time, it gets easier.

Enough talking. Let's close by sharing a moment's quiet."

Susan closed her eyes, and I followed suit. As I sat in the stillness, I was aware of being filled with a huge amount of love.

We stood, and Susan drew me into a hug. She was like a teacher, a mother and a friend, all rolled into one.

Feeling very happy and blessed, I left Geoff's house. I was looking forward to sharing this love and joy with Hina.

Chapter 24

When I arrived at Hina's apartment, to my surprise, it was Fitz who opened the door. He ushered me inside and took me into the living room. It was clear that Hina was not at home.

Without waiting for any question from me, Fitz immediately put me in the picture.

"First thing, Zac. Hina is OK, but she's had an accident," he explained, and seeing me begin to tense up, he quickly continued. "Hear me out! She's going to be fine. Let me tell you what happened.

Hina phoned and asked me to come here as quickly as I could; she'd explain why when I arrived. I found her tearful and unusually shaken. She'd had an unexpected blackout; in other words, a temporary loss of consciousness. She told me that when she awoke, she was on the living room floor, next to the dining table, but didn't remember how she got there, or how long she'd been out. Her right cheek was bruised, and her neck ached. She assumed she must have fallen, and maybe hit the table on the way down.

I gave her some water, and we just sat quietly for a while. There are different reasons why someone might experience a blackout, some quite serious, others less so. To be on the safe side, I immediately offered to take Hina to a nearby private hospital, where she could get a proper check-up. She agreed, and we went.

It's an excellent hospital. They agreed to give her an MRI brain scan tomorrow morning – it's a pain-free process, which means she'll be there overnight. After that, she should be able to return home."

"How was she when you left her?" I asked.

"She'd calmed down a lot by then, and she sent me back here to collect a couple of books for her."

"Thanks for helping her, Fitz. I'll get going now, so I can visit her before it's too late this evening."

"Let me take you there," Fitz offered, "I'll just drop you off, and you can take these books in with you."

Fitz gave me two small books, both of them works of Swami Vivekananda, one of India's best-known spiritual teachers of the twentieth century. He also passed over the keys to Hina's flat, so that I could return them to her.

It was small as hospitals go, and after enquiring at reception, I found my way to a private ward on the second floor. I went into the room slowly, endeavouring not to disturb her, in case she was asleep. She was wearing a hospital gown and lying quietly with her eyes closed, so I carefully and noiselessly moved a chair to her bedside and sat down. I noticed the slightly swollen area on her right cheek. She stirred shortly afterwards and opened her eyes. When she saw me, she reached out a hand, with a somewhat weak smile, and asked me to draw closer. I did so, kissing her gently, before sitting back and meeting her gaze.

"Hina, what have you done to yourself?" I blurted out. "Silly question, I know. Fitz has filled me in; he dropped me off here. Oh, and these are the books you asked for."

"Thanks. I wasn't sure if you'd come," Hina said.

"Why wouldn't I? I'm your *darling*, remember. Nothing else matters, right now, except you getting better."

Hina didn't feel up to a lot of talking, so I just sat with her for a while, until she started to doze off. Before leaving, I whispered that I'd be back to see her tomorrow, not knowing how much she had heard.

Once outside the ward, I sought out one of the nurses who was looking after her. She assured me that Hina had eaten a little, and when I enquired about tomorrow, she advised me to come back in the afternoon, but not before 1.30 pm, since the morning would be taken up with getting Hina prepared for her scan, followed by the procedure itself.

I agreed to that, and asked if she wouldn't mind making sure that Hina was told in the morning to expect me in the afternoon.

Chapter 25

Fitz phoned me early the next morning and asked about my visit to Hina at the hospital. I told him about my brief time with her, and that I'd visit her in the afternoon, and all being well, I'd accompany her home. Glad of that, he said he'd catch up with us later in the day.

As I still had Hina's keys, I did some shopping before visiting her flat and placing some essentials in her fridge and larder, as well as topping up a bowl of fruit I'd noticed she kept in the living room. I went into each room, making sure that everything was clean and in good order for her homecoming.

As I had some time to spare, I returned to the high street for a bite and to investigate some of the clothes shops. I ended up coming away with a maroon cashmere cardigan, which I hoped was the right size for Hina; I had described her to the shop assistant, who then helped me to make the choice. She'd assured me, as she wrapped and placed it in a bag, that it could be returned and exchanged for a different size if necessary.

I arrived at the hospital just before 2.00 pm. Hina was now dressed in her own clothes and sitting on the bed, with one of the books I'd delivered to her yesterday open beside her. Before she could get off the bed to greet me, I'd reached her side and wrapped her in my arms.

"Go easy," she gasped, "I'm delicate! No, don't you dare go easy; carry on!"

We laughed because of the simple joy of just being together.

Once we'd disentangled, I showed her the bag from the shop. She whooped with delight as she took out the garment and spread it out on the bed.

"It's lovely, and one of my favourite colours. Zac, you shouldn't've, it must have cost a fortune!"

"I didn't look at the price. For a priceless princess, that would have been a sin!"

Our mood soon shifted away from the banter, and we began discussing the current situation and making arrangements for the afternoon.

"Tell me about the scan," I asked.

"It wasn't difficult, Zac; I just lay down on a kind of conveyor belt, and it gradually glided into the scanner. My head went slowly into a kind of tube, while photos were taken of my brain. It lasted about half an hour. It was a bit noisy, but otherwise OK. I was told that I should have the results by Wednesday."

"In that case, as that's all over and done with, are you able to leave?"

"Can't wait – I'm packed and ready to go."

I called a taxi, and on the way to Hina's place, I suggested she collect what she needed and come and stay with me for a few days. Hina told me she was taking the week off from work, something the medical staff at the hospital had suggested would help with her recuperation.

Once at my home, I was boyfriend turned into carer! I told Hina that her job was to rest, mine to fuss over her for the time being. She quite liked the idea; said I was an angel!

During the evening, Fitz phoned to check on how Hina was doing. Hina didn't feel like speaking, so I explained to him that she was a little tired, physically and emotionally, but otherwise seemed OK. Fitz said he would call round in the morning to see us, which I welcomed, knowing that his calmness and wisdom were an asset whatever the circumstances.

Hina retired for the night quite soon after Fitz's call; I told her that I would join her a little later. I wanted to sit quietly for a while and reflect a little on this current situation. A single phrase kept recurring in my mind while I was sitting in the silence: *Nothing happens without a reason*. Did this apply to Hina's unexpected blackout?

Perhaps Fitz would shed some light on this during his visit.

Chapter 26

I was late to bed and early to rise. When Hina finally surfaced, her breakfast was ready. She smiled as she saw me notice that she was wearing the cardigan I had bought for her. The prolonged rest seemed to have worked wonders; she looked fresher and brighter. I'd already eaten, but I sat down and joined her while she tucked into her porridge.

"Zac, thanks; this is just what I need," she said gratefully.

"Sorry, it's not up to your culinary skills, Hina; just basic food."

"Basic is good, right now."

Once breakfast was over, I insisted on clearing everything up myself, knowing we would be getting a visit shortly from Fitz. Hina seemed content to give way for now, but I had a feeling that the fully vibrant Hina would be back quite soon.

Fitz phoned to say he'd give us the morning, and he turned up not long after we'd had a light lunch. Hina and I were delighted to see him, and we all sat down together in the living room.

After sharing a little about her experience at the hospital, the scan, and how she'd been for the rest of yesterday, I could see Hina looking rather inquisitively at Fitz, as if she were probing his thoughts.

Fitz smiled. "Yes, something is churning within these 'little grey cells' as the great Poirot might say. I have a sense of what may be happening with you, Hina – what this blackout is all about – but I don't wish to voice it right now. That would not be appropriate.

I'd prefer, if you agree to it, that we work with a form of spiritual enquiry that I've used a few times before. In other words, we would be working together to find the truth that lies behind this turn of events. It is the truth that liberates, that brings about healing. Nothing is guaranteed, of course, but also nothing is lost.

What do you say, Hina?"

"Yes, please. I know you have a nose for these things, and I trust you. Can we do it now?"

"Not now. I'd like to give you another day at least, whilst you are recovering. You still need that. Also, I'd prefer that we use a neutral setting; I'm sure Geoff would be happy for us to use his place."

Hina said she was happy on both counts.

I then thought it appropriate to share with them the recurring phrase that had visited me the night before.

"I kept getting this thought last night – that *nothing happens without a reason*. Is this relevant to the spiritual enquiry you mentioned?"

"It is," Fitz said. "One of the so-called great Christian mystics, Meister Eckhart, wrote: 'Divinity aims at the greatest good of all things.' Whatever comes to you unexpectedly has a purpose, and that purpose, however it might appear at the time, is for soul growth, for greater consciousness.

Hina, keep tomorrow free. I'll get back to you about a suggested time, most probably at Geoff's."

"Can Zac come with me?" Hina asked.

"That's entirely up to you. As long as you can give yourself fully to the process. I suggest you discuss it after I leave."

Once Fitz had left, I reassured Hina that I was completely OK with her meeting him at Geoff's place without me being present. But Hina insisted that she'd like me to be there, certain that it wouldn't be a hindrance. Instead, it would give her added strength to face whatever was going to come up during the enquiry process.

Chapter 27

As it happened, we had to wait an extra day for Hina's session with Fitz because Geoff's house was in use on Tuesday for a family gathering. Fitz collected us on Wednesday afternoon and drove us to Geoff's house. Hina was in good spirits; four days had elapsed since her blackout and fall, and she was becoming more and more like the vivacious young woman we knew and loved.

During the morning, we received the results of Hina's brain scan from the hospital. The results were negative, meaning that nothing abnormal had shown up. It suggested that Hina's blackout episode most likely had a psychological basis to it, something that Fitz had hinted at during his visit on Monday. This, of course, put me in a good mood. I had faith that Fitz would find a way to uncover both the cause of this incident and a pathway towards healing. What emerged was a big surprise for me, less so for Hina, and no surprise at all for Fitz.

We used the same room where Susan and I had met the previous Saturday. Fitz placed a chair at the back of the room for me, and two chairs centrally for him and Hina, with a box of tissues strategically placed on an adjacent table.

His instruction to me was to simply sit still, say nothing, and, his exact words, "be a beacon of presence." He intimated that this would be a helpful contribution energetically to his work with Hina.

Once he and Hina were settled, Fitz took a few moments to guide Hina into a level of stillness in preparation for the process he had in mind for her. He told her to keep her eyes closed. When he felt she was sufficiently centred, he began with a question:

"Hina, can you go back in your mind to last Saturday, to the moment you awoke in your living room after the blackout?"

"Yes."

"Good. Now go back to what you were doing in the time leading up to that."

"I don't remember the actual moment of blacking out."

"No, you wouldn't. Tell me what you *do* remember of that afternoon, before the blackout."

"I'd been shopping. I got home, put the food away, changed into fresh clothes ... and then I sat down in the living room. I can't remember anything else after that."

"That's great. Now, that last thing, sitting down in the living room. Can you remember what you were thinking?"

"I was thinking about Zac – Zac coming round later – Zac being with Susan ... and ... and ..." Hina burst into tears.

"Stay with me, Hina; this is important," Fitz said in a firm yet kindly manner, as he handed her a paper tissue.

Once Hina had calmed down, Fitz continued the questioning:

"When you were thinking about Zac being with Susan, what were you feeling? Bring your attention to the place in your body where this feeling is strongest. Can you do that?"

Hina took a few deep breaths. "Yes ... there's a really tight knot around my solar plexus ... there's also a sick feeling there ..."

"Right there, where you are feeling sick, what if you could name the emotion lodged in the sickness ... take your time ... can you describe it?"

"I can't believe it; I love Susan ... I was feeling jealous ... that jealousy is still here, mixed up with anger, and fear ... fear of losing Zac ... it's so stupid ..."

"Hina," Fitz interrupted, "don't analyse it, keep your mind at bay. What is important is the pure emotion that you are experiencing right now. Stay with that. What was the strongest feeling present?"

"A kind of dread; of being discarded, being abandoned ... feeling unworthy ..."

"Stay with this, Hina ... Is that feeling here now?"

"Yes ... yes, it is."

"Listen carefully. Have you ever experienced this mix of emotions before? Don't rush; see if there was a similar experience previously ... Allow the memory to surface naturally. It will ..."

"Yes, yes. I remember. I was fifteen ... still at school. I had a boyfriend, from the same school, a little older than me, but we kept it secret because he was from a strict family who generally arranged marriages for their children.

His name was Ashwin; he swore he loved me, and I believed him. He was tall, strong, and clever. I felt protected. He said that nothing his family tried would stop us from being together. I gave my heart to him ..."

Hina stopped for a while and made use of more paper tissues.

"What happened, Hina?" Fitz asked encouragingly.

"One day, he didn't turn up at school. I texted him several times, but got no reply. I phoned, but each time his mobile was switched off. After a few days, I spoke to Jamie, one of his friends at school. What Jamie told me ... my world just fell apart.

His parents had lined up a girl for him, the daughter of one of his father's business associates. If he married this girl, he would be given a secure place in the business. He would be provided with a house and a car of his choice. If he refused, he would get nothing, and because of the embarrassment caused, he'd never get any family support again ... Jamie's words were, 'He just caved in.'"

"What's important is how this affected you inwardly," Fitz said.

"I was devastated. At home, I spent as much time in my room as I could get away with. Each day, I seemed to be pining away, hardly eating. After a few days of this, I told my mum I felt ill and wanted time off school. And I refused to see a doctor.

One evening, I felt powerful waves of despair engulfing me ... that's the last thing I remember before I blacked out. Fortunately, when I regained consciousness, I was on my bed and unhurt. And although at first I felt disorientated, that sense of despair had waned, and I allowed myself to fall asleep. I told no one about the blackout. This is the first time I've spoken about it."

From then on, Fitz encouraged Hina to allow that experience of despair and abandonment to be fully felt in the present. He called on her to allow that emotion to be as strong as it wanted to be, to not resist it. As she complied, Hina described how that feeling gave way to a fierce anger, and Fitz asked her to respond in the same way to the anger, giving it full range, until it too subsided, to be followed by an aggravating sense of hurt.

All through this process, going through these layers of emotion, Fitz's love and care for Hina were evident, and her trust in him was strong enough not to give up before the completion of their work together.

After the layer of hurt, something of a change occurred.

"Tell me what is present now?" Fitz asked.

"I feel completely empty, there's nothing. It all seems very dark. There's a sense of resignation ..."

"Excellent," said Fitz.

I marvelled at Fitz's skill in keeping Hina on track, and never deviating from being wholeheartedly with whatever showed up as well as, when necessary, keeping her away from the story associated with the changing emotions.

Fitz encouraged Hina to completely welcome this onset of emptiness, and as she did so, she described a feeling of relief starting to fill the space of the dark emptiness. I noticed how, as she said this, there were signs of relaxation in her body; she even shifted into a more comfortable position. With Fitz's continued encouragement, Hina began to describe how the relief she was feeling began transforming into waves of peace, which were now gradually filling the emptiness.

Fitz was not content to let it stop there.

"What's at the very heart of this peace?" he asked. "Just dive in, free fall into this beautiful peace ... I wonder what you will discover."

"There is so much love here," Hina replied.

"Keep opening more and more into this love ..."

"Oh my gosh, there is so much love. It seems unending. It's everywhere ..."

"Does this love have any limits?"

"No, it's vast, boundless ..."

"And you, where do you fit into this boundless love?"

"There's no separation at all. I *am* this love, always, always ...

"That's right, you *are* infinite love ... staying centred in this love, *as* this love, what do you unquestionably know?"

"That I am totally free, beyond all harm, aware of an incredible presence that's impossible to describe, but it overlooks everything with this unconditional love; everything is held in it, always, always ..."

"Tell me, how are you in relation to this indescribable reality whose unconditional love holds everything within it?"

"I am it! I am infinite love, pure, ever-free."

For a while, Fitz and Hina remained silent.

Then Fitz began a new line of questioning.

"Can this love ever leave you?"

"Never," Hina replied forcefully. "It's impossible. How could I leave myself? I *am* love, as I've already said."

"You are. What about if Zac left you?"

"He can go. He'd have my blessing."

"Where would that leave you?"

"The same. Being love, giving love, open to love."

"OK. Now bring to mind Ashwin, the boyfriend from your schooldays. What would you say to him if he was here now?"

"I'd understand. At that time in his life, Ashwin didn't have the strength to resist the pressure from his family. In reality, he was still a boy. It was as if he was staring down a bottomless abyss unless he conformed. I feel compassion for him. Now I can let it all go."

"Speak to him as if he were here. In a way, he is, energetically. Express your sincere forgiveness now."

"Ashwin, I forgive you completely. I know that to some extent you did love me, but it wasn't enough to stand against your family. You did your best. I hope you find a way to be happy, wherever you are."

"Now, Hina, gently open your eyes ... take a few moments to re-orientate yourself, here, now, in this room with me and Zac."

Turning to me, Fitz said, "Just stay seated where you are for a moment, there's one more thing, and then we are finished."

Fitz then turned back to Hina.

"Hina, bring to mind the thoughts and emotions that were present just before Saturday's blackout. Just as a memory, there's no need to manufacture them or bring them back. But whilst bearing in mind those thoughts and emotions, speak to Zac.

Zac, you just listen without interruption."

Hina looked at me, and as she did so my heart seemed to burst with love; but trusting Fitz, I stayed still and simply listened.

"Zac, I'm so sorry that I gave in to feelings of jealousy about you being with Susan. I now realise that it was that little hurt teenage girl who still somehow haunted me, carrying with her that old fear of being abandoned. I really love Susan. I love you. That fear has been completely swept away now; it can never return.

Please forgive me, Zac, for allowing that feeling to overwhelm me, making me mistrust what we share."

Fitz said to me, "OK, Zac, you can speak now to Hina."

"Hina, there's nothing to forgive. We all carry baggage from the past. I'm just so glad that you've disposed of this particular burden. I know what you are, and in the last hour or so, you've shown it so clearly. If you agree, I wish to continue walking with you, discovering more about love, and if it comes to it, being brave enough and truthful enough, with you, to deal with anything that dares to rear its ugly head and threaten our love ... which of course is impossible."

At that, Fitz stood up, and in his customary manner said:

"Right. Time for me to go. You two, stay as long as you like, then let yourself out ..."

Before he could reach the door, Hina and I simultaneously rushed him and wrapped him in a strong embrace, almost knocking him over, as we laughed and celebrated what had been a very healing outcome.

“Fitz, I love you too,” Hina chimed, and I concurred.

Finally, Fitz was released, an amused look on his face, as he left us alone in the room.

Chapter 28

After Fitz had departed, Hina indicated that right now we didn't need to talk about what had just happened. We had both been present, we both knew what was true about the two of us, and it was important to allow plenty of time for integration.

Too often, she pointed out, the mind interferes, clouds over, and complicates the simplicity of the precious moment of realisation. The rest of the day should be treated like a sabbath so that we could remain present to what is *now*.

During the next few days, we did indeed manage to avoid talking about our relationship. Hina stayed with me for the rest of the week, returning to her place on the Sunday. She wanted to get herself organised for her work back at the bookshop on Monday. Spending time together, with such ease, it was apparent that our lives were now intertwined; we were *walking together in love* as I had expressed it at the end of Hina's healing session.

And yet we also knew it was important not to stifle one another. Being together did not mean that we had to do *everything* together.

I was reminded of a passage in one of my books, *The Prophet*, by the poet Kahlil Gibran, in a section on Marriage:

> Let there be spaces in your togetherness.
> And let the winds of the heavens dance between you.
> Love one another, but make not a bond of love.

Let it rather be a moving sea between the shores of your souls.

We could read different books, be inspired by different teachers, meet separately with different friends, and so on. We did not need to keep tabs on each other, although we'd naturally enjoy sharing what each of us was up to. Both of us were committed to our relationship being healthy, knowing that sometimes we might have to face difficult choices. We also believed that "love conquers all!"

Of course, we enjoyed being together. But we also had commitments to attend to independently. Apart from her work in the bookshop, Hina had meetings to do with setting up her counselling practice, and also making preparations with Fitz and Elizabeth for the opening of the School of Spiritual Philosophy.

I made several trips to my school. There were resources to obtain, especially for my GCSE and A Level classes. The English Department also liked to meet during this quiet period to review the syllabus for the lower school.

One thing we made sure we did together was to attend the next group meeting on the first Saturday in August. We also considered taking a break somewhere special together for a few days during the following weeks.

Once we were at Geoff's house, we discovered that Susan was visiting family abroad, so Fitz stepped in to lead the afternoon's teaching. Others were also missing for holidays, but I estimated that there were still about 9 or 10 of us present.

Once Fitz had taken his place, he invited us to meditate for about 20 minutes, after which he intended to give the afternoon's teaching. At the end of the meditation period, he kept us in the silence for a minute or two, while he slowly swept his gaze around, making eye contact with each of us individually. Once he'd connected with everyone, he began to teach.

"I've been asked to speak about *non-attachment*. I will do that, but I'll come at it indirectly. There is a bigger picture in which attachment and non-attachment form a part. Attachment comes about through a particular condition that afflicts virtually the entire human race. That condition is *identification*.

It is a condition that is so deeply entrenched in nearly everyone that most people are unaware of it, believing themselves to be quite normal and free. The identification is with the body and the mind. As a result of this identification, the simple knowing of our true Self, who we are essentially, is clouded over, obscured, and we think we are this body and this mind. By the way, I'm using the word 'mind' as shorthand for the stream of ever-shifting thoughts, images, attitudes, beliefs, and so on, that we take to be 'me'. It is this imaginary, limited self with its fears, desires and ambitions that we have become slaves to every day. It is an *imaginary* self in the sense that it keeps changing, and in moments of clarity, it is not there at all. Then, when the shifting thought patterns return, that moment of clarity is relegated to a memory, which is just another thought.

Over time, this condition of identification has invaded our language, the way we speak. For example, concerning the body, someone would most likely say, 'I'm cold', and not 'my *body* is cold'. With regard to the mind, someone might say, 'I'm thinking', rather than 'this *thought* is here'. Generally, people do not realise that most thoughts just enter the mental space unsought! Thinking happens!

All the dysfunctional forms of behaviour that we see going on around us are due to this identification with body and mind. Jealousy, hatred, fears of all kinds, pride, greed, and every other negative emotion you can think of are all effects of this identification. In their extreme form, they give rise to social conflict and wars between nations. Identification breeds fanaticism in religion and politics; identification leads to obsessions and addictions.

It is important to observe this, especially in oneself, and be honest enough to acknowledge it. Unless we do, we will not do anything about it, and nothing will change.

This identification is, in some traditions, likened to sleep, a 'waking sleep', in which we react to people and events in a conditioned manner, like machines or robots.

On the spiritual path, there are tools to help us 'wake up' and let go of this conditioning which forms the layers of identification veiling the Self. One very important tool is that of *discernment*, known for thousands of years in both Eastern and Western traditions.

In the East, the most well-known example is described by the Indian sage *Shankara* in a work entitled *The Crest-Jewel of Discernment*. *Shankara* uses the Sanskrit word *viveka,* which is translated sometimes as 'discernment', sometimes 'discrimination'."

Fitz picked up a book from a small pile on the table beside him.

"Here are a few verses from that text:

Under the veil of five sheaths, the Self is concealed,
like water covered by an accumulation of sedge.
On the removal of that sedge, the perfectly pure water
that quenches the thirst appears, unobstructed,
giving immediate joy.
When the five sheaths are eliminated, the Self will appear –

pure, being the essence of constant bliss, supreme
and shining with its own splendour.
To be free from bondage, the wise disciple must discern
between the Self and the not-Self.
This alone is the way to joyfully recognise
the real Self as Being-Consciousness-Bliss.

Then there is the Western tradition. This goes back to the Greek philosophical teachings whose influence can be seen in the writings of the early Christian Desert Fathers.

For example, in the fourth century, St Anthony regarded discernment – in the original Greek, *diakrisis* – as the greatest of all virtues. He called it the 'eye and lamp of the soul', embodying wisdom, intelligence and perceptiveness. In some of those early writings, discernment was associated with 'the guarding of the heart', 'attention' and 'watchfulness.'

After the break, we will consider how to *practice* discernment."

Before leaving the room, Fitz approached Hina and me and invited us to remain after the meeting had finished for a short "catch-up."

Chapter 29

Once we had reconvened in the main room, Fitz advised us that, as well as the regular sitting practice of meditation, our spiritual armoury would be much strengthened if we adopted the practice of *discernment*, separating the *not*-Self from our real Self.

"It is a practice which has stood the test of time," he assured us. "Those of you who've been introduced to this practice before, please allow today's introduction to serve as a useful reminder.

As you practice discernment, you are *dis-identifying* with what is observed, which brings about *non-attachment* naturally. You start by observing the sensations of the body. Be clear; you are not *rejecting* the body or its sensations. You are observing them and at the same time knowing that you are *not* the body or its sensations. As an aid, you might employ the words '*not this*' to what is observed.

As the practice progresses, you start to bring in the level of thoughts. Allow yourself, without any real effort, to observe every thought that passes through your mind. Be a detached observer. As an analogy, it's like someone looking through a window at passers-by on the street outside. In this case, what passes by is all the mental traffic.

Make no effort to manipulate or change what is happening. Just watch! Thoughts will come, linger, or pass and be replaced by new incoming thoughts. You may find yourself commenting on the thoughts: seeing them as good or bad, urgent or trifling. Such comments are just more thoughts, thoughts about thoughts; see them, and let them pass.

Gradually, you will notice that you are *not* your thoughts. Thoughts happen in you, the observer, or the awareness itself. Again, if it helps, you can use the words '*not this*' as a way of detaching yourself from what you are observing.

More difficult to detect are ingrained attitudes or predispositions towards things, situations, or people; you just need to notice these as you observe from deeper and deeper within your watchful presence. When you are at one in that presence, you know that you are not those attitudes or predispositions.

Whatever arises, however subtle, it is separate from who you are. Render it powerless with '*not this*'. Not just the words, but their meaning.

The object of our work, *The Work,* is to bring greater consciousness into ourselves, so that we can *see* the vast inner traffic of thoughts and feelings within. Then we can become *selective.* What we give our attention to, we enliven and strengthen; what we withdraw our attention from, weakens and eventually dies.

Suppose you notice moods, thoughts, and feelings that depress you, that eat you, making you negative, or self-righteous, and the like. Are you going to give such moods, such states, your consciousness, your strength? Or are you going to separate from them and allow your true Self to show itself?

Through regular practice, you gradually free yourself from the entanglements of various degrees of identification. You then begin to be more in tune with your deeper, wiser nature, and with finer levels of intention or motivation, more compassionate and universal in quality.

What are you doing? You are letting go into the boundless landscape of being, that which does not come and does not go! Through such *discernment*, you become more 'in tune with the infinite'!"

Having described the practice, Fitz then guided us into what he said was just one way of going about it. He first made it clear that he wanted us to understand the *principle* of the practice, so that our own innate wisdom could work with it in a variety of ways, depending on the changing circumstances.

After suggesting we sit in a balanced, erect, and comfortable position, with eyes closed, Fitz led us through a discernment process which began with the body and its sensations, and continued through whatever thoughts appeared, to the more subtle levels of attitude and predispositions. He stressed that these latter might not be apparent now, but would certainly come under the spotlight over time as the practice was refined.

Towards the end of the practice, he invited us to rest in and as the pure, ever-free being, unborn and undying, the one Self in all.

Fitz closed the session by pointing out that, unlike the regular practice of meditation in which we are seated, the *discernment* practice, once we inwardly make it our own, could be practised at any time, even in the midst of action. This was its great value.

Until the whole of life becomes a "work of art!"

Chapter 30

Once the group had dispersed, Fitz ushered me and Hina into one of the smaller rooms where we could converse in comfort. It had been two weeks since Hina's blackout, and Fitz was keen to check on her welfare. Hina was adamant that she had now fully recovered and that the healing gained with Fitz's help a few days ago had been life-changing. Time would tell. I was interested to see what deep insights Fitz would offer us; I was sure they would be forthcoming.

Fitz suggested that the blackout had been a perfect demonstration of the protective power of nature and that it had effectively prevented Hina from sabotaging her relationship with me.

"The subsequent healing work we undertook was also important," he added, speaking to Hina, "as it now means you're able to see Zac without any emotional demons from the past intervening when you least expect it."

Fitz then turned to both of us and continued:

"In a way, it's a lesson for all of us to be on our guard whenever any form of disagreement or friction appears within a relationship, not to give space for it to grow, but to explore it, uncover its cause, see what it's made of, and discern its nature. It can be anything from a genuine insight that one needs to take note of and act on, to some old emotional history needing to be seen and dissolved, similar to what we dealt with the other day."

Fitz now seemed to be happy about Hina's well-being, and our conversation turned to other matters. He and Hina made some further arrangements to meet up with Elizabeth during the coming week, before Hina and I departed to spend the rest of the day together.

I asked Hina what she would like to do, and she said we should go back to her place first, because she had a surprise in store for me. We could then decide how to spend the rest of the evening.

At Hina's place, we relaxed for a while with hot drinks, and then Hina left me in the living room while she went to get changed.

At this stage, it was a mystery to me what this "surprise" might be, but I was happy to play along and see what happened. When Hina returned to me, she was wearing a beautiful red-coloured sari that I'd not seen before. It was decorated with numerous small flowers arranged in geometric patterns.

"Do you like it?" she asked.

"It's beautiful ... suits you ..." I began, looking into her eyes, which were soft and moist, and not knowing what else to say.

"It belonged to *ammaji*, that is to say, my grandma," she rejoined. "I first wanted to make this connection with my family before speaking with you. I'm not sure why, but it seemed important."

"Well, I must admit, I'm enjoying the way you look. Is this the surprise you referred to?"

"Only the beginning. Zac, please just listen to what I have to say. Come closer, hold my hands, I'm a little nervous ..."

We sat together while I cradled her hands in mine. *Where is this going?*

"Zac, ever since we met, I've been aware that, after any period of absence, there's a wonderful feeling of renewal whenever you return to my side. It's happened enough times now for me to be certain that we are meant for each other."

Hina hesitated, took a deep breath, and then continued:

"Phew! Here we go! I know that Asian etiquette is about to be shamelessly blown away … But I don't care.

Zac, please marry me! Let's share our lives completely!"

Tears came to my eyes as it dawned on me what was happening and why I was feeling overjoyed. I drew Hina even closer to me and took a few breaths before I replied.

"The most wonderful, and the best surprise I've ever had! Seriously, though, I feel as if we're already married; our hearts are one, Hina. Yes! No question, yes! You beat me to it … you're so brave, darling."

We held each other, without speaking, for a while. Usually, it was Hina who would say a wise thing or two about any situation we were in, but on this occasion, I found myself doing the honours.

"Hina, let's keep this to ourselves for a day or two; let's savour this moment! There'll be things to discuss soon enough, like changing our living arrangements, sharing with our families and friends, how to celebrate … and much more. I don't know about you, but this is such a precious gift … Ah, Hina, your look says it all; I don't need to say any more."

"No, lovely *fiancée*! You read me well. And I agree: I'd also prefer to share this moment alone with you. First of all, Zac, practical things. It seems ages since we've eaten. There's not much food here, I'm afraid. Should we go out, or order a takeaway?"

I laughed. "Our first big decision! If you're happy, I'd prefer to spend the evening here, alone with you. I'll get on the phone; tell me what you fancy."

That settled it. It was our first evening as an engaged couple, and I hoped all our decision-making in the future would be just as easy, knowing that to be most unlikely in the years ahead. *Doesn't Life have a way of throwing up all sorts of challenges to test what we are made of?*

It was the end of a very special day, talking late into the night, learning more about each other, and eventually giving way to tiredness in each other's arms, until the new day beckoned.

Chapter 31

During the next few days, Hina and I slowly drew the threads of our new status together. Among other things, we decided that we owed it to our parents to put them in the picture first. Hina phoned ahead, and we visited Mr and Mrs Jaiswal on the Thursday of that week. They were so lovely. They welcomed me like a long-lost son returning to the fold.

My own parents, living in the outer reaches of Dorset, had to make do, for the time being, with a WhatsApp video call. I'd already told them about Hina a few weeks earlier, and they were delighted with this more direct opportunity to connect with their future daughter-in-law.

We decided Fitz would be the next person to inform and that we'd do this in person. So Hina invited him over, and he happily accepted; he'd visit us the following morning. Before his arrival, we'd settled on a number of things that we wished to bring to his attention, knowing that we would undoubtedly benefit from his wisdom.

He arrived the next morning with a cardboard box in tow, which he mysteriously left by the door as he entered. After the customary greetings among friends and a round of herbal tea, Fitz was soon into his usual direct approach to things.

"Well, don't keep me waiting. You've clearly invited me here for a reason. Fire away!"

Hina looked at me, then took the lead: "Fitz, we are engaged! I completely broke with all proper Indian decorum, and ... I asked Zac to marry me! Oh my God, this lovely man has agreed to be my husband. It's been a whirlwind journey, I know; just over a month since we met. Ridiculous. But both of us are completely certain we are meant for each other."

"Congratulations," Fitz replied, looking both delighted and serious at the same time. "Of course, I could sense this was happening a few weeks ago. That's a slight hint of an apology, Hina, about moving so fast – just let it go. I've known couples who acted far too soon after years; the situation is different for you. You're both very mature. Life has prepared you, and when you were ready, your paths crossed, and your two destinies drew together.

When destinies align, as in your case, there is an injection of power, spiritual power. Everyone must follow their own path, but two paths may draw close and strengthen each other. That is what is happening here."

"Thank you," I said. "That means a lot. You've clearly described what we both feel about this. You've brilliantly put into words what I know intuitively." Hina nodded in agreement.

"Just hold on a minute," Fitz said, getting up. He went back and retrieved the cardboard box. "This is your engagement present," he said, handing it to Hina.

"But how did you know?" she exclaimed.

"I notice things, that's all. Just open the box."

Hina worked away at the box and soon had the lid off, lifting out something heavily wrapped in coloured paper. Once all the layers had been removed, a beautiful statuette, about ten inches in height, of a female figure emerged.

"It's *Lakshmi*!" Hina cried. "My God, it's beautiful."

"*Lakshmi* represents what I wish for both of you," Fitz explained. "She's usually referred to as the Goddess of Wealth or Abundance. However, if you're in tune with your divine nature, you know that you lack nothing; you are complete. Hina and Zac, may your life together be one of increasing inner riches."

"Such a lovely gesture, Fitz," I said, hugging him. "We'll put *Lakshmi* in a special place in our home, wherever that turns out to be. Early days, though. Hina and I haven't got that far yet. What's it made of?"

"It's a bronze."

Before I could ask more about the gift, Hina placed the statuette on a side table, clearly deciding that it was time to ask Fitz some of the questions we had for him.

"Fitz. So … Where to begin? OK! We wanted to wait a while, enjoying this new path we've chosen, but then we realised that we have to start thinking about the wedding, because they can take ages to plan. We don't want a traditional church affair. After all, Zac and I are from different religious backgrounds. We'd much prefer a meaningful expression of the love we share, and for our marriage to be blessed, but in a more universal way."

"Shouldn't be a problem," Fitz stated in a matter-of-fact tone. "You create your own celebration. You write your own vows, so that you mean what you say to each other, rather than parroting the words from a prayer book service.

You can incorporate rituals, music, and readings from different spiritual sources – whatever your hearts resonate with."

Hina and I looked at each other. "We can design our own wedding?" Hina queried.

"Of course! It's your love, your life, your special day. You make arrangements with the local registry office. Tick all the legal boxes, say, the day before. Two witnesses required. Then you are married in the eyes of the law.

After that, you *celebrate* your marriage, which I observe already exists in reality, with your family and friends. It can end with a blessing from someone of your choosing. Bear in mind, even that, the blessing, is simply demonstrating what you already enjoy by virtue of your loving union. It's a blessing which also happens to overflow to those who care about you both."

We continued to pursue Fitz with our questions and, unsurprisingly, all his suggestions were in perfect alignment with how Hina and I wanted things to happen. It included the possibility, assuming our numbers weren't too large, of celebrating our marriage at Geoff's house. Fitz was certain that Geoff would be delighted to support us this way.

Fitz also had a friend who was an Interfaith Minister, experienced in helping to create and lead wedding ceremonies for couples from diverse backgrounds. He offered to pay her fee as a wedding present. *Talk about abundance!*

We eventually noticed that the afternoon had crept upon us, and we invited Fitz to stay and eat with us. However, he excused himself, saying he had some duties to attend to and he would catch up with us in a few days.

After he'd gone, Hina and I sat down to catch our breath. We then decided to go out for lunch.

Chapter 32

The next week or so flew past in a blur of activity. Hina and I decided to take advantage of the fact that I was on holiday, and not due back at school until early September. At some point, we would make decisions about where we would set up home, but in the meantime, it made sense for Hina to move in with me. I had enough space, but we had to buy extra furniture to accommodate her clothes and belongings.

Although that wasn't the main reason, it also made financial sense, relieving Hina of the monthly rent for her flat. It also meant that I could give Hina some extra support as she built up her spiritual counselling practice.

Hina continued to meet with Fitz and Elizabeth regarding her two new projects, both due to begin in September. I had my own tasks to attend to, including arrangements for the upcoming new school year. This included drafting a programme for the proposed after-school meditation sessions. Whilst I was confident that I could draw on my experience for the meditation practice itself, I also wanted to introduce, in small doses at a time, aspects of the wisdom teaching which, for me, were so life-changing.

On one of the days when Hina was away at meetings, I decided to visit the local library to see what books were available on meditation. Maybe I would find a suitable book for beginners that I could recommend to the after-school group. Who knows, such a book or books might also help to clarify ideas that were already forming within me about how to proceed in a practical step-by-step way.

The library was something of a community centre. In addition to the rooms full of fiction and non-fiction, there was a children's section, meeting rooms, a reference section on the first floor, and a decent café. I wandered over to the non-fiction books, and eventually found a shelf containing self-help books, among them a few with titles that drew my attention. There was *Practical Meditation*, *Start Meditating*, and next to those two, I saw a title that made me smile: *Meditation for Dummies*.

Taking the latter off the shelf, I gave it a look-through, and was surprised by just how wide-ranging its contents were. Glancing at his introduction, I noticed that the author claimed to offer "simple, easy-to- follow meditation instructions" as well as "time-honoured wisdom from the great teachers of old." That sold it for me. *Never judge a book by its cover*, I thought. *Or its title!* I made my choice and used the automatic check-out to borrow it.

As I turned to leave the building, I found myself face-to-face with someone who looked familiar; he was just about to enter the library. We both stopped in front of each other. At first, I was mystified, and then the recognition dawned on me. It was Ben, Hina's one-time tormentor, whom I'd last seen in Harmony Park, having left him sprawling down on the path. The delayed reaction was due to the fact that he seemed different. Firstly, he appeared to be sober, and secondly, he looked friendly, although also quite nervous.

It was Ben who broke the silence

"Christ! I was hoping to bump into you sometime. And here you are ... I need to speak to you ... I know that ... that you think I'm ..."

"Wait a minute," I interrupted, becoming more aware of his uncomfortable disposition. "Ben, just stop there! Why don't we sit down somewhere?"

It was easy to read his body language. Although he hadn't yet said as much, contrition was written all over his face, and I had a feeling he wanted to make some amends, but with no idea how to carry it out. His uncertainty was palpable.

We found a table in the library's café and ordered drinks.

"Let's clear up one thing," I said, "we are *not* enemies. What did you want to say to me?"

"Thanks. You are making this a little easier than I thought. Look, I admit … I behaved like a complete idiot in the park. It … I was completely out of order. And Liam pulling that stunt with the knife … hell, it freaked me out. He and I don't hang out together anymore."

"Glad to hear it. Keeping *good* company is so important, unless of course you're strong enough to know and hold to your highest standards, whoever you're with."

"I get what you're saying," Ben replied, looking somewhat dejected. He took a deep breath and then asked, "What makes you the way *you* are? I've never seen anyone do what you did that day. You didn't show any fear, and you dealt with me and Liam as if you were brushing away a fly."

"Look, Ben, honestly, I can't account for the way I am or how I behave. Let me assure you, I'm still striving to be better, and being with Hina is helping me in that department. We're all a work in progress."

"I feel I can apologise to you, but it's Hina I need to say I'm sorry to … I can see now that over the years, going back to our school days, I've been so bloody awful. She didn't deserve all that crap. What an arsehole! Believe me, I now so hate the way I was, and regret that I didn't completely throw off that whole stupid bullying attitude sooner."

"Ben, listen to me. We've all done things we regret. You are *not* that bully. Maybe what happened in the park was a wake-up call for you, meaning it's now time for you to tap into your true potential. You are the man I see in front of me *now*. You are *not* your past. I sense I am looking at a good bloke. It seems you're now ready to turn over a new leaf – to look into what truly brings you fulfilment."

"But how?"

I remained silent for a few moments to assess what was happening. I believed that Ben was quite genuine; he needed help, and was asking it of me. I knew one thing that would help him, but I couldn't share that with him yet. I needed to speak to Hina first.

"OK, Ben, let me think about this for a day or two; then I'll get back to you. What's your mobile number?"

We exchanged contact details and then shook hands before I left. Ben stayed in the library.

Chapter 33

Later in the day, I reconnected with Hina. She'd suggested I meet her at Elizabeth's Natural Health Centre so she could show me around. Upon approaching the building, I was greeted by a large noticeboard set into the front courtyard.

MAPLE NATURAL HEALTH
Complementary Therapies

I was standing in front of an attractive two-storeyed semi-detached house, set back from the main road. To its left was a broad drive leading to a parking area at the back, no doubt for visiting clients and the Centre's therapists.

Entrance was via a side door which led directly into a reception area and waiting room. Hina was sitting on one of the chairs, writing in a notebook; she immediately stood up and came over to me with a welcoming smile and embrace.

"Hi, darling, I was just starting to compose a leaflet about my counselling practice, but I can finish that later.

Let me show you around. I can show you the room I'll be using and one of the therapy rooms that's not currently in use. We need to be quiet so as not to disturb any treatment."

I followed Hina along a passageway, and she took me into a well-appointed room. A raised therapy-couch caught my eye, as well as the sink unit and some shelving containing towels and other items. There was a simplicity about the décor that breathed tranquillity. It was pleasing to see natural objects, such as potted plants and diverse crystals, on display.

"Looks great," I said. "Who usually works here?"

"Rosemary, she does Reflexology and Reiki, but she's finished for the day. Let me show you the room Elizabeth has offered me."

Hina led me into a smaller room where two comfortable armchairs sat on either side of a coffee table. A side table boasted a lamp and a box of tissues within easy reach. We sat down briefly while Hina excitedly outlined the arrangements she'd made with Elizabeth.

"I start during the second week of September. I can use this room every Friday morning. For the first three months – Elizabeth's so kind – she's letting me have the room rent-free, but taking a percentage of my fees. After that, I'll pay the usual hourly rate. By then, I could have the two slots she originally promised.

I've got a short window within which to get myself known. Elizabeth is helping me design business cards and leaflets, and she'll be adding my profile to the Centre's website."

"That's wonderful," I said, reaching for her hand. "You deserve it. You've got what it takes to help a lot of people. I know I'm biased. But I've already benefited so much from your natural wisdom, so I know what I'm talking about."

"Come on, let's go; before you make me cry ... I've more to tell you when we get home."

Home was, of course, "our" home now that Hina had moved in with me. She was no longer a visitor; we were going home together, and I was one happy, very grateful soul for what she was now bringing into my life!

Once we'd settled down after arriving home, Hina began to fill me in about her other project.

"As I was at the Centre with Elizabeth, Fitz called by so that the three of us could continue planning for the School of Spiritual Philosophy. We met in Elizabeth's flat on the first floor – all the therapy rooms are at the ground level.

We'll begin teaching in October, and the course will run over ten weekly sessions. We start advertising next week with adverts in the local papers, and posters and leaflets that we can distribute around the area. You can help with that!

Depending on the numbers on our first evening, there will be one or two classes. If one, Elizabeth will teach, and I will sit in with her. If there are two, I'll take the second class, and Jill and Angelo from the group will support us. And, for this first course, we'll be in Geoff's house. Geoff and Fitz have offered to help each evening with anything practical, such as manning the door and offering refreshments during the mid-session break. There may be one or two other volunteers."

"What are you calling the course?"

"The main heading will be *The Eternal Wisdom*; there'll also be a subheading: *Making Philosophy Practical.*"

"Sounds right up my street!"

"Zac, that's enough about me; tell me about *your* day!"

Chapter 34

After I'd told her about my visit to the library and the encounter with Ben, Hina excused herself and went upstairs to the bedroom. I knew instinctively not to follow her; to give her the space to reflect on what I had told her. I did not want to give her any advice on what to do. I would be here to support her, and I'd only add my take on the situation if it was asked for.

Eventually, Hina came downstairs and rejoined me. I waited for her to speak.

"Before you ask," she said, "I'm OK. I'd like to talk about this with you, but can we go somewhere else, say, in the open, please?"

"Come on," I replied, wrapping her close. "I know just the place. Let's go."

I took Hina to the woods I'd last visited after that profound meditation in Fitz's house, when Hina was in her mentoring role. We came to the clearing next to the pond and sat down together on the wooden bench, enjoying the serene environment.

Hina nestled into me, and we stayed silent for a while. Eventually, Hina took my hand.

"I love you, Zac. You are so tuned into me. I can feel your care so strongly. It's helping me to make my own decisions from a good place, whatever I might be going through emotionally."

"And of course," I suggested, "you don't have to make any decision right now."

"It's already made. I know what I have to do. On the one hand, I'm very unsure, as I sense the old hurt and resentment towards Ben, which started in my school days and carried on over the years, getting more and more entrenched.

On the other hand, I know in my heart that, in truth, we are all one. I cannot turn my back on all I've learned on the spiritual path. So it is to my heart that I must listen, not to the hurt child.

From the heart of oneness, it is possible to see beyond anyone's damaged persona to their essential nature. That's what you managed in the library, Zac. You affirmed Ben's goodness, not holding him to his past dysfunctional behaviour.

By offering him forgiveness, he and I are both liberated – he from his guilt and self-hatred, and me from one more old attachment to pain and imagined separation. Just as you told Ben that you and he were not enemies, so, in the same way, neither are Ben and I enemies. We both have to let go to make it true in our experience.

Remind me what you said to him after he reached out to you for help, just before you left the library."

"I didn't make any promises, nor did I tell him that I'd be speaking to you first. All I said was that I'd get back to him in a day or two."

"OK. That's perfect. I'll arrange to meet Ben. Don't worry, it'll be somewhere public. The library should do; it's as good a place as any."

As we walked home together, I sensed that Hina was feeling lighter, as if some of that old weight had already begun to drop away.

It made me muse that we might have more of this "stuff" to jettison to be fully free. And I did not doubt that Life would present us with plenty of opportunities, such gifts even, as we travelled the path of liberation.

Chapter 35

The next day, I phoned Ben as promised and told him that Hina had agreed to meet him. He seemed relieved, saying that he'd been quite "churned up" waiting for my call. I encouraged him to go easy on himself and suggested the library as the venue for their meeting. He agreed, and we set it up for the following Saturday afternoon, in the library café, since that was the place Hina had mentioned.

It was important for them to meet without me being present, and I was fairly confident that it would pose no problem. But I told Hina I'd not be far away, in a café nearby. She was happy with that.

When the day arrived, I walked with Hina to the library and left her with a hug and a kiss at the entrance. A few minutes later, I was sitting on a bench seat in the nearby café, clutching my Americano, and using the time to be inwardly still and mindful; simply enjoying the "sacred presence", and letting go of any consideration about what might transpire in the library. As I thought of Hina, I inwardly reminded myself of her strengths.

I believe in you, and your ability to rise to any challenge!

I was still drinking my second cup when Hina walked in, located where I was sitting, and joined me. I was reassured by her smile that all had gone well.

She took my hand while saying, "It went better than expected. More than better! I'll share with you later, not here." We sat for a while until I'd finished my drink. Hina declined my offer to get a drink for her, and we left shortly afterwards.

Back home, Hina brought me up to date regarding her meeting in the library.

"When I got to the library café, Ben was waiting for me. He'd bagged a table in a quiet corner so we could talk discreetly. The first few minutes were a bit awkward, as I waited for him to speak first. That seemed the right approach, since he was the one who'd wanted the meeting.

It took a while for him to look me in the eye, and then, somehow, he plucked up some courage and spoke to me.

His first few words surprised me. He said he was glad to see how well and strong I looked. That made it easier for him to apologise. He said he wished he could take back every word he'd uttered and everything he'd done to make my life a misery. He said he'd understand if I couldn't forgive him.

'However,' he then added, 'that's what I'm asking, if you could find it in you to forgive me.'

Zac, looking back on this with you helps me to see what was going on. As I sat down with him, I was determined not to project onto the Ben in front of me images of the Ben as I'd experienced him in the past. I wanted to meet him 'as if for the first time', as Susan had often encouraged us to do.

So, I was able to see that Ben was *asking* – he wasn't pleading. There was even something noble in his manner, and I was able to maintain a defenceless attitude throughout our meeting.

Before I could respond to his request for forgiveness, something wonderful happened, Zac. I was aware of a brilliant light pouring from Ben's eyes; it then encompassed him completely, before filling the entire room.

At precisely that moment, Ben said to me, 'What is that light coming from your eyes?'

Without any effort, I told him: 'The same light I see in you, Ben.'

It was extraordinary. We were sharing a timeless moment in which I knew that nothing but truth could exist. All the tension in his face had disappeared; I saw his true strength and gentleness. It was as if the Ben of old had been replaced by someone new! And my earlier intention had been granted – I was now seeing him as if for the first time!

There was such a rightness about what was now between us that I found myself taking his hand.

I told him that he and I should let all of the past go; the lot! That forgiveness had happened; that we were both held in the presence of Divine Grace. That we were both freer than we'd ever been. However, to put the seal on it, so to speak, I did tell him that I was forgiving him from the bottom of my heart."

I'd been listening to Hina's account with rapt attention, not wanting to interrupt, but at this point I felt so joyous at the way all this had unfolded that I let out a loud whoop of delight.

Hina smiled. "There's more," she said.

"I'm sure that Ben was in his best ever place, mentally and emotionally. He calmly said, several times, 'I see it all so clearly now'. He told me that nothing like this had ever happened to him before. He could now see that his past behaviour was just a veneer of bravado which his ego had made use of to hide a fearful and low self-esteem. He'd mixed with the wrong crowd – with those who bolstered his false image of himself. And all the while he was trying to talk big, whilst inside he was forever unhappy, and often feeling empty and hopeless.

He said he was grateful to you, and now to me, for helping him to see through the masks he'd been wearing. He now needed to make a fresh start, to find a way of discovering who he was. He told me there was no going back to his old ways or his previous companions. He remembered you talking to him about the importance of good company.

At the mention of 'good company', I had a sudden inspiration. I told Ben about the School of Spiritual Philosophy that Elizabeth and I are starting soon. If he did sign up, I made it clear, he'd go into Elizabeth's class. I gave him all the details and got the sense he was interested.

I then knew that the purpose of our meeting had been fulfilled for both of us, so I wished him well and came straight to you in the café."

This was a groundbreaking experience for Hina. I was delighted with how the meeting with Ben had gone, and said so; and that seemed enough, as we avoided the temptation of further comment. We decided not to go over it, with the danger of pulling it all apart through over-analysis.

Instead, we opted for a relaxing night, which included watching an old *Sherlock Holmes* film on the television.

Chapter 36

August gave way to September, and I was soon back in full throttle at school, getting to grips with the new intake in addition to new GCSE and A Level classes. For that reason, I decided to give it a few weeks before starting the after-school meditation class.

This was also an important month for Hina. On her first Friday at Maple Natural Health, she was introduced to two clients, one of them through Elizabeth's referral; a promising start. I was sure Hina would soon be fully booked on those Friday mornings.

The next day, after what seemed like a lifetime, Hina and I made our way to Geoff's house for the group meeting, something we were more than ready for after the long summer break. Susan had returned from her family visit abroad and took up her usual position in front of the group. She welcomed a new member, Ralph Newcombe, who I later discovered was a therapist at Elizabeth's Centre, and had joined through her invitation.

Susan then guided us in a short period of stillness, as preparation for the afternoon's teaching. Afterwards, she stood and wrote on the flipchart:

> **God is like a circle whose centre is everywhere,**
> **and whose circumference is nowhere**

Susan then sat down before continuing.

"What you are looking at is a statement attributed to an ancient Greek philosopher.

To me, this represents thousands of years of philosophy wrapped up in a single sentence.

If God's centre is everywhere, then the inner reality of everything we behold is divine, not excluding the observer, of course. It's best if we understand this not in the mind, but in the heart; for that's where such an insight is known; it is known where our being is most deep – that it is one centre, *the* one centre, which is in you, him, her, it and me.

It is not a bit of God here and a bit there, for the divine reality is indivisible – there is only the whole of divinity. It means that every aspect of creation becomes a doorway into the infinite.

Where do I go to find God? Answer: You can stay where you are. But open your heart, mind, and soul, look with fresh eyes, lay down all expectations, beliefs, ideas, and the like, and be totally innocent, like a child, fully engaged with the eternal Now."

Susan picked up a slim volume and opened it to where it had been bookmarked. She then continued:

"This is from the Gospel of Thomas:

Look at what is before your face;
and what is hidden from you
will be revealed to you.

It means that God is expressing Itself wherever you are, at all times. The key question is: Am I prepared to stop, be still, look, listen, let go of all distractions, and accept the never-ending invitation to be embraced and filled with the full measure of divine nectar?

Oh, if only we had eyes to see, and ears to hear! However, Divinity is not invasive ... it is very respectful. When fully welcomed, it enters us, fills us up; if our attention prefers to be elsewhere, no problem, that is perfectly allowable.

Everyone is invited to the Banquet, but we are always free to respond – or not.

Everything comes into being from Love, is held in Love, and ultimately returns to Love. We play the game of worldly activity at the circumference, as embodied souls. Yet, at the same time, our essential life is eternally hidden in the One Life, at the centre, 'the point with no dimensions', the infinite, eternal reality.

What is our Work, then?

To wake up to this reality. And then, where possible, to support others in their journey of awakening."

Once Susan had finished speaking, I could sense the profound joy and wonder that permeated the room. Throughout her presentation, you could have heard a pin drop. We stayed in that presence for a few moments; it was clear that nobody wanted to ask a question or speak about what they had just heard.

Susan, like Fitz, had a way of teaching that conveyed to the listener what was self-evident. It occurred to me: The truth is *always* self-evident when *heard*.

Often, whenever I was the recipient of such teaching, a kind of flame would be ignited within me, evoking a love of truth and a yearning to serve. On this occasion, an almost overwhelming sense of deep gratitude filled me. I looked at Hina and felt that something similar was going on in her. Our eyes met and we shared a moment of wordless understanding.

Our love was a strength, and there arose naturally within me a resolve to be as diligent as possible in The Work, and to use whatever abilities I had at my disposal to support others on the path.

It was clear that Susan was in tune with the general mood; she remained sitting in silence with us for around ten minutes, as far as I could tell. She then stood up and quietly left the room.

Even during the refreshment break, there was less than the usual sounds of conversation. Fitz sought me out and asked if he could meet with me and Hina the next day. I was delighted with the prospect and invited him to come to our home.

We agreed to meet mid-afternoon. Knowing Fitz, I was sure that this would be more than just a social visit.

Once we had returned to our seats in the main room, Susan said she wanted to share some news with us.

"It has been such a privilege to share the highest spiritual teachings with you good people. But it is time for me to make way for someone else. As some of you may already know, Geoff and I have been partners for a while, and we have now decided to do two things at the same time. Firstly, to share a home; and secondly, to create that home together abroad.

We will shortly be moving to Malta. Geoff has family in Valletta, the capital. In the first instance, we will live in their home while we seek a suitable property for ourselves. Of course, we will be continuing The Work on that lovely island. We aim eventually to host regular retreats in a location near the coast, which we hope some of you will be able to attend, and maybe when you do visit, combine that with a well-earned holiday.

Now let us come together in meditation."

Chapter 37

After a lengthy period of meditation, Susan stepped back into her teaching role.

"Although you might read wonderful spiritual literature, attend a spiritual group like this, diligently practice meditation, lead a good and fulfilling life, in other words, appear to be doing all the right things, are you still prone to periods of dissatisfaction? Because you rarely feel truly connected to your essential nature, that *You* which you really are?"

Susan laughed before continuing:

"No need to answer that – we're all in the same boat.

But I would like to suggest that, despite it appearing otherwise, a deeper, more authentic level of being is *always* awake to the non-relative nature of existence, even if your apparent separate individuality doesn't seem to be aware of it. And now and again, it reveals itself in all its glory, and you wonder – *good heavens, where did that come from?*

It is your true nature, and it is always here!

It is ever awake, no matter how things may appear to the ego at any moment.

Everything else is part of the play of consciousness, an unending drama that is always relative. Being that Self is easy, natural, complete, and always already perfect. In effect, nothing is missing and action is effortless ... *Everything else* can be very challenging indeed!

To experience Being, the time process needs to be transcended, and this occurs through the simple act of releasing attention from identification with anything that arises in awareness, beginning and ending with the arising of thought. As we cease to identify with objects, the timeless, spaceless, empty, infinite ground begins to emerge as the very presence of our unborn Being.

All sense of boundary, any sense of limitation, including all memory and desire, dissolves in an effulgent sea of fullness and completeness that always exists before the universe was created.

Is this so? Is this true in your experience?

I would like to further suggest that no matter how cut off we may seem, we are *never truly* cut off! The Self is not just the core of my – and your – Being. It is, at the same time, the total manifestation."

Susan returned to the book she had read from earlier.

"Again, from the Gospel of Thomas:

Lift the stone, cleave wood, I AM there!

The 'I AM' is, of course, the pure consciousness that permeates all.

I could easily add some alternative pointers, such as

Iron your shirts – I AM there!
In the supermarket – I AM there!
Changing the baby's nappy – I AM there!
Think of any situation – I AM there!

So, while we are all together, let us apply this *now*.

Right now, while you are listening – I AM here!"

Susan fell quiet and looked around at the group, and seeming satisfied that we were all with her, she carried on.

"Keep your attention fully in *this* present moment ... staying connected to the senses ... seeing, hearing ... noticing thoughts arising in the mind ...

Now ask yourself this question: 'Where has this attention come from?'

Observe – the attention arises out of the awareness that is always present as the ground of all our experience. Without it, there would be no experience. All experience is predicated upon the underlying awareness. It must always be present! Check this out for yourself.

This means that, however *low* I feel, whatever the *desperate situation* I am in, nothing prevents me from tapping into the presence of my essential Being. Making this connection, the *lowness* that I feel is an experience within this awareness – I am the beginningless, endless awareness in which states such as *lowness* come and go.

Regarding any *desperate situation*, I am the beginningless, endless awareness in which every *situation, desperate or otherwise,* begins and ends.

What is required is a small shift, or change in attitude, from identification with the *object*, such as feelings like lowness or desperation, to the underlying *subject,* which we might call *the witness.*

As we relax into this, the *witness* itself merges into its source, the underlying unchanging awareness, and suddenly we are free. The external sensations of the body, emotional states, and circumstances may still be around, but I am no longer attached to them. I am resting in the awareness in which all these are played out.

So, my dear companions on the path, whatever our situation, whatever emotions or thoughts are present to us now, this is the perfect platform from which to dive into the freedom of our immediately present Being, which is ever pure, supremely intelligent, and bliss-*full*! There needs to be a willing acceptance of *what is now*.

What is *now* – not what we'd prefer or wish otherwise – is *the* stepping stone into the fullness of Being."

Later that day, Hina and I found ourselves reflecting on the teaching given by Susan during the second half of the meeting. We agreed, first of all, that it was very reassuring, quite apart from being inspiring. The teaching was clear: no matter what we are going through, however difficult, it is possible to open up to the awareness of our true being. Divinity, by its very nature, could never *not* be present.

We also agreed that it was important, when things were going well, when everything seemed to flow, not to be complacent, but as much as possible to use each moment as a sacred gift in which to "walk in the spirit"; or put another way, each moment provides an opportunity to be wholly centred in one's authentic Self.

Turning to another aspect of the day's experience, Hina solemnly confessed that she would sorely miss Susan, who was not only her cherished teacher but also one of her best friends.

"You'll have to take me on a holiday to Malta," she announced.

"I'll see; it'll all depend on how good you are," I countered, not quite achieving the light-hearted touch that was meant.

"Hey! What does that mean?" Hina objected, skilfully putting on a forlorn appearance.

"Well, since you're always very good," I replied, "you've nothing to worry about, have you?"

Hina slapped me playfully on the arm, and we left it at that.

Chapter 38

We welcomed Fitz into our home the next day, and as we had come to expect, he quickly launched into the purpose of his visit.

"Susan and Geoff won't be leaving for Malta until next month, so we'll still be able to enjoy one last session of her teaching before they go. This leads me to a few other matters I need to share with you.

First off, Geoff will be donating his house for The Work. He has always been very generous, and I was not unduly surprised when he made this offer. We are looking into how this can be done properly. Do we set up a trust or create a charity? Or is there another way? We'll get some advice about these options before we take any action.

Now, for the main reason that I'm talking to you two.

Susan, Geoff and I have considered the many new challenges this change causes. We agree that there needs to be someone living at the property. Apart from the caretaking needs, we want the main centre for our Work to retain the qualities of a home for our family of fellow travellers. And again, we thought that you were the ideal couple to live there.

Before you ask any questions, let me say a bit more. Whoever takes up residence at the property will live there rent-free, but be responsible for all the services – heating, lighting, water, phone, Wi-Fi, and the like. We've set up a separate fund to take care of any major repairs; however, the house is in good order. Even with keeping the meeting room free for the group, you already know, I'm sure, that the rest of the living space covers a substantially bigger area than your present home.

The residents, which we hope will be you, will be responsible for the upkeep of the garden, and maintaining cleanliness throughout the house, something you'd do in your own home anyway. Any paid help, to keep on top of the garden's needs, for example, would be a decision for you to make."

"Wow! What can I say? You've left me speechless," I said eventually. "This is a decision we have to make as a couple. Hina and I will need a bit of space on this."

I looked at Hina, and her face told me that she was deeply moved by the offer, as I was.

"It's such a wonderful offer," Hina said. "We'll need some time to talk this over."

"Of course," Fitz replied. "I didn't expect an immediate answer. I'm sure you'd have to consider all the implications of this change of circumstances, should you accept.

I'll leave you to it; we'll talk again in a few days."

After Fitz had left, we felt we needed some time for the offer of what was once Geoff's house to sink in. We decided to go for a walk and sit quietly together. We wanted any decision we made to come from a deeper source than the surface mind. We sat for a while by the pond in the clearing of the nearby woods, something we had begun to do regularly.

Deep down, I knew we were going to accept the offer, but I wanted Hina's response to be completely free of any influence from me. Yes, it was technically my home that we'd be moving from, but I wanted Hina to see it as "*we* are moving to *our* new home."

On the way back to the house, Hina broke the silence.

"We're going to accept the offer." *Real matter of fact!*

"Yes, we are." *Another matter of fact!*

We walked in silence for the rest of the way. We would discuss later the nuts and bolts of this unexpected development that had just dropped into our lives. Our decisions would spring from that place of unity which we shared.

In the end, our decision emerged with extraordinary ease. The opportunity we were being given was a way of supporting the continuation of the group we both valued. We agreed that nothing about the move would impede any of our important life choices. Our current home could be let to a family, and the right person, or persons, would show up. In that way, we would retain possession of a property that we might need at some time in the future.

Even though all these changes in my life were happening at such a fast pace, I could not help noticing that I remained inwardly steady throughout it all.

Underneath all the changes, all the activity, was a new and growing sense of an inner strength and a firm faith in the divine intelligence that indwells and governs everything.

Chapter 39

I was back at school the next day, knowing I would be leading the first session of the meditation class later in the afternoon. During the lunch break, I was sought out by one of my colleagues, Jason Hewett, who taught Religious Studies.

"Zac, good luck with the new meditation class. Look, I was wondering if I might come along, or is it strictly students only?"

"You know, Jason," I replied, "It's not something I've thought about, but I don't see why not. Have you had any experience with meditation?"

"Some. Seeing your poster in the sixth form common room has rekindled an interest. I know I could do with it, Zac."

"Let's go for it," I said, sensing the importance of affirming him, and not allowing my mind to get into a tangle by trying to assess the pros and cons of such a decision. "If anyone objects, that'll be their issue, and just too bad."

I was confident that none of the students who came to the class would mind. Jason was a popular teacher and very good at a variety of sports. He looked after one of the school cricket teams, which meant often giving his time freely after hours, and on some weekends.

As I didn't have any teaching scheduled for the final lesson of the day, I used the time to prepare the space where I'd be holding the meditation class. I'd claimed a small room adjacent to the library where I knew we wouldn't be disturbed.

Grant and Shona, the two A Level students I'd approached last term, were the first to arrive. Shona brought her 12-year-old brother Conrad along; she said he'd insisted on being mature enough to join the class. She hadn't been able to shake him off.

"That's the spirit," I said to Conrad. "You're very welcome."

"Hugh Jackman meditates," young Conrad announced. "He's the one who plays Wolverine, you know, one of the mutants!"

"That's very important," I said, managing a fist-bump with the lad. "I'm sure meditation helps with his acting."

Just then, three more of my older students turned up – Geri, Robert and Elaine – along with Jason. Six students and one teacher, then. I was happy with that; we were starting small. I smiled as I remembered reading an old, once popular book on economics called *Small is Beautiful!*

I had set out ten chairs in a crescent shape facing mine, so I removed three of them before inviting everyone to sit down.

I decided not to make the session too spiritual to start with, so I began by outlining some of the benefits of meditation. I referred to various studies I'd looked up, including those mentioned in *Meditation for Dummies.* I spoke about the research findings of the 1980s, which compared those who meditated regularly over a long period with non-meditators. These showed that the former enjoyed less stress, improved concentration, a stronger immune system, tended to live longer, and were much less prone to conditions like cardiovascular disease or cancer.

I did make it clear, though, that often these benefits were seen as merely by-products of meditation, and not the main reason why many people chose to adopt the practice. There were other, deeper reasons, and I would go into that in future sessions.

I told them we would start with a short practice of about 12 – 15 minutes. After a few simple instructions about posture, I invited them to close their eyes. I kept the main part of the practice as simple as possible, but it was nevertheless very much in line with how I had been meditating since Hina had taken me in hand.

Once I'd brought the meditation to a close, and they had all opened their eyes, and after I'd allowed a short time of continued silence, I asked if anyone wanted to share how they had found the experience.

Shona commented that, at one point during her practice, she felt bigger than her body, but she confessed to feeling somewhat strange in admitting it. I reassured her that her experience was perfectly normal; that through meditation, our perspective regarding the body can change.

Turning to the class as a whole, I said:

"With the help of meditation, we may begin to view the body from a point of greater awareness and, yes, see ourselves *containing* the body, not the other way round.

Through practice, our understanding will deepen further."

Jason said it felt like "coming home". He was certain he would now practice meditation more regularly.

The rest of the class looked relaxed and happy, but did not make any contribution. I was happy with that; teenagers sometimes take a while to open up, I told myself.

Before closing the session, I gave a brief teaching about meditation as a form of self-enquiry, leading to a greater knowledge of who we are. I also emphasised how the practice could assist us in opening up to inner resources to help us negotiate the demands of everyday life.

We decided to meet again in two weeks. Elaine asked if she could bring her boyfriend, who attended a different school. I told her that he would be welcome.

On the way home, I took a diversion to the clearing in the woods for some quiet time of reflection. My first attempt at teaching meditation – how did it go? I was pleasantly surprised by how easily the session flowed. The teaching that followed the meditation was spoken with an authority I didn't know I had, and seemingly without effort.

Furthermore, I could tell that the session had been a positive experience for all those who attended, for some more than others. Shona's contribution seemed to have been accepted without any quibble. It suggested to me that this group could easily be offered more advanced teaching next time.

I looked forward to sharing all this with Fitz. After all, he was the one who encouraged me to step into this role.

Chapter 40

Fitz was available to share a catch-up with me a few days later. It was a Friday afternoon, following the end of the school day. We decided to meet up in the café which had been home to our first meeting. Once we'd settled down with our drinks, I gave Fitz a full account of my first experience of teaching meditation. I then told him that I was open to any feedback he could give me, and, in addition, asked if he'd consider suggesting any alternative approaches. He listened without interruption.

"First of all, Zac," he began, once he'd ascertained that I had nothing further to add, "this is a great initiative of yours; steering meditation in through those iron school gates!"

I laughed. "Well, it was you who put me up to it!"

"Yes, but you wasted no time in getting on with it. If the students left looking happy, having agreed to a follow-up session, that spells success to me.

Let's consider the question of authority. You mentioned that you spoke with an authority that you didn't realise you possessed.

In one of the Gospels, St. Matthew's, you'll find the Sermon on the Mount; it's the core teaching of Jesus. When he had finished speaking, so the writer tells us, the people there were astonished 'for he taught as one having authority, and not like the scribes.'

The power of his teaching was that he was one with it, and that was his *authority*. The original Greek word here for *authority* is *exousia,* which means, literally, 'out of being'; *ex* means 'out' and *ousia* means 'being'.

If you live what you teach, *that* is your authority; it comes from your being, not your head. Because of that, your students heard the ring of truth in your words and responded accordingly. One of your students even experienced an expansion of consciousness, and she felt able to share it with you and the others in language that was available to her at that time.

She said she felt bigger than her body, and you cottoned onto exactly what she was attempting to describe, so that your response to her and the rest of the class was carefully measured – enough to open them to a deeper sense of their nature, but without over-stressing it. Again, knowing when *not* to say too much – that's also a skill.

From what you've said, I reckon you could now bring more spiritual teaching into the class. Not too much, but trust your judgement on that. If you follow the inner guidance that comes to you in the sacred moment, then you can't go wrong. The principle is this: Knowledge arises to meet a need. Trust. If you are speaking from an inner stillness, free of any personal agenda, then what you say will meet the needs of those listening to you.

Here's a prediction: your next meditation class will be larger."

I thanked Fitz for his kind and supportive words.

"You're welcome," he replied. "Now for something entirely different. A short while ago, you and Hina shared with me possibilities and aspirations about your future marriage celebration. You might remember that I told you about my friend, the Interfaith Minister, who could work with you to create *your own* ceremony. She's very experienced in working with couples from diverse backgrounds.

I've had a word with her, and she'd be delighted to meet you both. She gave me her business card to pass on to you."

With that, Fitz gave me the card, and I thanked him, saying I'd contact her to arrange a meeting once I'd checked in with Hina to see when we'd both be able to meet her.

Before parting, Fitz said that if not before, we'd see each other again at the next group meeting, Susan's last before jetting off to Malta.

Chapter 41

Later that evening, Hina and I caught up with each other. I shared with her my conversation with Fitz about the school meditation class. In turn, Hina told me how pleased she was with her morning, having progressed to seeing three clients at Elizabeth's Natural Health Centre. She was also growing in confidence, reassured by how the sessions turned out, that she was truly following her heart.

A little later, I remembered the business card Fitz had given me for the Interfaith Minister and passed it to Hina.

"Great," she exclaimed, and without more ado, she phoned the number.

"Right," said Hina, after the call had been completed. "We're meeting with the Reverend Stephanie Bamford on Sunday. Here at two o'clock. She sounds lovely. And fun."

"Not wasting any time then, I notice," I said, tongue in cheek.

"No, you're well and truly hooked, young man!" I deserved that. And I must admit, I didn't mind at all.

On Sunday, Reverend Stephanie Bamford breezed in at exactly two o'clock.

She did not fit my preconceived idea of a minister, no doubt a good thing. She looked to be in her mid-to-late thirties, an attractive blonde, dressed casually in t-shirt, cardigan and dark red jeans.

"Just call me Steph," she said as she sat down.

Having completed introductions, we enjoyed some drinks before she moved to the matter in hand. She told us that she had graduated from the Universal Interfaith Seminary four years ago, and her specialty was working with couples like us who came from different backgrounds. She guided, suggested, and worked alongside her clients; together they would create a unique ceremony which reflected both of their cultural and religious origins and, of course, their particular preferences.

"Now, before we start considering the marriage service as a whole, with all its parts, let me ask you both a question. What do you see as the most important part of the service?"

Hina and I replied simultaneously; Hina saying, "vows," while I said, "the promises."

"Exactly," confirmed Steph. "You two are going to be so easy-peasy to work with!

The vows or promises you offer one another are at the heart of the Marriage Ceremony – they express in words what is in your hearts. That's why I encourage you to create your own vows. They are then a true reflection of *your* vision of *your* life together – no one else's!

I've prepared some questions to help you do this. They're to make you think deeply about the relationship you already enjoy, and also to help you express the deepest potential for your life together.

I *suggest* that you consider these questions on your own, and only later come together to share and discuss them.

Then you might want to start writing your vows. Again, do so individually. Once you've completed them, you'll likely want to share what you've created."

Stephanie offered us each a copy of the questions:

What does marriage mean to you?

What do you love and appreciate about your partner?

What is the highest purpose of your relationship?

What gifts are you bringing to one another and the marriage?

Where do you feel strong together as a couple?

Where would you like to become stronger? How?

"It's only when you have both written your vows and are satisfied with them, that we can start to create the whole service, placing around the vows the rituals, the readings, music, the blessing, the exchange of rings, and so on. Are you happy with that?"

We said we were.

"Then, let's meet again in a couple of weeks. You don't need to worry about my fee; Fitz is looking after that. We should also try to agree on a date and place for the ceremony quite soon. OK. It's been lovely meeting you."

"And you also," said Hina. "We'll look at diaries next time. I'm sure we have a venue. Thank you for coming to see us."

After Steph had gone, Hina and I embraced each other. We were both delighted with our minister and agreed that her approach suited us perfectly, allowing us to have a major say in our own ceremony, rather than the more restrictive form that would have prevailed if we'd gone through the established religion route.

During the week, Hina and I did our vows homework separately as advised. By Wednesday, we were ready to discuss our progress, at the same time agreeing that all our "hard work" deserved to be rewarded. We went to one of the local Italian restaurants to discuss our vows over a good meal.

"Can I go first?" Hina asked. I said that was fine by me, and then Hina, with a somewhat resolute expression on her face, laid down her knife and fork and took my hand. *A surprise was on the cards, that was certain.*

"Zac, I don't want to prepare my vow; I don't *need* to. I know my love for you and what your love means to me. And what it means for our life together. I want my declaration of love and my commitment to come from my heart spontaneously, at whatever point in the service it is due.

This is what *I* want, Zac, but I won't mind if you choose to repeat your vow after Steph, or read it. Honestly, Zac, you can ..."

"Hold on, hold on," I said, interrupting her flow. "No justification required. You know that. You continually amaze me, which, of course, makes you so adorable."

There were tears in her eyes as I continued:

"OK. Let's both be convention-crushers – is that a word? I also don't need any cues when we come to the vows. Why didn't I think of that? You're an inspiration! We'll *both* speak our vows in that way.

At the last wedding I attended, the bride and groom each repeated their vows after the vicar, one phrase at a time. They were the standard vows in the prayer book, which are set for every church wedding. On reflection, it felt a bit too staged, but everyone was happy, so it was OK.

Steph's approach is certainly better and very helpful for a lot of couples, I'm sure. But *your* way, Hina – *our* way – is what's right for us."

The following day, I phoned Steph and told her about the decision Hina and I had arrived at regarding the vows. Steph stated that this would be quite a new experience for her, but that she respected our wishes and we had her support. She said she was aware of the depth of our love for each other during her visit.

Having made a date for our next meeting, Steph said she would send us a sample Interfaith Marriage Ceremony that contained all the possible nuts and bolts of the ritual; we could use it as the basis for our ceremony, chopping and changing elements as we saw fit.

She intimated that it would be good if we could make some progress before the next meeting. I expressed my appreciation and said that at the next meeting we should be able to finalise the date and venue of the ceremony.

Chapter 42

A few days later, Hina and I attended the next group meeting, aware that it was Susan's last from the Teacher's chair. Fitz began the afternoon session by warmly thanking her on behalf of all of us for her faithful and enlightened service. After a short meditation, Susan took a deep breath and began to speak.

"This is my last meeting with you before I take off for Malta; Geoff is already in Valletta making arrangements for our temporary stay with his family. I ask this of you all: please see us both as continuing members of this group. We may soon be geographically far apart, but the Spirit has no walls, no distance, and no barriers of time. I promise, we will stay in touch. And we will visit from time to time.

I am grateful for the opportunity to share with you what I value about our group. We've always had a sense of family. We've treated each other the same as we would a brother or a sister.

What are we then, you and I? We are a spiritual community.

In this place, we see each other in the here and now, free of judgement or expectation. We are not in the game of seeking to change anyone. But of course, we may watch with delight as we see our companions throw off the shackles that have burdened them for too long, watching people mature over time, and begin to shine with their inner potential.

We are not a sect. When we first set up this group, we didn't give it a name. We began to call it *The Group* purely for convenience.

We do not insist on any dogma. True, we present a teaching that we declare to be universal. One that is ancient, yet ever new. But each one of you is asked to be a spiritual explorer, satisfying your own intelligence about what you hear. To trust the 'inner teacher', which is your most important teacher.

Furthermore, our respect for one another transcends all differences of viewpoint, at the same time as we endeavour to bring to light our own prejudices, for the sole purpose of consigning them to history.

We meet with open minds and open hearts.

Community. The word means literally *gathering into one*. '*One*' does not mean uniformity. It is a oneness of Spirit that is at ease in the midst of diversity.

This community that we enjoy is, of course, part of the larger community of humanity as a whole. Therefore, all that I've said about our group, endeavour to understand how it might apply in all other circumstances. The basic principles remain the same.

Each one of us is an individual. Yet whatever you do that makes you blossom, as a unique offspring of the Eternal, is a gift to the group and a gift to all humanity.

Indeed, the greatest service you can provide for humanity is your own self-realisation."

Susan stopped a moment for a sip of water, while looking around at each one of us before continuing:

"Here's what I suggest we do for the rest of the afternoon. It'll be an opportunity to get to know each other better. It involves working with a partner. There are people that we usually gravitate to socially, but on this occasion, I'd like you to seek out members of the group that you've had little or no contact with before.

See this as a spiritual exercise. Sit facing your partner. Spend about five minutes or so sharing something of your different backgrounds, your interests, your work, your family, what brought you here, and suchlike. Then gently move from the personal to the impersonal. That means being together, in Spirit, in consciousness. It could be that neither of you says a word, you simply enjoy the silence of being, the oneness. There will still be communication, but without words. Notice what that is like. Let your inner understanding tell you when it's time to stop; thank one another, and then pair up with someone else. Again, if possible, with another member you've had little contact with previously.

Keep it as informal as you can. We'll break now for refreshments, which you can take with you wherever you choose to meet."

We all converged on the adjoining room where, as usual, teas and simple snacks were laid out. Once I'd armed myself with a cup of herbal tea and a coconut biscuit, I looked around for someone to pair up with.

"Hi Zac!" It was a soft female voice with an Eastern European-sounding accent. As I turned to her, she added, "We haven't yet met properly. I'm Karolina."

Karolina was a tall, striking woman with shoulder-length auburn hair.

"Well then, Karolina, here's our chance," I replied. "Let's see if we can find somewhere to sit together."

We found an unoccupied bench on the garden patio just through the French windows, within reach of any call to return to the main meeting room.

Karolina suggested that we speak for a couple of minutes each, while the other just listened without interrupting, before moving into the following ten minutes of silence. I got the impression that she had experienced this exercise before. She then asked me if I wouldn't mind going first. I said I didn't mind and proceeded to share very openly with her about my upbringing, my work as a teacher, my introduction to the group, my subsequent relationship with Hina, which led to our engagement, and the meditation class I'd started at my school.

After I'd shared with her what I thought was most important, Karolina thanked me and congratulated me on getting engaged to Hina. She admitted to already knowing about it! We then swapped roles; I became the listener, she the speaker.

Her full name was Karolina Kucerova; her family moved to the UK when she was 19 years old, about 20 years ago. After helping her parents set up a Polish delicatessen in the high street, she trained as a hairdresser, eventually finding employment in a salon near their shop. In time, she progressed to senior stylist; soon afterwards, Susan became one of her regular clients.

Karolina told me she always looked forward to Susan's visits to her salon.

"I loved the conversations we had, which made me think back to my teenage years in Krakow, where I used to attend a monthly Buddhist class, and learnt to meditate. Susan knew a lot more than me about Buddhism, and I marvelled at her spiritual knowledge, which was so extensive and deep. I always plied her with a barrage of questions. Eventually, she invited me to join this group.

It was Susan who encouraged me to train as a teacher – she insisted that she could see my potential. And she predicted that I would 'become a great teacher', her words.

I'm now in my second year of teacher training. Meeting Susan has been truly wonderful." *Like me meeting Fitz, I thought.*

"Oh, and I've recently started dating one of our members," she quickly added, leaving me in suspense as to who that might be.

I thanked Karolina for what she'd shared, and then, without any fuss, we stayed in eye contact whilst observing silence.

It didn't take long before I found myself communing with her at a deep level. It was so natural, as if both of us had done this many times before.

At first, I sensed a sadness within her, but without any resignation or bitterness attached. Somehow, I knew that it was not a sadness to do with her personal situation. I had the clear sense of it being born of a universal love of humanity, leading to expressions of compassion through her work and relationships, leaving me in awe of what I was seeing.

I also saw in her a powerful innocence – an innocence that was a strength, not a weakness. Her compassion – I could well see this quality being at work in her future school teaching.

We lost all sense of time until our attention was caught by the voice of Fitz speaking inside the house, asking everyone to end their current exercise and find an alternative partner.

We both stood up. Karolina drew me into a gentle hug before we re-entered the house to find new partners.

Chapter 43

I allowed myself a few moments before going into the house; there was part of me that just wanted to linger with the experience of that deep sharing with Karolina.

Once inside the house, I discovered that everyone else had partnered up. Before I could work out what to do, Fitz materialised beside me.

"Have you drawn the short straw?" he asked, light-heartedly.

"Seems so," I replied. "I was supposed to find someone I'd least known here, wasn't I? Looks like I was too late."

"Not a problem. We could try something else. Let's go to the back of the garden where we won't be disturbed."

Once we had settled, Fitz suggested an exercise he had often found useful.

"I'm going to ask you a question. You answer it truthfully without reference to your analytical mind. Let your answer come out of your mouth without the interference of preconceived ideas. Once you've answered, I'll thank you, and then I'll ask you the *same* question again. You must allow the answer that's there to be spoken, however unexpected, even if it appears illogical. OK?"

I agreed to go along with this to the best of my ability. Fitz encouraged me to relax, and then he waited quietly before posing the question:

"What is it that stands between you and the knowledge of God?"

I could feel an immediate influx of confusion upon hearing those words. The word "God" rankled with me.

Why not use words like "The Eternal" or "Ground of Being" – the more non-personal terms I preferred? These and other related thoughts were coming in thick and fast, but I was determined to answer truthfully, which meant staying with what was present, here and now.

"I'm not sure; certainly, a little anxiety ... embarrassment even at the confusion," I eventually blurted out.

"Thank you ... *What is it that stands between you and the knowledge of God?"*

The repeated question left me somewhat numb, and at this point, making no sense of what was going on within me, my mind in a fog, I didn't answer. After a while, Fitz spoke again:

"Thank you ... *What is it that stands between you and the knowledge of God?"*

This time I answered immediately.

"My ever-active mind."

A short pause, then: "Thank you ... *What is it that stands between you and the knowledge of God?"*

With this next repetition of the question, I found that the thought processes, my so-called "ever-active mind", were beginning to fall away; quite quickly, the whole massive cloud, the accumulation of years of ego-based baggage, had somehow dissolved, leaving no sense of a separate self, no Zac. There was a boundless, spacious being in which all was one. *The* One which is the Being of every being.

"Nothing," I replied. "Nothing stands between 'me' and God. There's no 'me and God'. There's not two, just oneness."

Whilst saying this, I was looking at Fitz, and he too was of this oneness, in which he and I were not separate.

I felt moved to add: "Neither is there a *me* and a *you*. I am you, and you are me. And I am everyone, as are you, as is everyone ..."

“Thank you,” said Fitz. After a minute or so, he said, “Let’s go and join the others.”

Chapter 44

Fitz and I were the last to arrive back in the main room. Once we'd settled into our seats, Susan quickly glanced around the group before proceeding.

"Now that we're all here, I'd love to hear how you got on with the exercise you were given."

It was only a short time before a hand went up.

"Yes, Sandra," said Susan.

"It was like basking in love." I turned towards the speaker; Sandra was someone I'd also had no real connection with yet.

"Indeed. Anything else to add?" encouraged Susan.

"Only that my usual sense of self, me, Sandra, was absent."

"That's gratifying, isn't it?" Sandra simply nodded. Tamara, who was sitting next to her, gave her a brief sideways hug!

Karolina then shared her experiences, which included the one with me. She spoke of the privilege of being in the presence of someone who was completely open and transparent and how this was the foundation for a true relationship. There were murmurings of approval.

Daniel was the next to offer an observation.

"In the second exercise, I accidentally ended up partnering with my wife," he confessed, drawing amusement from some. Daniel's wife was Elizabeth, Fitz's daughter.

"We often meditate together, but not in the way you outlined for us today. Anyway, we dispensed with the *getting-to-know-you* part and went straight into the silent *being-with-one-another* exercise. It was wonderful. I asked myself, 'Who is this extraordinary woman facing me?'

Through this exercise, I was in touch with something very new, yet eternally present for 'eyes that see' ... and – I'm going to say this; my heart won't let me keep it back – I was in the presence of a goddess."

There were tears of joy in Daniel's eyes as he finished speaking. As far as I could tell, there was no one, including myself, unmoved by what they'd heard.

"Thank you, Daniel," Susan said. "What you saw was – *is* – the truth of everyone here – you *are* gods and goddesses. And you are right, when we have 'eyes that see', the curtain of illusion is drawn aside, and we behold the light of pure being.

Good. Let's leave it at that. It's been a truly rich afternoon. Each one of your insights has been received by us all as if it were our own. That's how a spiritual group works.

More than enough for you to absorb right now. Take all these insights as an *inner knowing* within you. Stay well, continue to inspire each other – you will. And ... *Au Revoir*!"

As Susan stood up, Fitz rushed to her, lifting her tiny frame off the floor while giving her a mighty hug. The rest of us stood as one, clapping and cheering. As the applause subsided, some of us approached Susan for one last goodbye. Hina was among them. She stood before Susan, with her hands placed together prayerfully.

"*Namaste*, darling," she managed through her tears, before embracing her dear friend.

I did not feel the need to join in; so, I took the opportunity to quietly leave the room and make my way out to the front of the house, waiting for Hina to join me when she was ready. Ralph was the next to emerge, approaching me with a smile and a warm handshake.

"Zac, isn't it? Maybe we could meet up some time over a coffee or a beer, your choice," he suggested.

"That'd be great," I agreed. We didn't make any immediate arrangements to meet, being content to exchange contact details.

Back home, Hina and I shared highlights of our respective one-to-one exercises. Hina affirmed that she'd experienced Fitz's repeat-question exercise several times previously, although the question used was different each time. She told me that if the one being questioned remained open and truthful, the question carried the power to pierce through whatever seemed to block the way to realisation.

Hina was particularly pleased that she'd been able to work with Jenny, who had joined the group at the same time as me.

"I'm sure she's our youngest member, and yet so wise," Hina said. "When we were sitting in silence together, I started to feel sleepy, even nodding off. She gently took my hand, so I glanced up and was met with such a loving light, I almost cried. She then shuffled closer to me, and I seemed to get a shot of renewed energy. She then whispered to me as the exercise ended, 'You are a beautiful soul.'

I mean, Zac, the community we are part of – aren't we blessed?"

After a light supper of pasta, mushrooms, and leeks, we settled down for a quiet evening. Hina suggested that Sunday might be an opportune time to make some progress in the planning of our marriage service. I agreed, but added that I'd also like to draw on her expertise for the meditation class I was preparing for Monday after school. Hina was happy with that and said it might help if we practiced together whatever meditation exercise we settled on.

"Well then," said Hina finally, "I think we may well need an early night."

"You're usually right on such matters," I agreed.

Chapter 45

We awoke to a bright sunny morning, so we decided, before anything else, to go somewhere outdoors. After a late breakfast, we revisited Harmony Park, Hina insisting that there was much more to the place than what we took in last time we were there, due to our somewhat hasty retreat.

As before, we entered the geometrically laid out park, walking past the small pond where we'd sat during our last visit. We soon came to a stone fountain at the centre of four paths, water gently flowing into an octagonal trough from the mouths of what appeared to be a four-sided lion's head.

Hina laughed as she noted my inquisitive nature, watching me slowly circle the feature, examining the fine detail.

"Look at those four faces," I said. "They're lions alright, but each one has quite a distinct personality, don't you think?"

Hina's assent took the form of a bright-eyed smile and a whispered, "I love you!"

We stopped for a while, enjoying the melodic sound of the cascading water. Looking around, I could see a bowling green with groups of mainly elderly people enjoying a game. From there, across the path, was a playground dominated by a beautifully constructed wooden climbing frame, which a few children were carefully exploring, while parents or carers stood by.

"Something for every generation," I mused, as we slowly

walked on, appreciating the wonderful gift of such outdoor resources.

As we turned a corner past some landscaped flowerbeds, a rather ornate building came into view. It reminded me of a certain seaside pavilion with its ornate dome, though this was on a smaller scale.

"That's the park's café," Hina pointed out. "You can sit inside, or on a day like today, we could sit outside on the balcony. They serve an all-day breakfast, a variety of cakes and scones, and excellent coffee ..."

Upon hearing the word "coffee", I quickened my pace, to Hina's amusement, pretending not to know that she'd set me up. Hina had come to recognise my partiality for that particular pick-me-up.

The words "Harmony Café" appeared above the front entrance in beautiful calligraphy.

"One of the local artists did that," Hina said, noticing how I was looking up at the sign. "The owners love to support local talent, and often display any number of works around the place. Sometimes they sponsor an exhibition based on a particular theme."

After checking out the full and varied menu, we decided to stop for an early lunch and eat outside at a table on the balcony. After making our order and while waiting for our food, a thought occurred to me, which I wasted no time putting to Hina.

"Why don't we discuss the marriage service while we're here? This place seems to lend itself to creativity, doesn't it? Should've brought a notebook and pen to write things down."

"A good idea," Hina agreed. "Look, we don't need pen and paper – we're sure to remember whatever we agree on. We can write it up when we get home."

The one thing we had already agreed upon was the vows, so we started our conversation by considering how marriage services usually began. We acknowledged that in most weddings we'd been to in this country, the groom stood up front near the minister, and the bride was escorted in by her father to be "given away."

"Not for me. I'm not being given away by my dad!" Hina insisted. "After all, I've *chosen* to give myself to you. And that's what should be reflected in the ritual. Right, Zac?"

"Yes, please," I agreed, getting a firm nudge, before adding, "And of course, I'm giving myself to you, Hina."

"Thank you. Which means we should walk in together."

"Done. And we need to agree on the music that goes with our entrance."

"And since I was the one who proposed to you, we should enter the room to some classical Indian music."

I was not sure about her logic, but I was happy to agree. As we were on the subject of music, I suggested we choose something joyful to close the ceremony.

I thought for a moment, inwardly asking myself what I'd like? My mind took me back to a concert in which I'd been mesmerised by Mozart's *Clarinet Quintet*. I made the suggestion, which Hina said she liked the sound of, but that she didn't know the piece. I offered to play it for her when we returned home.

The opening and closing music virtually decided, we next turned our attention to possible readings.

"How about letting Fitz read something of his choice?" Hina suggested. "It's bound to be something perfect for the occasion."

"Yes, I'd be confident on that score. What next?"

"Speaking of other contributions, there's my brother, Mahendra; I'm sure he'd like to be involved. What about your family, Zac?

"Probably my mum; she'd be keen. My dad, not sure – he usually avoids that sort of thing."

"I think we've now got enough to be going on with; we could get in touch with Steph again. I'd like her to know what we've decided. She'll no doubt be giving the marriage blessing; we could ask her about that too."

"That usually includes the blessing of the rings, doesn't it?"

"Indian weddings don't always include rings, although some foreign practices have seeped into the traditional ways. Can we give some thought to this another time, Zac? I'm not sure my mind can process much more now."

With that, we terminated our discussion about the marriage service and headed back home.

Chapter 46

After our evening meal, Hina wrote down the notes about our conversation in the park, while I searched for Mozart's *Clarinet Quintet* in my CD collection. Once we were comfortably settled, we listened together to the music. I was so happy to witness Hina, eyes closed, drinking it all in! We listened to all four movements. In the end, we both agreed that the final movement provided just the right note with which to close the service, an exquisite balance between joyful and solemn.

"Now," Hina said, after I'd turned off the CD player, "you wanted some inspiration for tomorrow's meditation class, right?"

"Yes, but only if you feel up to it tonight, Hina."

"I do, and I'm more than up for it because I have a little experiment in mind; it's been brewing for a while, and I feel this is the perfect opportunity to try it out. Honest!"

"OK. Let's give it a go."

"I've not done this before, but I have a good feel about it. This is what's needed; it's so easy. We sit in meditation together, facing each other, but with our eyes closed. You *stay* with the practice all the time while I ask you a series of questions. And although you will answer me, it's important that you continue with the meditation, not getting sucked into the ego-mind."

I could see immediately what Hina was driving at, and having agreed to go along with her "experiment", we got into our respective positions, preparing the body, relaxing, opening to the silence, in meditation.

After a minute or two, Hina asked: "What are you doing?"

Without shifting from the practice, remaining inwardly centred, I found it was possible to answer her:

"Relaxing ... stepping back, metaphorically speaking, from thought processes ... letting go."

A few moments later, Hina spoke again: "And what are you doing now?"

"Still letting go ... I'm more strongly aware of *witnessing* the mental stuff ... and I'm less engrossed than before."

Again, after a little while, Hina simply asked: "And now?"

"Not doing anything, as such ... there's an attitude of acceptance, really ... the thoughts are still performing their merry dance ... but I don't mind one way, or the other ... I feel very spacious, which makes all the mental activity appear like very minor stuff going on, as if it's far, far away."

After what seemed a longer period, Hina questioned me again: "What now?"

"There's no doing ... thought processes are still around ... and, in a way, so what? I'm simply sitting here, accepting whatever *is* as perfect ... nothing needs to change; nothing is disturbing my peace and contentment right now ..."

"In other words, you are simply *allowing everything to be as it is*," Hina commented.

"That's right."

"And how *is* that for you?"

I laughed. "Extremely liberating. Hina. Thank you; this will now be my approach tomorrow after school. I'm not sure how, but I know it'll come to me."

We sat for a while, just being together, until Hina indicated that she wanted to say something.

"Susan once said to me that once we truly master what meditation is *for*, it ceases to be a practice. We are no longer 'meditating'; we are just *allowing everything to be as it is.* This attitude increasingly establishes itself in all aspects of our life. We still do what we have to do, we still meet the obligations of our work, and so on – but we are inwardly free, and our composure can't be shaken. You've come into this Work, Zac, with so much of that unshakeable attitude already a part of you.

Were you a *guru* in a previous life?"

I just shook my head. "Hina, honestly, I haven't got a clue about any former lives. But I must've done something good for the gods of *karma* to propel you slap bang, right into my path."

Hina leaned over and kissed me. "Put some more music on, Zac; I want to know more of what you love."

This time, I put on Vivaldi's *The Four Seasons*, and we listened to some of it before retiring for the night.

Chapter 47

Fitz had been right in his prediction that the next meditation class at the school would be larger. It was good to see those who were present last time turning up again. In addition, four more of my older pupils arrived: Jana, Holly, Violet and Barry. Elaine brought along her boyfriend, Greg, and Jason Hewitt introduced me to his wife, Anara. She and her family had moved to the UK from Kazakhstan, he informed me as we were introduced, and the two had met at a charity fundraising event.

If the class continued to grow, I thought, we would have to move to a bigger room.

Once everyone had found a seat and appeared comfortable and ready, I began the session.

"This afternoon, I'd like us to consider this: that if we could transcend the level of personality, with all its desires and expectations, we would find that our core nature, which is our *real* Self, remained perfectly content with what *is*. There'd be no resistance, no grasping; in fact, there'd be no need for either.

The meditation I'm now proposing we follow is intended to directly demonstrate this to you all. Any questions before we start?"

There were no questions, so without more ado, I began to take the class gently into the practice, starting with the preliminary relaxation of the body, whilst sitting in a balanced, upright position. I then invited them to shift their attention from whatever thoughts were present to the natural coming and going of the breath.

"Now we'll keep this as simple as possible," I continued. "Remain sitting quietly, eyes closed, and let everything be just the way it is ... Don't focus on anything in particular – that now includes the breath; just let everything be, without trying to change, avoid or eliminate anything ... *Allow everything to be as it is* ... No effort is required, no trying ... This is an invitation to rest in pure openness ... the openness that is a quality of your essential nature ...

Whatever thoughts and images appear in the mind, make no effort to resist them ... let them be there ... let them come, and let them pass ... In this way, you are welcoming *this* moment, accepting this moment, as it is ...

You are watching the show ... so be one with what is watching ... one with the consciousness or awareness – the pure intelligence at the heart of all you perceive ..."

I continued to guide the group in this manner, which consisted in quietly repeating the instructions, though not necessarily using the exact words, and allowing plenty of space between each injection of words, whilst keeping myself in the same frame of awareness that I was asking of them.

I intuitively knew when it was time to bring the meditation to a close, and did so, sitting quietly with everyone until it was clear that the right moment had come to speak.

"Good ... How was that for you? Would anyone like to share?"

It was Anara who spoke first:

"I've so missed this. Back in Kazakhstan, I belonged to a Sufi group which taught a beautiful mystic philosophy and, of course, there was regular meditation."

"And just now," I prompted, drawing her back to the here and now, "What was happening for you during *this* practice?"

"Just the peacefulness of being, with no expectations, which I know I usually impose upon myself ... Glad to see that it's not at all necessary."

"Wonderful! That's an important insight. What about anyone else?"

"I liked the meditation," Violet said. "But I didn't manage to let go of thoughts – they just kept coming, queuing up, somehow ... a right old mental fog!"

"I can sympathise," I said. "It's often that way with me, too.

Two things. Firstly, you don't need to *let go* of thoughts – it's more like *letting them be*, 'watching the show' as I called it earlier.

Secondly, the 'fog'. OK, consider this analogy about the sun. On some cloudy days, you can't even tell if there's a sun at all. But you know it's there; the sun never stops shining, the same as when there are no clouds. In the same way, that fog of thoughts simply obscures your essential pure being. The light of your true Self is always shining; it is always there as the silent background to whatever is going on. Hold to this, keep practicing ... in time, you will surely come to see this."

I noticed that Conrad was itching to say something, but looked a little nervous.

"Go ahead, Conrad," I said, encouragingly, "I'd love to hear what you experienced."

"Well ... might sound a little weird," he said in a hesitant voice, "but during the meditation, I felt like I wasn't me!"

"Not weird at all. It's the other way round, Conrad. The more you practice meditation, the more you'll realise that what you thought of as you, *isn't* you; and the you that doesn't feel like you *is* who you really are. Funny stuff, eh? It's what we are all working on together: getting to know this *real* me. Do you get that?"

Conrad nodded, whilst managing a wry smile.

The class remained silent for a short time. After a while, Grant indicated that he had something he wanted to say.

"When I was growing up, my dad often said, 'If at first you don't succeed, try, try again.' I've heard others say the same. This 'not trying' or 'letting it be' is a whole different ball game. Are you saying that we shouldn't try succeeding in meditation?"

"A very good point. There has to be some intention, Grant, or you'd never sit down, close your eyes, and start to practice. But then you let things be as I've described; but you are still inquisitive; you are watching, taking it all in. You become innocent. It's what I think Jesus meant when he said, 'Unless you become like a child, you can't enter the Kingdom.' This doesn't mean you have to regress to your nursery days" – there was some laughter at this particular expression – "but even as adults, we needn't have lost that wonderful innocence ... which is a great quality to have in opening to truth."

I then turned to the whole class.

"Yes, this is a meditation class. And in meditating, we discover that we are on a path of self-enquiry. It will have repercussions for every aspect of our lives. So be prepared. We need to be brave. Hey? What we are ditching in the process are all our old habits, our fears, our prejudices, even, as Conrad showed, our beliefs about who we are. And the world out there is likely to present us with just the challenges we need to help us rediscover our glorious true Self.

If you find this approach OK for you, come back and join us in two weeks."

As the class dispersed, I could sense that there was a buzz of quiet satisfaction in the air, and I found this encouraging. Jason and Anara stayed back, however, to have a word with me.

"Thanks for this session, Zac," said Jason. "Anara and I have been pretty much sharing the spiritual path since we met, but probably in a somewhat casual way. What you've given us, I think, will help us go much further."

"Yes," Anara added. "I feel grateful already. And Zac, we'd love for you and your partner to join us for a meal one evening."

I thanked them and said that Hina and I would undoubtedly enjoy that. They left the room with their arms around each other. After they'd gone, I found myself thinking about Jason. He and I had been colleagues for a while at the school, but I felt we were becoming more than colleagues.

Although we didn't see each other much outside the context of the school, we were indeed friends, and I made a mental note to invite him and Anara to our marriage ceremony, whenever Hina and I had settled on a firm date.

Chapter 48

The following evening, Fitz telephoned, inviting Hina and me to a meeting at his place at the weekend. No reason was given, but knowing Fitz, we knew that it would not be a purely social get-together.

When we arrived on the Saturday afternoon, Fitz already had company. His daughter Elizabeth and Karolina, whom I'd partnered with at the previous group meeting, both warmly greeted us.

Shortly afterwards, Fitz came into the living room from his kitchen with a tray of drinks and shortbread biscuits, and then sat down with us.

"Good. You are all here now," he said matter-of-factly. "As you probably know, I look upon every member of our group as a teacher. There are different types of teachers. Some teach through their art; others by the simple beauty of the way they live – in other words, by example. Wisdom can be expressed and appreciated in a variety of ways.

I've specifically brought you four here because each of you has a *particular* gift that you share. A gift I've had the privilege of witnessing for some time. In your case, Zac, I've seen enough over a relatively shorter period.

It's this: you all have the ability to articulate spiritual teaching extremely well. Or to put it colloquially, you all have the *gift of the gab!*

It's why I encouraged you, Zac, to start the meditation group at your school. It's why you two, Elizabeth and Hina, are perfect for the new School of Spiritual Philosophy, which opens this coming Wednesday. And it's why Susan saw the potential in you, Karolina; we're both so delighted that you grasped the opportunity to train as a classroom teacher – but it won't be long before you'll be guiding the spiritual seeker as well.

For now, Elizabeth and Hina will focus on developing a beautiful step-by-step course in Philosophy; in time, I would like to see you both taking the chair in front of the group.

More immediately, with Susan's departure, I am looking for one or two, other than myself, to facilitate future group meetings. Apart from the fact that I may not always be able to attend due to other commitments, I do not want to assume any ownership of the role when other capable people could easily be available.

Karolina, not only do you have a beautiful way of expressing things, but your compassionate nature adds so much more, shining through to reach your listeners' hearts."

"That's so kind of you," said Karolina. "And your confidence in me means a lot. I have no idea how I'd fare in front of the group. All I can say is that I trust you, Fitz, and treasure your friendship."

"Bless you for that. You'll be more than fine."

Fitz then turned his attention toward me.

"Zac, it seems only yesterday that we met. But it's been more than three months. The time, however, is irrelevant. I know what I've seen ... what I *see*. You've been ready for a long time, longer than you realise. Our meeting was no accident. The universe has now kindly provided the right conditions for you to step forward. So, Zac, I hope, like Karolina, you'd be open to the challenge."

After holding eye contact with Fitz for a moment or two, I found I was able to respond: "Well, like Karolina, I feel a lot of gratitude for what you've just said, and I'm sure you know I've trusted you since day one. Count me in; after all, it's just one more jump into the unknown, isn't it?"

Fitz laughed before saying, "And the unknown will surely catch you safely!"

We all joined in the conviviality, before Fitz asked:

"Anyone want to ask a question, or say something about this?"

"I've always wanted to ask you this," Hina said, "But it never felt appropriate until now. Do you have a teacher, something like a *guru*, Fitz?"

"I've had quite a few teachers since I was a teenager," Fitz replied. "And this is a good question to ask right now, because I gained a lot about teaching from all of them. It would take too long to tell you about them all, but let's see who springs to mind.

My very first was, in fact, a teacher at my school. She taught History. But it was what she taught *about* her subject that stayed with me. She confessed that everything we learned about the past had to be partial, and probably misleading, because no history book was long enough to include all the nuances of the period it covered. We needed to be aware of what any historian might even deliberately choose *not* to mention. We had to be open, to take nothing for granted, although she stressed, with a wicked smile, we shouldn't let on to that attitude when answering questions in any public exam! What struck me most about her was that she was truthful to the core. She inspired me, and I resolved to be like her as much as possible.

Some years later, while stationed in Spain as part of my work, I met someone I'll refer to as Ruth, since she preferred to remain anonymous. She was from a Jewish family, but extremely versed in many different spiritualities. When I visited her home, I noticed a large framed coloured diagram on her living room wall and asked her about it. She told me that it represented the Tree of Life, which Kabbalists used as a guide to the different manifestations of the One. She introduced me to some teachings and practices from the Toledano tradition of Kabbalah. During the time the Moors ruled Spain, there was a merging of ancient Hebrew wisdom with Neo-Platonic and other philosophies; it was a time when there was a true understanding between the esoteric systems of Christianity, Judaism and Islam, and a free interplay between their adherents.

Ruth taught that there was only one true Teaching, the apparent multiplicity of teachings being due to a universal law, which is that the further one moves from the Divine source, the more diverse, limited and tenuous becomes the grasp on reality. A complete understanding only comes through union with the Divine itself.

From Ruth, I also learned how to see different levels of meaning in sacred texts, particularly those of Judaism and Christianity. Kabbalists teach that there are four levels of meaning corresponding to the four worlds: physical, psychological, spiritual and divine.

Ruth claimed that she was not a teacher, just a 'non-stop student'. Nevertheless, she led a Kabbalah group in her home, which I had the pleasure of attending whenever I was free. Her younger brother, Simon, usually sat beside her and often contributed with his own seemingly abundant wisdom.

The next significant teacher came much later. During my travels in the Far East, I met a teacher, an Indian swami, who was an initiate of the ancient Vedanta School. His teacher had been the Shankaracharya of the Jyotir Math ashram in North India. He called himself *Sangala*, he told me – the word means 'channel' – because he was merely a conduit for the universal teaching, the *sanatana dharma*, and because he himself 'knew nothing'.

This man who 'knew nothing' taught me so much. He once narrated an ancient legend that had greatly influenced him, about a saint who had twenty-four *gurus*, each of whom taught him a key aspect of truth. The inference was that everything in creation is a source of teaching if one is awake to it. The man himself was called *Dattatreya*. Part of his greatness lay in the fact that he never regarded himself as a teacher, and always introduced himself as a student. He appeared to wander about the country without any belongings. No one knew where he was going, and neither did he!"

We all showed our appreciation of what Fitz had shared with us, acknowledging that his outline of what had inspired him was, in fact, an inspiration to all of us.

Karolina was the next to raise a question with Fitz.

"Fitz, when teaching, do you ever have a moment when your mind goes blank? You are sitting there in front of a group, and you don't know what to say. Does that happen, and if so, what can be done about it?"

"This is a matter I mentioned to Zac when discussing his meditation class. The principle: that *knowledge arises to meet a need*. The teacher has no personal agenda. When in front of your group, you do not leave the depth of inner stillness. If you stop speaking, it could be that you've finished! Or there's a need for a pause; if the latter, stay unperturbed, remain at one with those who sit in front of you. Through that natural attunement, what needs to be said will be forthcoming. If you start speaking to fill the void, it will lower the energy because of the interference of the ego-mind, which carries the doubt.

Have no fear of pauses, moments of seeming emptiness, and the like. Non-stop speaking may well be a sign that you have left your true centre.

Another thing, a pause can happen because someone wants to ask a question. Never feel you are being interrupted. The student always comes first.

Does that help, Karolina?"

We were all happy with that answer, after which Fitz said he felt he'd said enough about teaching for now, and that we should share a short meditation before we departed.

Chapter 49

The first session of the School of Spiritual Philosophy began the following Wednesday evening at Geoff's house. Hina described how the evening went when she was back home. With fourteen students signing up for the ten sessions, only one class was needed. As had been agreed, Elizabeth took on the role of main tutor, but just before the class got underway, she asked Hina to consider herself the co-tutor.

"Elizabeth felt that for some areas of the course, she'd like me to take the lead," Hina explained. "Such as when we touched on aspects of Indian philosophy, of course. She also wanted me to be the main facilitator for meditation. Fitz had suggested it to her, but also said it would remain her decision."

"It's right you've been given that responsibility," I said. "As Fitz pointed out last Saturday, you're a natural."

Hina thanked me and then took a sheet of paper out of her shoulder bag, which she handed over to me.

"I thought you might like to see this; it's the basic outline of the first course, which we'd worked out with Fitz."

SCHOOL OF SPIRITUAL PHILOSOPHY
INTRODUCTORY COURSE

Week 1	Philosophy: Love of Wisdom. "Know Thyself."
Week 2	Who am I? Personality and Essence. Discernment.

Week 3 Levels of consciousness. Self-observation.

....

Week 4 The Sacred Present. Challenges or opportunities?
Non-attachment.

Week 5 Meditation. Knowledge and Action.

Week 6 Philosophy in the West. Plato: Allegory of the Cave.

Week 7 Philosophy in the East. Vedanta and Yoga.
Shankara: Self and not-Self.

Week 8 Insights from Sufism. Rumi and Ibn-Arabi.

Week 9 Happiness. Harmony in relationships. Life's purpose?

Week 10 All is one! Meditation as a way of life.

(Suggestions for reading before the next course).

"Why have you placed a line between weeks three and four?" I asked.

"Ah! We felt that by week three, we'd have got the measure of the class; we'll ask ourselves whether we're pitching the teaching at the right level. We're prepared to give extra time to some things if we agree that it would be more beneficial for the students.

For the same reason, we might also make some changes to the subject-matter, or even the order of the teaching – we aim to be very flexible. And anyway, anything we didn't manage to cover could be carried over to the next ten sessions.

Elizabeth did all the teaching this evening; she was fantastic – as if she'd been doing this all her life."

"Great! What about Ben? Did he turn up?"

"He did, but although he gave me a genuine smile, we didn't get to speak to one another. He sat quietly throughout the session and was one of the few not to ask any questions.

Before leaving, he spoke with Elizabeth, but I don't know what it was about. I'll meet her at the Clinic on Friday, after I've seen my clients, to review tonight's session and make plans for the next; she'll either share what was said with me, or not – I'll happily leave that to her."

Having been updated about the new philosophy course, my thoughts now turned to our marriage ceremony, since Steph was visiting us again the very next evening. When I reminded Hina about this, she said that she'd typed up notes for Steph based on what we'd agreed so far.

We were now looking forward to completing the arrangements, at least enough to start sending out invitations.

Chapter 50

Steph was not just our minister for the ceremony, she was turning into a lovely friend. After we'd met with her, we felt completely reassured about what we'd signed up for. She seemed to read both of us, as if she could see into the very soul of our relationship.

The shape and contents of the ceremony were now settled, although we still needed to speak to those we'd designated as contributors. The venue would be Geoff's house, in the garden, weather permitting. And for the date, we chose the last Saturday before Christmas. It meant that we needed to get moving with the invitations – they'd be going out from early next week, although some we would give out at the next group meeting, which was only two days away.

In addition to the group members, we wanted to keep the ceremony for close friends and close family only, especially if we were using Geoff's house. With the main room set up theatre-style, we reckoned we could sit a maximum of forty guests. We made it a priority to invite both our sets of parents, and Hina's brother, Mahendra, with his wife, Fiona

We would book the registry office to get legally married a day or two before, for which we needed two witnesses. We intended to keep this as low-key as possible. For us, the ceremony at Geoff's house was the real wedding, since we understood that nothing spiritual was allowed during the short registry office "formality".

In the end, Hina was happy for us to exchange rings during the blessing. Her attitude was a kind of shrug: "Why not?" and "Aren't we in England? Let's do it!" We decided to visit a jewellery shop at the next opportunity, which meant the coming Saturday morning.

As for the marriage blessing itself, we didn't want Steph to give us a heads-up. We both trusted her to be in tune with the occasion. We wanted the blessing to be new to us as we received it. Again, as with our approach to the vows, Steph told us this would be another first for her; she felt blessed to be a part of it!

The following evening, Hina shared with me a little of the conversation she'd had with Elizabeth earlier in the day, at the clinic. Among other things, they'd considered what Ben had said to Elizabeth after the class.

"Ben wondered why we'd chosen the title 'School of *Spiritual* Philosophy' for our project! He thought the word 'spiritual' was unnecessary and might put off some potential students. Elizabeth listened to him carefully and felt that he was being sincere and intending to be helpful.

His point was that philosophy, meaning *the love of wisdom*, was inherently spiritual, and therefore, why the emphasis? Furthermore, *School of Philosophy* was a more appropriate name; it was more straightforward and sounded better! You know what, after we'd discussed this a bit and reflected quietly together, we found that we too agreed with Ben. We're going to make the change for our next courses!"

"Well done, Ben," I said, "and well done you and Elizabeth. It's good to be open to suggestions wherever they come from, however surprising. Sound advice can come from anywhere, and one needn't be too proud or precious to listen. Have you put Fitz in the picture?"

"Not yet. But Fitz will be happy to leave it to me and Elizabeth; I'm confident of that."

When Hina was thrilled about something, she seemed to glow with an ethereal light. And lucky me, I got to bathe in that radiance. Although, of course, Fitz would insist that there was no such thing as 'luck': it was the law of *karma,* naturally threading its way with perfect intelligence into every corner of the universe.

Chapter 51

On Saturday morning, we set off early to visit some high street jewellery shops. We'd decided that wedding rings were symbolic and we weren't going to spend a fortune on them. Happily, we found rings that we liked in the first shop that we came to. We were told that often rings had to be ordered if they didn't have the size the customer needed, but luckily for us, our sizes were available, and we bought them – or rather, I bought them – without too much fuss.

We also set off earlier than usual to our next group meeting so that before everyone arrived, we could place an invitation to our marriage ceremony on every chair. Fitz was also there early and once he'd noticed me, he immediately drew me aside.

"Zac, this is short notice, I know, but I hope you don't mind. Angelo's mother died, or rather, made her transition, a few days ago. She and Angelo were very close. He'll be attending the group this afternoon, and although deep down, he's very much aware that life goes on, he'll still be somewhat raw in the early stages of grief.

Before I get down to any teaching, I'd like you to share with everyone the near-death experience you had. The way you shared it with me, when we met for the second time, way back in June."

"I'd be happy to, Fitz. Just call me out when you want me," I replied, adopting a confident manner, despite the onset of stomach butterflies. Knowing Fitz, he probably noticed this, but he didn't say anything.

"Thanks, Zac. As it happens, it'll be your first time addressing the group, but not the last."

Once the group session began, Fitz spent a few moments paying homage to Angelo's mother, whom he knew personally, and offering his love and support to Angelo and his family.

He then called me out front to speak, and I gave a slightly shorter version of my experience, focusing mainly on what happened once I'd fallen into the pool. When I'd finished, Fitz thanked me, and once I'd returned to my seat, he then asked for a short period of silence before speaking again.

"Let me take this opportunity to speak to you about the experience of grief. It is perfectly natural to experience grief when somebody you love makes the transition from this life to the next. In truth, life is a continuum, but the separation at the physical level can sometimes appear to create a dark hole, and the temptation is to give way to despair.

The reason for this is the commonly held belief that death signifies a loss that is somehow final and irreversible.

The best way to deal with grief is not to resist it. Let it engulf you; allow it to wash right through you. If you do this, you will find that this experience often gives way to a period of inner peace.

In the stillness that follows, we may access a deeper knowing within us. Our soul knows, has always known, its origin within the divine consciousness. And this is true for the loved one being mourned. No one goes before their time, and when they do, it is the continuation of the journey to our eternal Home.

Our origin, where we come from, and our destiny, where we are being drawn back to, are one and the same. This is true for everyone, without exception."

Fitz took a few moments to look around, giving Angelo a big smile in the process, before continuing with the teaching.

"We can never be separate from those we love. We are bound together, beyond all the external changes that go on in the physical realm. In consciousness, we are forever one. Everything is held, one and inseparable, within the Divine Heart.

What we call 'death' can be an invitation to find space in our lives for a deep surrender to that which is unchanging in the depths of our heart, where we'll know with absolute certainty that our loved one's highest good is being met in the realms beyond.

We'll take a break now and regather in about twenty minutes."

Once we'd returned to our seats, Fitz told us that he'd been very pleased by how well the one-to-one exercises had gone when we last met. Add to that, the bonus: the unity amongst us was increasingly evident. He acknowledged that the teaching before the refreshment break had been quite intense, although in a good way, and suggested that we now do something practical.

This time, instead of each of us looking for a partner to work with, he had worked out in advance how we were to be paired up, linking, as far as it was possible, those he felt knew each other the least.

"Although this is certainly not an exact science," he added. "Just enjoy working with your allotted member, even if you've worked with them before.

OK, this is the exercise for this afternoon. You have about an hour, but you needn't use the whole time. There are three stages:

Firstly, one of you guides the other in a meditation practice. Any practice, be creative. The *form* is secondary to the consciousness that you invest in the task.

Secondly, you swap roles. The same principle applies.

Thirdly, give each other feedback, honestly and fairly.

Be true to the inspiration of the moment; then whatever practice you adopt will be transformational, for both the giver and the recipient.

And of course, this is something you should all enjoy."

Fitz had paired me up with Jasmine, whom I remembered meeting briefly several months previously. I'd been introduced to her by Hina during a refreshment break. She was David's aunt, and someone I'd been looking forward to meeting again.

We found a quiet corner and placed two chairs opposite each other, before sitting down. I told Jasmine how pleased I was to be working with her and invited her to take the lead first.

"You know, today's teaching has reminded me of a Sufi saying, *Die before you die, and you shall never die*," she began. "It's the death of the ego that's meant; the death of clinging to all that's transient. No ego means there's no one to be afraid of dying. There is only oneness; infinite being.

Shall we apply this now, in a meditation practice?"

"Of course," I said. "I'm happy to place myself in your hands!"

Jasmine smiled and then proceeded to take me through the preliminary postural and relaxation steps. I made a mental note of the fact that she offered a lot more space between each instruction than I generally allowed.

"Now that you've settled, be totally and effortlessly present …

This is the only moment, right now ...

Let go of any attempt to control ... anything.

Is there someone or something you are holding onto?

Let go ...

Let go of that thought, or memory ... let it go ... let it go ...

Let go of your self-image, possessions, your work, any plans ...

Allow everything to be resolved in the unborn ground of your inherent, infinite nature ...

Whatever comes to mind ... let it be ...

Remain centred in this moment ...

Accept yourself ... totally ...

Accept all others for what they are ...

With each breath, let go of expectation, regret ...

Let go of the need for approval ...

Let go of old judgements and opinions ...

Die to all that ... enjoy the natural freedom ...

Let go ... Let be ... at home ...at ease ..."

After a while, and not hearing any further instructions, I opened my eyes. A shining Jasmine sat before me.

"How is it for you now?" she asked.

"Extraordinarily spacious," was all I could manage; I appeared to contain everything that was in my field of perception. I was reminded of Conrad's observation at the last meditation class: "I felt like I wasn't me!" I shared this with Jasmine, who appreciated the irony of the situation.

"Yes," she countered. "The ego keeps us locked in a very limited perception of reality. When ego-free, we see things closer to how they are; usually the opposite of the commonly held view.

OK, Zac. I'd like you to be the facilitator now, please."

We switched roles, and finding that I was still in that spacious awareness, I guided Jasmine into a meditation that unfurled itself effortlessly, moment by moment. It was similar to what I'd led at the last meditation class, only using fewer words and, taking a leaf out of Jasmine's book, allowing more space between each step in the guidance.

At the end of the practice, we decided to share feedback whilst walking together in the garden, agreeing to speak softly so as not to disturb those who might still be working together there. As it happens, the two couples in the garden seemed to be conversing, having also completed their two practices.

I commended Jasmine on her unhurried approach. She said that it depended on the person sitting in front of her, and that this would vary according to her inner guidance at the time.

She, in turn, appreciated the intonation of my voice, which she said helped to carry her into a deep, restful place. Speaking more generally, she said that, when in front of a group, if the teacher is truly attuned, the voice will naturally adapt to the situation; and there will also be whatever is required of humour, seriousness, or any other aspect of a teacher's devices.

"I can see the importance of enjoying every moment and every experience," I then found myself saying, "but without grasping, or trying to hold on ... including even our loved ones. Being able to love *and* let go. I truly want – though *want* is probably the wrong word – anyway, I can't think of another; so yes, I really want to love, including love for Hina – to love, without any degree of possessiveness, allowing her perfect freedom to be herself ..."

"That ideal is right at the heart of *The Work*," Jasmine replied, her words carrying genuine support. "It reminds me of a short but very wise poem by William Blake:

He who binds to himself a joy
Does the winged life destroy;
He who kisses the joy as it flies
Lives in eternity's sunrise."

"That just about sums it up," I said, as we made our way back to the others in the main room.

Chapter 52

The following Monday evening, Hina and I visited the home of Jason and Anara, a pleasant semi-detached house in a secluded cul-de-sac. Having been received like old friends and offered drinks, we settled down in their modest living room.

I couldn't help but notice a prominently placed framed painting on the wall directly facing me. It was a portrait, head and shoulders only, of a noble-looking bearded man. I asked our hosts about it.

"That's Khoja Ahmed Yasawi," Anara answered, in a reverent tone. "He's the founder of a major branch of Sufism in Kazakhstan. His tomb is a well-known focus for pilgrims. It gets visited not only from within Kazakhstan but also by people like me who've moved abroad. Sufis from other countries are also attracted to the site.

He lived in the twelfth century, and his influence spread way beyond his country. Sufism was heavily suppressed during the Soviet period, but it picked up later, mainly through Kazakhs returning from abroad, and now the number of Sufi groups is increasing in most parts of the country."

"That's just so heartening," Hina commented. "There are Sufi groups in this country, I'm glad to say."

"There is so much of value in the Sufi way," I added, "and I love Rumi's poetry."

"We've recently joined a local Sufi group," Jason told us. "They're quite active, and very open to Sufi teachings and practices from different branches of the tradition, as well as inspirations from other quarters."

Just then, we heard what sounded like movement on a floor above us.

"Do you have other family staying here with you?" I gently asked.

"Oh no," Anara said, smiling. "We have *guests*; well, that's what we call them."

"They came to us through our work with the *Refugee Trust*," Jason added. "Anahita is an Iranian woman with an eleven-year-old daughter, Zarina, although she prefers to be called Zari. They came to this country as asylum seekers a few years ago, but they've now been granted permission to stay indefinitely, which is fantastic. Our charity helps with finding good accommodation, work or study opportunities, access to health care, and schooling for the children.

Anahita hopes eventually to gain British citizenship. They're a little squashed, up there in our converted loft, but it'll have to do for the time being – until they can find a more suitable and affordable place, and that won't be too easy."

Hina and I looked at each other, and she gave me an almost imperceptible nod. I knew immediately that we were at one with what I was about to say:

"Well, as it happens, Hina and I are moving to a new home very shortly, but we'll be keeping our existing house, which we hope to let out to some family ... once we've given it a good spring clean. Maybe your 'guests' would like to consider our place ..."

"We'd love to offer them a home," Hina pitched in eagerly. "Could we meet them this evening? If that works for you, of course."

Looking at Hina as she spoke was like witnessing pure compassion in action! Even as I was feeling proud of her,

I'm sure that, at the same time, my love for her went up another notch!

"I'll go and see if they'd like to join us," Anara said, as she stood up and left the room.

While she made her way upstairs, Jason filled us in with a little more background:

"It's extremely tough being a female in Iran, especially if you belong to one of the minority faiths like Anahita. She is from a Baha'i family. Her husband stayed behind; apparently, he's a serial optimist and believes that things *can* change for the better. Anahita hopes that one day her husband will be able to join her here, but she fled Iran to give her daughter a better chance at an education and more freedom to follow her dreams. She's a loving mother who's been very brave."

"We'd love to help them," Hina began, but stopped as Anara brought her lodgers into the living room.

For a mother of an eleven-year-old daughter, Anahita looked quite young, but looks could be deceptive, I told myself. They were both in Western casual attire – t-shirts, jeans and trainers.

We spoke for a little while about their circumstances and learned that Anahita worked part-time at a local supermarket, which she enjoyed, and Zari attended school, where she was making friends and doing well.

After a while, it became clear to us that Anahita was more than a "guest"; she had become a close friend of Anara and Jason. We were told that from time to time, she accompanied them to their Sufi group, where she found, to her delight, that her Baha'i faith was not out of place.

We shared details of our home with Anahita and invited her and her daughter to visit.

"If you decide to move there," I said, "we won't charge you any rent for the first three months; then when we do, we'll take advice from the refugee charity so that it's a fair rent for those in your position. How does that sound?"

"You are very kind," Anahita said tearfully, before turning to Anara and asking what she thought of the offer.

"It's up to you, darling," Anara replied. "If you should move to Zac's house, your landlords will then be our friends, people that we trust, and that's so much better than ending up somewhere where there might be more uncertain conditions."

It was eventually agreed that Anahita and Zari would visit the house with Anara sometime in the next few weeks.

Jason invited them to join us for the evening meal, but Anahita said that she and Zari had already eaten, and after thanking us profusely, they returned to their upstairs accommodation.

"Right, we'd better serve up supper," said Anara. "Come and sit down in our kitchen-diner."

We enjoyed a delicious meal, a vegetarian lentil stew, followed by a dessert of apple and rhubarb crumble. We also enjoyed their company. Jason and I endeavoured to stay off educational matters; instead, our conversation focused on our spiritual interests, and Hina and I discovered that we had a lot in common with our hosts. We had made some wonderful new friends, and without hesitation, we invited them to our marriage ceremony.

I was also aware, as the evening progressed, of a desire to invite Jason and Anara to join our group. At the same time, I could see that two things were holding me back. One was the fact that they already enjoyed attending a Sufi group, and I did not wish to appear disrespectful in any way.

Secondly, I wondered if the group was getting too large, and whether there was an energetic principle that governed the threshold beyond which a group might somehow be negatively affected. I made a mental note to question Fitz about this and so chose to refrain from any action until I'd gained more clarity.

Before leaving, Hina and I agreed to join Jason and Anara at one of the Refugee Trust's fundraising events. We both knew that being of service was itself a spiritual practice, and a way of helping others less fortunate than ourselves.

Chapter 53

I wasted little time before phoning Fitz, and we arranged to meet at his place a few days later.

Before we got down to any conversation, Fitz presented me with a small gift. It was a set of Tibetan bells, similar to those Susan used during group meetings. Fitz explained that, over the years, he'd twice received the same gift, but one set would suffice for him. I thanked him and was sure I could use them, beginning with the next meditation class at my school.

We soon turned our attention to the reason for my visit.

"Fitz, there are a few things I'd like to run by you," I began. "They're related. There are some people I've considered inviting to join the group. But I've held back, not because I'm uncertain about their suitability – they're very suitable – but I was wondering about the *size* of our group: could it already be too large?

Also, is there some natural law which governs the threshold beyond which a group might somehow become increasingly less effective in its purpose?"

"To come to your second question first, it's not something I've seriously considered," Fitz replied, "but there are some in this Work who look at the mathematics of group work quite seriously. They'd point out, for example, that Jesus had twelve major disciples, known as apostles, including an inner core of three: Peter, James and John.

Twelve is three times four.

The number three relates to action, the three forces needed for anything to happen. This is well described as the

Law of Three in the system Gurdjieff brought to the West. In *Vedanta* generally, and specifically in the *Bhagavad Gita*, the three *gunas* are described as the three forces that operate at every level of creation, from macrocosmic to microscopic. They are personified as the three great gods: *Brahma*, the creator; *Vishnu*, the sustainer; and *Shiva*, usually described as the destroyer, although nothing is really destroyed – it is simply dissolved back into its unmanifest origin.

If we consider a sequence of numbers, the third is what brings about the reconciliation of opposites, the synthesis, and so is associated with peace and justice, balance and harmony.

The number four, or *tetrad*, suggests stability. Three is dynamic; four is steady, grounded, and reliable. The four wheels of a car, the four legs of this settee we are sitting on, holding us. Stability. If you use these criteria, then the number twelve incorporates both dynamism and stability.

With regard to our own group, there has always been, if you like, an unofficial inner circle which meets occasionally when it's felt there's something we need to give our attention to. Up to now, those involved have been Susan, Jasmine and myself. Our last meeting was just before Susan left for Malta.

We would, when it was necessary, look at areas of teaching that we thought might be needed or welcome at any time; we'd sometimes discuss the care of any individual member who might be going through a difficult patch; or we might meet to share and deepen our own existing knowledge and awareness, which in turn would benefit the group."

"Then, with Susan gone, what is the situation now?" I asked.

"If you hadn't asked to see me, I would have been contacting you anyway, because this is precisely a matter I wanted to speak to you about.

You have to understand, when looking at the bigger picture, that groups come and go; the make-up of a group will also change occasionally. People die, or move abroad like Susan and Geoff, or choose to leave for a variety of other reasons. In some countries, political changes could force a group to stop meeting altogether, or even resort to meeting in secret. Fortunately, in this country, such groups as ours can meet quite freely.

Sometimes nothing changes for quite a while, and then suddenly a rush of changes may occur close to each other. That's why I'm speaking to you now. Another change will happen either by the end of this year or early next year.

I will be moving to the north of England, to York. I'm following an inner impulse, which I've sat with for a while, to ensure it's not a personal whim, but a genuinely divine prompting. Whenever I am faithful to that inner guidance, it always proves to be the right decision.

It will involve continuing The Work in that fine city. Jasmine is coming with me; we've been friends for a long time, and love each other's company. Whether our relationship takes a more intimate turn remains to be seen. We are both committed to being true to each other, so all will be well either way.

So, coming back to the group: by the end of this year, several senior members will have departed: Susan, Geoff, and possibly Jasmine and myself.

If there were an inner circle of three from here on in, who would be the members?"

"Well," I said, once I had caught my breath, even as I noticed the slight oncoming of a kind of sadness at the thought of Fitz's departure, "going back to our last meeting, which was about two weeks ago, you'd invited those of us who you said had a natural flair for teaching: Hina, Elizabeth, Karolina ... and myself!"

"That's right. And of you four, I'd currently whittle it down to three, leaving out Elizabeth; not because she's less capable – she's more than capable – but because her leadership of the School of Philosophy must currently be her prime responsibility.

Zac, I know you have been with us for a relatively short time, but that factor is irrelevant. I'd like you to consider yourself the senior teacher for our group. Hina and Karolina are both splendid teachers, with their own very gifted styles. But you also possess great leadership qualities, and often those qualities are needed.

Your commitment to truth is impeccable. I fully trust you to take over the mantle of leadership. For the group to continue to flourish, it needs someone exactly like you to oversee its well-being ... that's why you turned up when you did!"

We sat for a while in silence, during which I observed the usual demons of self-doubt wanting to assert themselves. But when I looked at Fitz, and tuned into his energy and consciousness, I was once again in touch with the inner strength and understanding of my core being. I knew that there was no going back; that this invitation had come to me without any seeking. It was, as Fitz would say, a divine appointment.

"Of course," I said. "Yes. Because, to coin a phrase, it's written in the stars. With divine assistance, I will ensure our group continues in good order."

"Wonderful. And regarding the group size?"

"Not a problem. With you and Jasmine going, its size will be reduced anyway. All it requires is to remain consciously sensitive at all times to the health of the group, and, if all is well, leave well alone!"

"Bravo. A man after my own heart. That's settled then; let's have some tea!"

Chapter 54

Over the next few weeks, Hina and I found ourselves dealing with new developments – all to the good.

Hina was able to reduce her hours at the bookshop to accommodate the increased demand for her services as a spiritual counsellor, for which Elizabeth offered a further half-day at her clinic. The School of Philosophy, as it had now been renamed, gave both of them a great deal of satisfaction.

Hina came home one evening, after a Wednesday class, itching to share the delight she felt.

"It's so wonderful, Zac," she said, bursting with joy, "to have such a mature group of people to teach. The course has attracted those who've all lived a bit; they've been challenged in one way or another, which has led them to ask themselves questions, such as *Why am I here? Does life have a purpose? Why am I afraid of love? Is there a God?* I could go on, but you get my drift. They are also discovering that there's a wisdom in each one of them, that they can tap into."

I was, of course, delighted for Hina as I witnessed her growing into the role. She had already started sharing in the teaching, and I felt grateful for Elizabeth's generosity, her selflessness, and lack of need to monopolise the role.

As for me, the meditation class at the school continued to thrive; I'd also moved it to a bigger room, one of the larger classrooms.

I was also getting to know some of the other group members more directly. Ralph and I had met for a coffee, and I could see why he'd been invited to join us. He exuded a *joie de vivre* which was quite infectious, and he was a great example of someone who chose to learn from his life experiences, understanding the power of challenges as opportunities to grow.

The school's half-term break provided a useful window for Hina and me to move into Geoff's house. For the time being, until we'd worked out how to best to make use of this "mansion" which had been offered to us, we commandeered the living spaces on the first floor, which were in effect the equivalent of a two-bedroom apartment, including an *en suite* bathroom, and a small kitchen. We would still use the downstairs kitchen when needed, but that and all the other ground floor spaces would mainly be reserved for the group and the new School of Philosophy.

We also decided to stop referring to the property as *Geoff's house*. After a discussion with Fitz and a few other members, it was agreed that we adopt the name *Unity House*; a plaque embossed with that name was soon attached to the brickwork near the front entrance.

Now that we'd made the move, we contacted my parents, who lived in Dorset, and invited them to stay with us for the weekend of our marriage ceremony. Likewise, there would be space for Mahendra and Fiona, who would be travelling down from Scotland. As for Hina's parents, they lived near enough to easily join us on the day itself, but we gave them the same option anyway, which they said they would consider.

During this period, we also visited the local registry office. We arranged for the legal marriage service to be conducted on the same day as our more spiritually-centred marriage ceremony, which would be held at Unity House.

That way, in the morning we'd be legally bound together, and in the afternoon our existing union, based on love and spiritual affinity, would be acknowledged and blessed. We were delighted that this would all happen on the same day.

At the registry office, we were told that we needed a minimum of two witnesses for the service to be legally binding. In the end, we found four friends who were more than willing to act as witnesses: Jason, Anara, Elizabeth and Daniel.

Once we were home, I found a message on the answerphone from Mum asking me to call her as soon as possible; I did so immediately. She didn't want to worry me, she insisted, as soon as she heard my voice, but she thought I should know that dad was in a local hospital being treated for a broken leg. She was quick to point out that he was in good spirits and otherwise healthy.

The "silly man" – her words – had fallen off a ladder in their garden, whilst trying to cut down an impossibly high branch that was threatening to damage an upstairs window in their home. He would love me to visit him, as he wanted to talk to me directly about one or two matters! Intriguing!

I decided without hesitation that I would go, and when I shared the news with Hina, she voiced a strong desire to accompany me. It would be a great opportunity for her to meet my parents well *before* we were married. I immediately made arrangements to travel to Poole in Dorset on Friday afternoon, soon after Hina had finished at the Clinic, and we'd then return on Sunday evening since I would be teaching again the next day.

After I'd booked the return rail tickets to Poole station and made a start on packing, I phoned Fitz to excuse myself and Hina from the next group meeting, explaining what had happened with dad.

“I’m sorry to miss the group,” I said. “It will be the first time since I joined, and those meetings are always so special.”

“Well, you cannot miss the truth,” he rejoined, “because it is in you. You must give your father the fullest attention and be open to the truth he will express to you during your visit. That is where you are meant to be.”

“Thanks, Fitz. I look forward to a catch-up with you when I get back.”

Chapter 55

It was a Friday, and Hina's regular morning at the Clinic, but she was able to rearrange the consultation booked with her third client so that we could leave as early as possible. I managed to set some work for my A Level class to get on with without me, enabling me to leave the school at lunchtime.

We took the underground to Waterloo, then changed onto the train for Poole. The journey took about two and a half hours, and we arrived just shy of three o'clock. To save time, we hired a taxi at the station to take us to the hospital.

At the hospital, a receptionist confirmed that my dad had been admitted to the orthopaedic ward and pointed us in the right direction. After a zig-zagging trek through dimly lit corridors and up two flights of stairs, we finally found ourselves in the right place and quietly entered the ward.

I spotted dad immediately; he was dressed in pyjamas and a dressing gown, and sitting on a chair adjacent to a standard hospital bed, his right leg in a plaster cast and resting on a metal stool. Mum was sitting on the bed next to him. As soon as she saw us, she ran towards us gleefully, embracing us both in turn.

"Wow! You got here so quickly, Zac, and with your lovely fiancé … So delighted to see you both together, for real."

"And I've been wanting to meet you and your husband too," Hina replied, entering into mum's joyful mood.

"How's dad doing, mum?" I asked.

"Go and ask him yourself," she suggested, "while Hina and I go down to the hospital café for our first proper chin-wag. We'll come back and rejoin you soon." And with that, the two of them disappeared through the doorway. I assumed dad must have asked for some time alone with me, and mum was taking Hina off in her usual considerate manner.

I went over to dad, took his hands and gently kissed his forehead.

"Hi, dad, how are things?"

"As you can see, the irresistible force has turned into an immovable object!"

It took me a few moments to catch his meaning before replying: "If my translation is correct, it means you have to sit like that until the nurse gives you permission to move. Am I right?"

"Spot on, Zac. Despite how it looks, however, I'm as fit as ever ... apart from this here leg. It's not as bad as it seems. I'm told that bones are living tissue, so quite capable of healing, but they need to be lined up and held in place long enough to ensure they heal in the right position. That's why this leg is currently in prison. It might be a week or two before this thing can be removed."

"I'm glad you're healing, and you sound in good spirits despite what's happened. Do you have any idea when you can go home?"

"I'll know later today, or tomorrow, when the leg is examined again. But enough of all that. Now you're here, there are things I want to say to you. I'm sure you know that your mum and I are delighted that you're getting married, that you've at last met the right girl. So, while it's just the two of us, I want to tell you what your mum and I have been considering. First of all, we want to give you a special wedding present, but to do so, I need your bank details."

"Dad, Hina and I are OK financially, we don't ..."

"Stop, Zac. I don't need to hear all that; I know you've always been careful in money matters. That's not the point.

Didn't St. Francis say, '*It is in giving that we receive*?' I've been in finance for too long, and I've acquired more wealth than anyone needs. None of it will be of any use to me when I go through those pearly gates to join the heavenly assembly, will it?

How much of a mortgage do you currently owe?"

"It's about £30,000, give or take a little ..."

"Listen," Dad said before I could continue, "your mother and I want to pay it off as a wedding present. Being free of a mortgage sets you up for your future married life; there's always the unexpected around the corner; new expenses are bound to come, especially if you have children! We'll transfer £50,000 into your bank account so you can pay off the mortgage, and have a tidy sum left over for you to set up home together. Rest assured, Zac, it'll hardly make any difference for your mum and me.

Right, the matter is now closed. Let me have your bank details before you go back to London."

"Dad, that's so generous. What can I say?"

"Nothing, Zac. There's more. Your mother also wants you to have something tangible, something that you can see and hold. We know how your love of books influenced your choice of career. That's why we're getting you a special collection of the fifty greatest classics, all in similar hardback editions. You know, Charles Dickens, George Orwell, Victor Hugo, Jane Austen, Leo Tolstoy, and many other great writers. You'll eventually be able to pass them on to your children.

And, in addition, your mother has something up her sleeve especially for Hina. No doubt she'll get onto that during their conversation in the café.

Now do me a favour, Zac. Go down to the café and bring me back a medium-sized Americano, with milk, no sugar; the stuff they bring round here on a trolley is virtually undrinkable."

I gave dad a big hug, carefully avoiding his leg, and made my way out of the ward and down to the café, which was a Costa franchise, so I was familiar with what was on offer. Before ordering, I looked around and saw mum and Hina. They were happily engrossed in conversation and didn't see me until I arrived at their table.

"Hi, you two," I said. "Dad sent me to get him a proper coffee. You seem to be enjoying yourselves."

"Us girls are doing just fine," mum replied. "What Hina's been telling me about her background and her work is fascinating; I can't get enough of it."

Hina laughed. "Your mum is so interesting, Zac. She and your dad are an amazing couple ..."

"You can call me Becky," mum said to Hina; then, turning to me, "Go and get your dad his coffee, and we'll come up to the ward shortly."

I could sense that mum wanted a little more time alone with Hina. I bought two coffees, then returned to the ward to see dad.

When the four of us had re-united next to dad's hospital bed, Hina wasted no time in asking dad how he was doing; was he getting the right nourishment, was he able to relax, and other related questions.

Dad's response was typical, an exercise in diversion. He hated talking about himself:

"Well, Zac, I see you'll be well looked after. Your wife-to-be is as caring as she's gorgeous. Now, Hina, don't you worry about me; I'll be rocking an' a-rolling in no time! I want to be dancing with you, Becky, and every other female that'll let me, on your wedding day."

"I look forward to that," Hina reassured him. We didn't mention that no dancing had been planned for the occasion!

"Becky has filled me in," Hina continued, "about your gifts for our wedding. It's wonderful, and I thank you both. What's also wonderful is your love for Zac, which I can see and feel so clearly. I also feel that you have accepted me unconditionally as part of your family – you haven't needed to express it verbally. I promise to be a good daughter-in-law to you both!"

Mum was moved to tears, and dad nearly so.

Just then, a nurse joined us and respectfully waited a few moments before speaking to dad.

"Hello, Clive dear," she said. "I've been in touch with the doctor, and he's informed me that he'll check how your leg is healing tomorrow morning. If all is well, and I see no reason why it wouldn't be, you'll be off back home in the afternoon."

"Thanks, Barbara," dad replied. "That's good news."

Nurse Barbara smiled and then made her way over to another patient.

Mum turned to dad. "Darling, we're going to leave you to get some rest. And these youngsters must be tired after their long journey. I'll need to settle them in at home and get some dinner prepared. We'll come back tomorrow afternoon, when I hope to take you home with us. I hope you have a good evening."

With that, she kissed him sweetly, and Hina and I expressed our best wishes for tomorrow's doctor's appointment. The three of us then left, and mum drove us in her Vauxhall Viva to the Marshal residence.

Chapter 56

Mum drove us into the quiet leafy cul-de-sac I was familiar with, before parking on the spacious front drive next to dad's Mercedes saloon. Once we were all in the house, she told us about the arrangements she'd made for our stay.

"You might as well put your luggage upstairs now. Zac, use your old room; I checked it earlier to make sure it was cosy and ready for you both. Then come down and join me in the living room. By the way, Hina, please view this place as your own home while you're here."

"Thank you so much," Hina chimed, as we picked up our luggage and made our way upstairs.

We came down to a delicious vegetarian stir fry, which included cashew nuts, broccoli florets, and marinated tofu, followed by a dessert of yoghurt and fresh berries. As mum said she wanted an early night, we jumped in and insisted on clearing the table and washing up. She gave us loving hugs and went up to her bedroom.

The next day, after a late breakfast, I suggested we take advantage of a sunny, if chilly day, to wander down to the beach.

"You two, go," mum said. "I'll be here when you get back; then we can have a snack before we go to the hospital."

So off we went, and on the way, passing an ice-cream van parked on the coastal road, temptation got the better of us. We ended up with differently flavoured ice-creams, tucked into cones. Hina's inner child was in full swing as she cooed over this simple delight.

Drawing nearer to the beach, we enjoyed looking out over the English Channel, observing the much fewer families, given the time of year, nevertheless enjoying the same experience, the younger members playing games in the sand. We continued walking until our ice-creams were no more, and then took ourselves to a bench with a wide, favourable view of this scene.

As we sat quietly, enjoying the sights and sounds of our coastal surroundings, I was moved to ask Hina about her work as a spiritual counsellor. I had been meaning to do this for some time, but other matters always seemed to step in and take precedence. Also, humility was one of Hina's attractive attributes as a young woman, and I was aware that we spent more time discussing my activities than hers. This was a chance to redress the balance.

"Tell me, Hina," I said, "while we've some time together, about your work as a spiritual counsellor. I know you did the training, but what interests me is what happens when you're actually with your client; what then? What do you rely on in the moment?"

Hina looked at me appreciatively. "What a question, Zac! Yes, I did the training and gained some valuable tools, plus the certificate, which allows me to practice. But at the same time as I was training, and ever since then, through meditation, and precious moments of reflection, and not forgetting helpful discussions with Fitz and Elizabeth, I've found there to be three basic things without which the counselling could not be considered 'spiritual'.

I regard these three principles as key to serving those who've chosen to come to me.

The first principle is *grace* ... 'allow room for *grace*,' someone said. It's a recognition that nothing can happen outside the divine compass. Even the working out of *karma* is held within the all-knowing and all-loving One. Behind everything that happens to us, whether *we* might consider it to be good or bad, there's the silent influence of grace. As Jesus said, 'Even a sparrow cannot fall to the ground apart from the will of God'.

It means you have to *let go and let God*, surrendering every counselling session to a greater purpose. Yes, you give of yourself, together with all the tools of your training and all your life experience – but you drop the *burden* of responsibility and leave the fruits of your work to the beautiful intelligence of universal Love. This is what I believe Krishna meant when he said that when we work, we should 'renounce all attachment to the fruits.'"

"Is that in the *Bhagavad Gita*?" I asked.

"Yes. And this attitude affects how the client is seen. Even before the client arrives at your door, you try to see them as already whole. The client is not the problem, the conflict, the stress, the story, the emotional baggage, or anything else of the kind that is brought before you. The client is an immortal soul, a child of God, who has reached out for your love and care. If you, the counsellor, can connect with the deeper Self of the client, then there is a greater chance that the client will open to the same realisation.

This naturally leads me to the second principle: *listening*. It is a listening that requires all your presence. Your heart is centred and open. Listening is a form of love, but I doubt any tutor will tell you that as you go through the training.

Having been on the receiving end of such listening myself, I have sometimes been able to see through whatever attachment is causing the problem, and let go into healing before the listener could respond. I have been brought to reconciliation with my situation without the listener saying a word – the listening was sufficient. That's the power of true listening.

Of course, if anything needs to be said to the client, then, because of that openness of heart, the words seem to look after themselves, being equally new to the speaker and the one receiving. The giver and the receiver are guided simultaneously! This quality of listening emerges from the fact that we are, in essence, one."

Hina stopped speaking and was watching some seagulls that were scrapping for some leftover food not too far away.

"That's terrific! You said there was a third principle," I said, breaking the silence.

Hina looked at me with a smile that seemed to say, "Just be patient."

"Gathering my thoughts, Zac, that's all. It's the first time I've spoken in this way about the work that's so important to me. And I'm really glad you asked me about it. It's part of my life's work, which you are also part of. I hope that makes sense.

OK: the third principle is *trust*. You're not going to work in the way I've described, unless you can trust and place the entire process before the Source of all that is. You will not be able to truly listen from the heart unless you can trust yourself, letting go of personal concerns, self-doubt, and even attachment to ideas regarding your abilities. Trust gives rise to inner freedom, humility, honesty, light-heartedness, and an ease that enables a wonderful empathy with the client to come about.

Trust enables you to avoid being distracted by the presenting 'problem' and to accept the inherent wholeness of the one who's come to you. Trust enables you to accept that this person has come to *you*, not someone else; they have got this far because they've been guided here, whether they are conscious of this or not. Therefore, you are up to the challenge and will be used as an instrument of healing, in some way or other, irrespective of your perceived view of your experience, qualifications, and the like.

Through trusting that oneness in which you are both already whole and from which all understanding comes, the session is in divine hands, and whatever is required will be provided.

Trust itself is a gift; it is an aspect of faith in God. This faith grows in the heart each time it is allowed to operate. Gradually, the instrument is refined. Each client who comes to the spiritual counsellor is a herald of grace and a source of teaching and healing.

This makes every session a reciprocal opportunity to move forward on the return path to oneness.

Zac, these principles are part of the natural human potential, and you have these qualities in abundance; don't forget that. It's partly why I love you. Every day, you inspire me to be more of who I am. Even your initial question – it was from your love, I know, to hear me speak of what I love."

"Now that you say it, I see it was just that. I love you, Hina; forgive me if I blow my own trumpet too much, and don't allow enough time for listening to you."

"Don't, Zac. I've no complaints whatsoever. Come on; it's time to get back to your mum."

Chapter 57

Back at the house, we found mum busy in the kitchen. "You've come at just the right time," she informed us. "I'm nearly ready to serve up something simple before we set off to the hospital."

Lunch consisted of Indian style vegetable samosas and pakoras, along with a side salad, consisting of sauerkraut, beetroot, gherkins and salad leaves. Knowing my mum, the Indian food element of the meal was most likely her way of honouring Hina's ethnic roots, and her caring way of saying, without words, *we welcome you*. Hina, being such a sensitive soul, I was sure she registered the sentiment.

"I'm afraid the samosas and pakoras are only from Sainsbury's," mum said apologetically. "I'm not aware of any Indian delicatessen in the neighbourhood."

"They're delicious," Hina said, reassuringly. "Who knows, they may have been prepared by an Indian family business, and Sainsbury's just put their label on it."

After lunch, we piled into mum's car and made our way back to the hospital.

Once at the hospital, I called in at the Costa coffee shop to get drinks for everyone, while mum and Hina went directly to the ward to see dad. When I rejoined them, I was pleased to see dad dressed in his day clothes.

"Dad, you can go home, I see," I said happily, as I handed him his Americano.

"Thanks, Zac; yes, the doctor has given me the all-clear, although I have to keep the cast on until my leg is checked again, this time when I turn up as an out-patient. It could be in a couple of weeks, at best; I hope not too much longer than that."

Mum then took control of the next few arrangements. "Right, when we've finished our drinks," she said, addressing dad, "I'll order a taxi for you to be taken home. With your leg outstretched like that, we'd have difficulty slotting you into my car. Zac will go with you. Hina can keep me company when we leave."

The four of us used the lift to the ground floor after dad had said goodbye and thanks to the nurses who were on duty. We were all in a celebratory mood. I sat with dad in the back of the taxi, but we didn't speak much; dad wanted to wait till we were all back together at the house.

We settled down in the living room around dad, who had parked himself in an armchair. Mum pulled up a footstool for his embattled leg to rest on.

As the afternoon unfolded, Hina and I brought my parents pretty much up to date with what was happening in our lives. And then they surprised us with some developments of their own, which I was hearing for the first time.

"You see," dad was explaining, "I've really had enough of the financial world, and all its boring shenanigans, and those few days in hospital have given me time to do a lot of thinking, thanks to this leg, here! It's time to venture out into the real world."

I had no idea where this was going, but I was overjoyed to see dad in such good spirits.

"Becky and I have enough capital to set up in business," he continued, "and it's a great opportunity for us to work together at something we both love. We've been a book-loving family, and I'm sure, Zac, that in some way, that has contributed to your journey into teaching English, no less, and passing on the love of good books to the kids at your school.

We plan to set up a book shop, with a built-in café if that works out too. I've given in my notice at the bank, and I'll be a free man at the end of the year. Becky has already stopped teaching, so we'll go full throttle towards our goal in the new year."

"Dad, that's so exciting," I responded. "This is a big surprise, but a great one. Mum, I didn't realise you'd stopped teaching. Is this definitely for you?"

"Of course," mum replied, with a slightly indignant tone. "Believe it or not, your dad and I actually like each other; we get on like a house on fire! I'm so looking forward to being surrounded by books and serving yummy cakes in the café, if that is also to be."

"Do you already have a location in mind?" Hina asked.

"No," said mum. "We're starting completely from scratch. It could be here in Poole, or we might even find a place in or near London. At this stage, we've no idea."

"Well, if there is any way we can be of help," I said, "just say the word."

I went over and hugged both my parents before suggesting that, to give mum a break, I'd order a takeaway meal for the evening. This was easily agreed on, and dad opted for Italian, so that's what it was to be.

Chapter 58

Sunday morning turned out to be the exact opposite of the previous day. No sunny amble down to the beach this time. There was no sign of the sun, and it was raining heavily. After breakfast, we perched ourselves lazily in the living room, and it was the Hina show. My parents plied her with questions about her family and background, and apart from what I already knew, I learnt a little more about her.

Her mother's name was Sushma, and her father's Rajendra, although most people close to him called him Raj. I learned that in the 1970s, her father, as a young man, helped to bring Indian families to the UK who were escaping from Uganda, which was then governed by the brutal dictator, Idi Amin.

After that, he was invited to work at the High Commission for India, which Hina preferred to call the Indian Embassy for short. He was particularly keen to help those families, mostly Hindu, find a way to be true to their religious faith, whilst at the same time learning to be proud citizens of their new nation.

I also learnt more about her mother. Her passion, Hina explained, was her work with a local interfaith group. They met monthly, each meeting usually covering a topic from a different faith. Sushma was currently the group's secretary. She often quoted the Vedic saying, "Truth is one; sages call it by different names." Hinduism was, by its nature, an interfaith religion, she would explain, which accepted that different types of people needed different ways to walk the path.

Hina also spoke about her mother's work as a fashion designer, and added that she was making her a special dress for the marriage ceremony. She'd be going for a first fitting very soon.

"I didn't know that!" I complained, using my best theatrical skills.

"Well, you don't know everything ... yet," Hina retorted. We all laughed.

"Anyway," she added, "I thought it was a British tradition for the wife-to-be to surprise her man on the big day."

Once I'd admitted that I was more than happy to be surprised, Hina was asked about her brother, Mahendra. She told us that Mahendra went to university in Edinburgh to study graphic design; he then stayed in the city after meeting and falling in love with Fiona, a fellow student. After they graduated, they travelled for a year around Europe and Asia. Whilst in Thailand, they both became inspired by a Buddhist monk who happened to be a visiting Australian. They came back to Scotland wanting to know more.

Mahendra discovered a Master of Arts Degree in Buddhist Studies being offered at the university in Edinburgh; he signed up for the two-year part-time version, so that he could start work at a graphic design studio without any delay. Mahendra and Fiona were now members of one of the many varieties of Buddhist groups in that city.

"What does Fiona do now?" mum asked.

"As far as I know, although she also graduated in graphic design, she is someone who loves all things women's clothes. She decided to go into retail, even if it meant starting at the bottom. Mahendra is very supportive of her. The last

I heard was that she was an assistant manager in a small women's fashion boutique in the city centre."

"What interesting folks," dad ventured. "After your visit, I feel that we are already paid-up members of your family!"

"I feel that too," said Hina, laughing. "So, when you come to us for the wedding, remember: treat our place as your own home to enjoy."

In the afternoon, we said our goodbyes, and mum gave us a lift to Poole station. During the train journey back to London, Hina filled me in on her "us girls" conversation with mum.

"Your mum insisted she wanted to enjoy a day out with me before the wedding, take me to some great restaurant, and get me top-of-the-range gear for my wardrobe. I couldn't refuse, could I? Apart from that, she's such fun company."

"When I was in the hospital with dad, he did hint that mum had something up her sleeve especially for you."

"I've so enjoyed meeting your parents, Zac. I can see where some of their magic has rubbed off on you."

After some time without conversation, I could sense that Hina was quietly considering something. Eventually, she broke the silence:

"Zac, I've been thinking about the way your parents are setting out on this new venture of theirs: the bookshop, the café. Do you think there'll come a time when we might do the same? Not necessarily a bookshop, but something we'd enjoy working together on?"

"Of course, I love the idea of working with you, Hina," I replied gently, putting an arm around her shoulder and easing her closer. "Our lives could move us in that direction.

But right now, you are at the beginning of your counselling career, and who knows how the School of Philosophy might develop. As for me, I love my work. That might evolve into being the Head of the English department, hopefully at the same school – I get on so well with everyone, from the head downwards.

I don't have to tell you that it's unlikely to be something we can force. Our aim is to live fully in each moment, meeting every challenge as it arises. I'm sure if we are destined to change direction at any time, it will become clear then. Any change that's worth it will come from our hearts being in alignment with each other, and with a purpose bigger than the two of us as individuals."

"Holy Krishna," Hina exclaimed. "That's you at your philosophical best, Zac Socrates! You've mirrored perfectly what I've been feeling inwardly for some time. But it's so reassuring to hear you putting it into words."

After that, we spoke very little, and Hina found a way to make me into a comfortable cushion to rest on. We reached Unity House, our new home, with sufficient time to start preparing for the working week that awaited us.

Chapter 59

The week that October turned into November was a busy one, each evening taken up with something that I or Hina, or both of us, were engaged in.

Monday was my next meditation class, which now seemed to have fallen into a natural rhythm of teaching, meditation, and time for questions, all in an easy, informal manner. I spoke with Jason and Anara when everyone else had left, and agreed to meet with them and Anahita the next day, after school, so that she could view the house as a prospective tenant.

On the day, I made sure I was there a little earlier to ensure the place was tidy. In the end, it was just Anara who turned up with Anahita and Zari; Jason was still at the school, engaged in some extracurricular activity.

Zari was very excited at the thought of having a bedroom all to herself, and so much more room to "hang out in"! It was an easy decision for Anahita, the improvement in their standard of living being so obvious. The deal was made verbally, then and there, and I promised to get the official rental agreement drawn up, "as soon as I find out how to do it," I admitted.

"But first, I'll need to get the whole place properly cleaned and presentable before you move in."

"Zac, you're very kind," Anahita said. "I wish you'd let *me* do that. It'll be like giving you back for the first three months that are free of rent."

Before I could reply, Anara took my arm. "Zac, please let her do it. It's her way of saying thank you. Honestly, it'll be her pleasure. You won't recognise the place when you visit – she is very creative. Please!"

"OK. Done. When would you like to move in, then, Anahita?"

"Would two weeks from now be good? I'll take some time off work."

"That's perfect. I'll get some extra keys cut for you. I'll pop round to talk you through the heating system, the boiler, the washing machine, and any other household things, as soon as I can. I'll be giving the keys to Jason when I see him at school, and he can pass them on to you."

Once again, Anara spoke to me. "Zac, before we go, Zari wants to ask you a question."

"Right, Zari, I'm all ears." When Zari looked a little nonplussed, Anara translated for her.

"He means he's going to listen to you carefully."

"Can me and mum use part of the garden to grow herbs?"

"What a great idea. Of course. Whatever you like."

For that, I was greeted with an impromptu hug, Anahita and Anara beaming.

When the three of them had left, clearly all very happy, I noticed a certain inner feeling of satisfaction, the sort that occurs when even simple acts of service are allowed to flow naturally.

When I got home, I discovered that Hina had been busy making phone calls. We sat down together while she brought me up to date.

"First off, Mahendra called," she informed me. "He asked if he could chant the *Gayatri Mantra* at our ceremony.

It's one of the most common prayers in Hinduism, and loads of Hindus know it off by heart. It's in the ancient *Sanskrit* language."

"If you're happy, I am," I replied. "Do you know it?"

She said that she did, and before I could ask her, she honoured me with a recitation. I found the sounds of the chant pleasingly uplifting without even knowing the meaning, so I asked Hina if she could give me a translation.

"Give me a minute," she said, rushing out of the room.

She returned with a notebook that looked like it had been around for a few years.

"Here it is," she proclaimed when she had found the right place. "I wrote this translation down some years ago when I found it. I'll read it to you:

May we attain to that adorable splendour
of the divine reality, Savitri.
May she enlighten our hearts
and direct our intelligence.

Savitri, Zac, is one of the many names for the sun in *Sanskrit*. This particular name is feminine. She is sometimes presented as a goddess, but it's important not to take this too literally. She personifies the radiant light of divinity, which is omnipresent, and therefore in you and me. In the chant, we are praying, 'may she enlighten our hearts'."

"That's lovely, Hina. Now that you've explained it so eloquently, I'm looking forward to hearing your brother recite it."

"I rang Steph. I thought it was important to let her know about Mahendra's offer. I knew you'd approve. She said she could suggest a reading for your mum if she was stuck. I said I'd get back to her."

"I'm sure mum will find an appropriate passage to read."

"Well … she already has! As soon as I'd finished the phone call with Steph, your mum rang me to arrange our day out together, which we've fixed for a Saturday in mid-November. While I had her on the line, I broached the subject of a reading, and she said, 'Oh yes, already chosen!'"

"And?"

"A passage on marriage by a Paul Ferrini."

"I'm not surprised. Mum has a collection of books by him; he's a modern spiritual teacher in America that she's quite taken with. Are there any more gaps to be filled?"

"I don't think so, but we'll have another chat with Steph soon."

"That's it then?"

"Not quite, Zac. I've spoken to *my* mum as well. We're invited to lunch on Saturday, and while we're there, mum will take me off to her studio to measure me up for the dress she's making me … while you talk to my dad, of course!

Now, you must be starving; we need to get that sorted immediately!"

Chapter 60

The final three weekdays and evenings were very busy. On Wednesday, it was Session 4 of the School of Philosophy, and as it now met where I lived, I offered my services, welcoming people at the door. Ben was one of the first to arrive, and I was pleased that we were able to meet each other without any reference to the past. He told me that every Wednesday evening was now the highlight of his week.

The following evening, I stayed on at school for a "special meeting" with the parents of A Level students. When it was the turn of Shona's parents, and after I had heaped praise on their daughter for her natural intelligence and dedicated approach to her studies, her dad took the conversation elsewhere.

"We've noticed a big change in Conrad," he said, "since he began attending your meditation class."

"He now actually reads books by choice," his wife added, as if this was a surprising development. "His favourite writers seem to be Alan Watts and Ram Dass. I've had a look through these books. Aren't they a bit too advanced for him?"

"I have to tell you that in the meditation class, Conrad is not out of place among those much older than he is. His contributions show a maturity beyond his years. I'm sure he'll get a lot from those books. You can be proud of him."

While Hina was out on the Friday evening at a planning meeting for the School of Philosophy with Fitz and

Elizabeth, I used the time to get my marking up to date, and to frame some lesson plans for the following weeks. This would free me up for the coming weekend to enjoy with Hina, including the visit to her parents.

The next day, after an early breakfast, we set off to see the Jaiswals. Their home was a few stops to the north by underground, and a pleasant walk along wide, tree-lined streets.

As we approached the house, the door was opened by Hina's mother, a tall regal looking woman who squealed with delight as she gave her daughter a big hug. She then turned to me and, much to my surprise, did exactly the same.

"You look surprised, Zac," she said with a giggle that reminded me of Hina. "You see, I'm a Hindu, but I'm also British! Come in, please. It's such a joy to see you again."

I followed Hina and her mother through a hallway into the house proper. I noticed a gold-leafed statuette of the loveable elephant-headed god *Ganesha*, resting in the centre of a mahogany console table. I expected to see more signs of the Hindu faith in the rest of the house, and I was not disappointed.

As we entered a spacious living room, Hina's father stood to greet us; a hug for Hina and a warm "British" handshake for me. Despite wearing casual clothes, he appeared very distinguished, with a smartly groomed beard and kind greenish eyes.

After a few pleasantries in which I was encouraged to call them Raj and Sushma, and not Mr. and Mrs. Jaiswal, Hina and I were left sitting together while they hurried into the kitchen.

Hina squeezed my hand. "You know what, I think they've taken to you," she whispered. "I even felt that during our first visit."

"I've taken to them," I replied. "Your mum's so gorgeous, and your dad seems very distinguished and kind."

A few moments later, they returned with trays of tea and various Indian sweetmeats. My previous experience of Indian confectionery was that it was ridiculously sweet, too sweet for me. As if reading my thoughts, Hina spoke up:

"Mum makes all these herself, and has found over time that less than half the sugar Indian bakers normally use is more than enough to end up with delicious cakes."

"Just eat what you want, Zac," Sushma said. "And please: I shan't be offended if anything is not to your taste. You don't have to do anything for *my* benefit."

As it happened, Sushma's baking was truly delicious, and I got the impression that she would only ever use the finest ingredients.

We spent a little while talking about the wedding ceremony. Hina's parents were delighted that there was going to be something from Hinduism included in the ceremony, and also that their son would be the one delivering it. They also seemed perfectly happy that Hina and I would make an entrance together rather than follow what was traditionally expected.

"In any case," said Raj, "it's more of a Christian thing, I think, for a dad to hand over ownership of his daughter to a new owner! I've never owned Hina, anyway. Just let anyone try!" We all laughed, and Hina went over and gave him a kiss.

"I've always loved you being my dad; and the loveliest of friends," Hina said tearfully.

Sushma then gently took Hina by her hand. "Hina, we'll just leave the men here while you and I go to my studio for some measuring up."

Chapter 61

Raj refilled our cups with the spiced tea and was then the first to speak.

"I gather, from the little Hina told me about you, that you are someone who thinks deeply about things. Hina is that way inclined too, I'm glad to say. Without some positive *weltanschauung*, a lot of young people today are simply adrift, and easily buffeted by which way the wind happens to be blowing. Someone with a strong outlook, a wide perspective on life, has an anchor and can hold firm whatever the outer circumstances."

"Sounds like you possess a *weltanschauung*," I replied. "If you don't mind me asking, what forms the basis of your outlook on life?"

"That's easy to answer, Zac. As you know, I grew up within a Hindu family. My uncle was a keen member of the Vedanta Society and a great admirer of Swami Vivekananda. He taught me to meditate when I was still a schoolboy, and introduced me to one of the visiting swamis from India.

What I liked about him was that he was not dogmatic at all. He insisted that while the principles of Vedanta provided 'a true science and technology for living', as he put it, it didn't mean that those same principles weren't to be found in other cultures and traditions. He was a firm believer in the gracious attributes of *karma*, and was full of stories of its wonderful workings out."

"You must have a favourite story," I suggested. "And if so, perhaps you still remember it."

"Well, there is one that I found quite moving, and I've shared it with Hina and others, but you might as well hear it from me:

> A young boy in India had lost both his parents and ended up living on the streets. He desperately wanted to go to school, but had no money for the fees and books. His situation seemed hopeless, and he was heartbroken.
>
> One day, seemingly by chance, he met a holy man who was passing through his village. The boy shared his plight with the holy man, who gave him some advice. He was told to write a letter to God, asking for the help he needed to get an education like other youngsters.
>
> 'But what should I write on the envelope?' the boy asked.
>
> 'Simply address it to God,' the holy man replied.
>
> He did as he was advised, writing the letter and addressing it simply to God. He then put it in the nearest post box.
>
> Later at the sorting office, a puzzled postal worker picked up a letter which was addressed to God, and being unsure what he should do, he took it to the postmaster. The postmaster decided to open the letter. As he read it, tears filled his eyes. He asked his employee to go into the nearby village, do a search, and bring the boy to him.
>
> The boy was brought to the postmaster, who adopted him and paid for his education. The boy flourished and in time achieved great distinction, eventually becoming an accomplished lawyer."

"What a great story," I said, "especially if it's true. I can see how it shines a perfect light on the importance of true intention being ultimately rewarded."

I decided to change the subject, as I wanted to hear more about Raj's connection with Fitz.

"Tell me how you got to know Fitz," I asked. "As you know, it was through him that I met your daughter."

"We first met at a function at the Indian High Commission, where I still work. Fitz was there as part of a foreign office delegation. We immediately hit it off and have been friends ever since. I'm sure Fitz's knowledge of Vedanta exceeds mine. He himself had a Vedantic teacher, a swami he met in the Far East. Fitz spoke very highly of him."

"Yes, Fitz has spoken about him, and other important teachers he's met along the way."

"Fitz absorbs spirituality like a sponge. He'll make a good teacher himself one day!" I laughed; I knew that Raj was saying that Fitz *was* a good teacher, but he was like me in often wanting to say something with *gravitas* in a light-hearted manner. I found Raj's company very refreshing, and I knew that we would be good friends in addition to being in-laws.

Hina and Sushma came back into the living room.

"Right, darling," said Sushma, addressing her husband. "Let's take these two beauties out to lunch." Not a word about what occurred in Sushma's studio!

The *Maharaja of Bond Street* was not in Bond Street, but just a short way down a turning off the High Street.

"They took this name," Raj explained, as we sat down at our table, "because the owners used to work in Bond Street, before coming here to open their restaurant."

"Makes sense," Hina added, tongue-in-cheek. "More importantly, the food here is great; I'm sure you'll like it, Zac. They do deserve the reputation which the name they've cooked up has generated."

Hina was right; the food was excellent, and the service impeccable. During the meal, conversation flowed easily, and I felt very much at home. Both of Hina's parents were very knowledgeable in different ways. Raj was more philosophical; Sushma possessed a more homely wisdom. Whereas Raj would be eloquent about some of the jewels of his tradition, Sushma was full of tales from schooldays, family events, and the workplace. They truly complemented each other and were equally inspiring.

We returned to the Jaiswal home after the meal, and we spent a delightful hour or so together before Hina took the initiative, and we finally bade farewell. Although we'd invited them to stay with us before the day of our wedding, they'd politely declined and said they'd prefer to arrive in good time on the day.

Later, Hina told me that it was what she'd expected; she couldn't ever remember her parents wanting to stay anywhere other than in their own familiar space, except when they were travelling for a holiday.

Chapter 62

When I arrived home from school the following Wednesday, I found Hina quietly making preparations in the main room for the next session of the School of Philosophy. She called me over, but I could tell it was not just for an intimate embrace.

"You want to ask me something, don't you?" I queried gently, once we'd separated and sat down on some chairs nearby.

"Observant as usual," Hina said. "Yes, Zac. Elizabeth isn't coming this evening; she's feeling a little unwell. As I was due to be doing the main teaching this evening, anyway, I told her that she should stay at home and look after herself, and I suggested that maybe I could ask you to sit with me instead.

Elizabeth said she was more than OK with that. Would you, Zac?"

"Anything to help," I said. "What do you want me to do?"

"Not much really. Elizabeth and I usually sit together, irrespective of which one of us is teaching. During the first half of this evening, I'm taking the subject of meditation forward to another level, I hope. Then, after refreshments, the door is being left open for questions about anything we've covered so far, or any other matters that a student feels relevant.

It's possible that you might be best placed to answer a particular question; if so, please don't stand on ceremony, feel free to take the initiative. Let's play it by ear."

With that, my evening was well and truly sorted. Hina had contacted Fitz to put him in the picture, and he had responded by coming over early, prepared to be the doorman, and then later a catering assistant, looking after us during the refreshment break.

Hina began the session by explaining Elizabeth's absence and then introducing me, before calling for a short opening period of silence.

Having secured everyone's attention with the Tibetan bells, Hina moved smoothly into teaching mode:

"Let us take a deeper look at meditation this evening. I like to think of meditation as a surrender of the entire being to Being Itself, to God, the Absolute, beyond words, thoughts, emotions, attitudes, and every other inner process.

It is a one-pointed withdrawal of consciousness to its Source, the Ground and Life, which is giving birth to each one of us in eternity, which is always *now*. That's why meditation is a fundamental tool for Self-Knowledge.

Through meditation, you enter the 'inner chamber' of the heart, beyond all mental processes. As you withdraw deeper into yourself, you begin to realise your universal nature, your oneness with all that is. Your name, your history, everything that belongs to your identity as an apparently separate individual, disappears. You know yourself as that which you have always been – eternal, unborn, ever-free, at one with the Source of All."

From my vantage point, sitting at Hina's side, I could see that Hina's words and her beautiful way of speaking had everyone totally gripped. I'd been a recipient of Hina's wisdom before, of course, but this was my first time witnessing her teach in this more formal setting.

"The way of meditation," she continued, "is a way of honour and courage, at the same time requiring an element of child-like innocence. When it's meditation time, it's a time to forget everything else – your duties, your worries, every single concern. Only one thing matters: letting go into the stillness. You are to *die before you die*, as a Sufi saying has it."

Hina said very little more before gently guiding everyone into a similar practice to the one she'd taken me through during our first couple of weeks together. As she led, I followed, appreciating the opportunity I'd been given, as I too let go into the stillness.

The meditation was brought to a close, probably about twenty minutes later, with the sound of the Tibetan bells.

"As you open your eyes," Hina said quietly, "keep them soft; allow colour and form and texture to come to you ... Stay free of any effort ... Stay open and relaxed ... Take note of whatever feeling you are left with, but let's not speak just now ... We'll talk after the break."

Fitz had now switched from doorman to caterer, happily serving drinks to one and all during the refreshment break. But he nevertheless found time to come over and have a quick chat with me.

He told me that he'd be teaching next Saturday at the group, and wondered whether he could make use of me for a simple demonstration. He went through what would be required, and I agreed once I'd realised its purpose.

Once we'd returned to our seats for the second half of the evening, Hina asked if there were any questions.

An older-looking woman raised her hand, and Hina invited her to speak.

"First of all," she said, and then paused briefly as if endeavouring to get clarity before continuing.

"Take your time, Amber," Hina encouraged.

"Firstly, I loved your explanation about meditation," Amber continued, "and you guided us so well, I wish we'd had longer. But I felt my heart wobble a bit when you said in your introduction that we have to *die before we die*. Was it a kind of throw-away remark? Could you say what you exactly meant by that?"

"Yes, of course, Amber," Hina said. "And first of all, those words, 'die before you die', are certainly not spoken lightly. They've been an important reference point for me throughout my own spiritual journey. They are a kind of shorthand for the complete letting go of every attachment, everything that feeds the illusion of a separate ego-identity.

The use of the word 'die' should not be misunderstood. It means dying every single moment ... *whilst living*.

Let's see if we can come at this another way. Let's use the word '*giving*' instead of '*dying*'. To give yourself totally and unconditionally in your life. To withhold nothing. This too must be understood in the right way: it is an attitude of surrender to the truth, to the needs of the moment, being utterly whole-hearted. You have to understand this with your heart, not with your head.

But bear in mind: what happens when you empty yourself in this way? ... Divinity fills the emptiness! Your divine Self. And the freedom that comes with that passes all possible imagination. I think this is what Jesus meant when he said, according to the Gospel of Thomas, '*Come into Being as you pass away.*'"

After a second or two, a young man indicated that he had a question.

"Yes, Jordan, fire away," Hina said.

"Thanks, Hina. I get what you've just said. But what I don't understand is how the ego – or separate self – could itself choose to begin meditation, or any spiritual work, when it's not in its interest to do so? Because if becoming whole again means that everything you identify with must go, why would you choose to self-destruct?"

Hina looked at me, and I knew she was inviting me to take on this one.

"That's a brilliant question!" I began. "Let's look at this from an entirely different perspective.

If your essential nature is universal, then the so-called outer self can never have complete sovereignty. A certain teacher once said, 'The greater can never be satisfied with the lesser.' The greater has a way of getting through to the lesser – 'the still, small voice' that beckons, or 'the voice crying in the wilderness'; in this case, the wilderness of the *psyche*.

To be locked into the separate self is to suffer discontent. However, the pull of the universal Self, even amidst the clamour of all those conditioned influences, eventually wins out.

As more of the universal is given room, the individual starts to understand the importance of working so that the latent, more conscious qualities may be awakened. Strangely enough, there comes a point when the so-called ego is happy to collaborate with its slow march towards redundancy.

Gradually, the path becomes more and more attractive, and the hold over the individual of those older influences begins to weaken.

Do any of you recognise this trend in your own journey?"

A few heads were nodding, together with a few voiced assents.

I continued. "That is why you are here, and still going strong halfway through this course."

Hina thanked me and said there was time for one more question.

A young woman spoke up.

"Where does making love fit into being on a spiritual path?"

"Thanks, Paula. No one *makes* love. You *are* love. Of course, I know what you mean. You're referring to the sharing of love in intimacy between two people who are special to each other. When that happens, when the intimacy is shared within a bond of true love, it is a truly great grace.

But consider this: you cannot ration love. You either love or you don't. It cannot be manufactured.

Are you in love with life? That special relationship between the two lovers does not exist in isolation.

Does making love fit into the spiritual path? The spiritual path is *itself* the path of love. Without love, there is no spirit! Please, everyone, love! Whoever you are, wherever you are, whatever you are doing, love. We can love every day, every moment, whether there is a special one to love or not. You are life; love life!

If you are truly in love, then you love one and all.

Then the special love between two individuals is transformational, not just for those two, but also for those who find themselves drawn into their sphere of life." *Hina, it is the love in you speaking, which is why your teaching is so effective!*

There was a profound silence in the room as Hina's words were absorbed. Eventually, Hina rounded up the evening by wishing everyone goodnight and saying how she looked forward to seeing them again the following week.

Slowly, people began to drift out of the room, many of them showing their appreciation as they left. As I surveyed the parting group, it was clear that many, if not all of them, had been very moved by the evening's teaching.

Once it was just the two of us, Hina and I went out to the dining area, and found that everything had been cleared away. There was no sign of Fitz; he'd left quietly once he'd completed his act of service.

"That's Fitz all over," Hina said. "This is the side of him that not everyone sees. He does whatever he has to do, without any need to draw attention to himself."

"Hina, you taught so well this evening; it was incredible," I enthused, changing the subject. "Your students love you. I'm so glad you asked me to join you."

Hina took my arm. "And I'm so glad you were with me, by my side. I felt I was being held in your quiet yet strong energy.

Come on, let's shut up shop for the evening."

Chapter 63

A few days later, it was time for the next group meeting. As we assembled in the main room, I noticed a chair had been placed separately from the semi-circle of chairs for everyone else. It reminded me that, at some point, Fitz would be asking me to come forward for the little demonstration we'd agreed on.

Fitz took us through the usual meditative few moments of silence before moving on to the afternoon's teaching:

"As some of you know, there are study groups that are linked with this group. One of them, the Christian Mystical Study Group, has invited me to give a talk on the mystical understanding of Creation at their next meeting, next Saturday. Angelo, who chairs the group, has asked me to tell you that anyone who's not a member is nevertheless invited to attend on that occasion. You'd be very welcome. Just let Angelo know if you are intending to go.

That invitation has inspired me to share my understanding of another theological principle: *The Holy Trinity*. It is usually associated solely with Christianity, but I'm going to demonstrate that its teaching is universal. The Trinity is a beautiful model of universal law.

First, let's do a little exercise based on English grammar. Zac, please would you step out here and join me."

I stepped forward and sat down on the prepared seat.

"Now, Zac, what are you doing?" Fitz asked.

"I am sitting on a chair," I replied as I'd been told to, keeping it simple. Fitz wrote *I* on the adjacent flipchart, which was slightly turned towards him.

Fitz, speaking to me, then said, "Yes, you are sitting on a chair." He then wrote *You* underneath the *I*.

Finally, he turned to the Group. "It is clear, is it not, that he is sitting on a chair?"

"He is!" someone blurted out to mild laughter, at which point I left the isolated seat and went to sit next to Hina.

While I was doing that, Fitz wrote *He* under the *You*. He then continued to write, before turning the flipchart stand around so that everyone had a clear view of it.

His efforts now read as follows:

	ZAC
FIRST PERSON	*I*
SECOND PERSON	*YOU*
THIRD PERSON	*HE*

Fitz continued: "In English grammar, there are three *persons*; within any sentence, each *person* depends on the perspective of the action. What is shown here is quite obvious, isn't it? *I, YOU,* and *HE,* in this little demonstration, all refer to Zac. Three different words; one reality, one Zac!

I ... when Zac is *speaking*.

You ... when Zac is *spoken to*.

He ... when Zac is *referred to*.

All three are Zac!

You may think I'm somewhat labouring over this, but it's so that I can present the Trinity using these same elements of English grammar. Just give me a moment."

With that, Fitz returned to the flipchart and began adding to what he had already written. When he had finished, the previous diagram had been augmented:

	ZAC	TRINITY	PUT ANOTHER WAY
FIRST PERSON	*I*	Spirit	The Self within
SECOND PERSON	*YOU*	Son (Word)	The Manifest Creation
THIRD PERSON	*HE*	Father	The Unmanifest Divinity

Fitz drew our attention to what he had written, and then continued:

"In orthodox theology, the Trinity is usually conceived in the form of three Persons: *The Father*, *The Son,* and *The Holy Spirit.* There is one reality, God, yet God may be understood from these three fundamental perspectives, with a specific name for the One according to the perspective being considered.

Now we should consider each of these *Persons* in turn:

The Father. The Father is a metaphor for God transcendent, the Unmanifest, the One Absolute Reality, eternal, unchanging, impersonal. It corresponds to the third person of grammar. Little can be said about the ineffable reality that transcends time and space.

The Son. The Son is a metaphor for the totality of the divine in manifestation. It corresponds to the second person in grammar. It is God expressing Itself. It is also called the *logos*, or 'Word', as in John's Gospel, but the term itself precedes Christianity, being used by Philo, among others. It was understood to stand for the source of Life and Light, containing the blueprint for the entire cosmos and every element within it.

Let me read to you one of the most beautiful descriptions I've come across of this aspect of the Three-in-One. It is from the twelfth-century mystic, Hildegard of Bingen."

Fitz picked up one of the books that was on the small table beside him and began to read:

"I am that living and fiery essence of the divine substance
that flows in the beauty of the fields.
I shine in the water; I burn in the sun, the moon and the stars.
I sustain the breath of all living.
I am the force that lies hid in the winds,
from me they take their source,
and as a man may move because he breathes,
so does a fire burn through my blast.
All these live because I am in them and am their life.
I permeate all things so that they may not die.
I am Life."

Fitz put down the book before continuing:

"In other words, whatever you behold, at any time, is the Divine expressing Itself. The entire creation, and everything in it, is a sacrament of the presence of God. The Sufis say something similar: 'Wherever you look is the face of *Allah*'.

Now for *The Spirit*. The Spirit is God within. Speaking more directly, it is your own pure divine Self. This corresponds to the first person in grammar.

You see, there is no escaping God. Look within, God is there. Look outwards: everything you are looking at is God.

This is a lot to take in, I know. To help you, I've printed copies of the substance of today's teaching, which you can collect later before you leave.

For now, let's have a break. We'll look a little more at this when we return in about half an hour."

Back in our seats, Fitz immediately carried on from

where he'd left off! He picked up another book.

"Here are a couple of statements from the Gospel of Thomas:

> The kingdom of the Father is spread over the entire earth, yet people do not see it.
>
> The kingdom is inside you, and it is outside you.

God, the Eternal Reality, is both the essence of who you are *and* shines through everything that you behold.

Now that I've taken you through these three perspectives on the One Reality, it seems appropriate to do something practical. And, as it happens, the weather is on our side today. This is an exercise which is intended to ground you more deeply in the appreciation of God Manifest, the Son, or Word, God expressing Itself; it is everything, everything *without exception*, that you meet.

Go outside into the garden – allow all your senses to be fully open; drink in whatever comes into your field of awareness. Be open, be like Hildegard ... Like her, are you able to just drink in the pure sensory experience?

In effect, I'm inviting you to meet the creation with full awareness. For the universe, and every single aspect of it, is shot through with divinity. Do all this in silence. Forget time. I'll call you back in due course."

We all made our way quietly into the garden. Once outside, some, including myself, decided to sit for the exercise, whilst others chose to slowly amble about. I gradually opened my attention and endeavoured to receive the simple, pure, raw experience without the intrusion of the usual analytical thought processes.

Sometimes those persistent intruders did gain the upper

hand, and then I had to bring my attention back fully to what was in front of me. Backwards and forwards, until the intrusive thoughts weakened, and I found the separation between me and what I was observing begin to blur.

Slowly, the observer and the observed, as separate and opposite points, merged. I was indeed one with the grass, the trees, the flowers, the sky, the breeze, the birds, my sitting and ambling companions. As a poetry lover, Thomas Traherne's words came back to me, words which had somehow stuck years ago, because I somehow knew them to be true:

> "You never enjoy the world aright, till the Sea itself flows in your veins, till you are clothed with the heavens, and crowned with the stars."

Indeed! I immediately filed away a resolve to look up the full poem when I got back home, whilst keeping my awareness tuned to the matter at hand.

For a short span of time, I was one with what I beheld, no separation. With this came an exhilarating feeling of pure joy, the sense that all things were possible; that Zac Marshal was simply a conduit for universal love, that a divine intelligent purpose was being enacted through everything and everyone.

When Fitz called us back to the house to complete the afternoon session, there was a wonderful sharing. Other members of the group spoke of experiences that were similar to mine. Fitz encouraged us to practice this exercise from time to time. He said that in time, it would no longer be an exercise because it would have become our natural state.

Someone asked how long it would be before that

happened. Fitz smiled and answered:

"No time at all, or a thousand lifetimes!"

With that cryptic comment, Fitz effectively brought the afternoon's teaching to a close.

Angelo made a point of finding me before Hina and I left. He'd wanted to tell me that he'd found the near-death account I'd given at a recent meeting, which contained the realisation of the continuum of life, very helpful following the loss of his mother.

"I say 'loss'," he added, "but it doesn't feel like that anymore."

"I'm glad of that," I said. "I feel that a true bond of love cannot be broken ... ever."

"Thanks. I'm happy I caught you before you left. About the Christian Mystical Study Group, which Fitz mentioned earlier. I've been going regularly. I invited Fitz to speak about the mystical understanding of creation next Saturday. A question about this was raised by one of our members, and it seemed like a no-brainer to bring in Fitz. You'd be very welcome if you'd like to come along."

I knew without question that I should take up Angelo's invitation; Fitz's spiritual knowledge and understanding often seemed limitless to me, and therefore, this was an opportunity not to be missed!

"I'll be there," I confirmed. "And I'll bring Hina too if she wants to join me."

Chapter 64

I was still somewhat joyfully overflowing with the special exercise that Fitz had given us at the last meeting, so when the meditation class at my school came round only two days later, I was determined to share it with my students. I didn't attempt to link it with teaching about the Trinity. I introduced it as an alternative practice; instead of going inwards in meditation, the attention was to be fully outwards.

As it was an evening class and it was too dark to go outside, I raided some classrooms and the science lab for potted plants, vases with flowers, large fossils, and a few crystals. It worked up to a point. Not all the students were able to let go of the inner chatter about what they were viewing; a few, however, did get the point of the exercise, and also a degree of the sense of oneness.

I learned something here: give a bit more thought before trying to transfer an experience from one set of circumstances to another that is not quite compatible. I suggested we might change one of our meetings to a Saturday morning to take advantage of the daylight, and most were happy with that.

The following day, Anahita & Zari moved into my house. They already had all the keys I'd given to Jason to pass on to them. Once school had ended for the day, I called round to see how they were doing. Anahita had wasted no time in settling in. The place looked very tidy, and I noticed that some of the furniture had been changed around here and there, which I didn't mind.

I could hear the sound of the washing machine, but I decided not to ask what was being cleaned. It was important for Anahita to feel in control of her environment, and I made my support clear when I spoke to her.

"This is now your home," I said to her. "You must feel free to live here exactly like that. It means you can invite people round, have family or friends staying over. You can put up pictures, for example, and, as already agreed, you can grow herbs and vegetables in the garden. If you are not sure about anything, just give me a call, OK?"

Zari looked so happy, and it warmed my heart. I could tell that I'd made a friend for life. Anahita said she'd like to cook for me and Hina – would we come round one evening? Yes, we'd be delighted, I assured her. I had a feeling that these two lovely souls would become much more than just tenants to me, and I left soon after our brief conversation.

For the next meeting of the School of Philosophy, Elizabeth was back and able once again to share the teaching with Hina. She arrived early so that she could speak with the two of us.

"I'm so looking forward to your marriage ceremony," she exclaimed excitedly. "I would love to contribute to the ceremony ..."

"Oh, that'd be fantastic," Hina almost shouted, cutting off Elizabeth before she could say anything more.

"I have a suggestion," I added a little more calmly. "Let me give you Steph's phone number. That's the Rev. Stephanie Bamford; she's our celebrant. The order of service is more or less sorted, but if you talk to her, I'm sure you'll both agree on something that will blend in with whatever's been arranged."

“Thanks, Zac. I already know Steph,” Elizabeth said. “She’s one of dad’s friends. I’ll call her tomorrow.”

We spent a little while reviewing the previous week’s teaching that Hina and I had shared. Elizabeth was delighted with our report and said she hoped it wouldn’t be the last time I got involved with the School.

The two of them then disappeared to get the main room prepared before people began arriving. I offered to help with the catering, along with Tamara and David, who had already volunteered for this evening’s class.

Chapter 65

Hina had been invited by my mum to meet her at the Victoria and Albert Museum in Kensington on Saturday afternoon, in its splendid Victorian-style café. A hotel had been booked nearby, and Sunday had been earmarked as a day for heavy retail therapy. Knowing my mum, I could foresee Hina arriving back later that day laden with shopping bags full of new and exquisite items for her wardrobe. With Hina otherwise engaged, I would be attending Angelo's study group on my own.

Arriving at the study group was amazingly easy. The group was held at Unity House, of course, and all I had to do was come downstairs a little before the start time. When I entered the main room, I found Fitz already there, along with Angelo, Jasmine, Karolina, and half a dozen others.

I was greeted warmly and offered a seat. Fitz took up a position in front of our small semicircle. I noticed beside him on a small table were notebooks and several volumes. He would, of course, be quoting various Christian mystical teachers during his address. There was also a flip chart standing by, ready to be used.

After a short meditation, Fitz began his talk:

"When considering creation, we need to give up thinking in terms of linear time. Creation is *now*. Therefore, let us be here *now*. Don't try to grasp what I'll be saying with your mind. You need to listen to what I'm saying in stillness, free of any preconceptions.

The beginning is *now*. To be – gin is to generate from being, as the word implies!"

Fitz stopped to write the following on the flip chart:

BE	**GIN**
Being	**generate**

"All the levels of creation are present right now," he continued, "from the state of absolute potential, through all the step-down phases of manifestation, to the fully embodied appearance of things we enjoy through the senses. This is true both for the macrocosm and for the microcosm.

What I've just shared with you is precisely the understanding expressed by some of the great mystics. Let's start with Meister Eckhart, with whom I'm sure many of you are familiar."

Fitz retrieved a volume from the table and opened it at one of the bookmarked pages.

"I'm reading from a selection of his writings:

> 'The loftiest part of the soul ... stands above time and knows nothing of time or of body. The happenings of a thousand years ago, days spent millenniums since, are in eternity no further off than this moment ...
>
> The now wherein God made the world is as near this time as the now I am speaking in this moment ...
>
> Follow then after this now. And reach this now and possess this eternal now.'

This teaching has important implications for each one of us. What happens if, as Eckhart suggests, we 'possess this eternal now'? Of course, finding language to describe this is always a challenge, because we are describing what essentially evades description, and which can only be known in direct oneness. However, I'll give it a go. This is based on Eckhart, but if you like, in my own words.

If you stand as one in *the* One, in the eternal now, then all the trappings of separation are stripped away, and you are God, in God. This means – and for this, let go of any adherence to ideas of linear time – that since creation is always now, you are participating in the creation, through your oneness in the divine.

Coming back to Eckhart, this is exactly what he understands."

Fitz took up another book from which to read.

"Eckhart again:

> 'In my birth all things were born and I was the cause of myself and of all things.'

He is speaking of himself as at one with the creative impulse – the cause of himself and all else! In other words, if you could return to the source of your being, you would have returned to the beginning of creation, which is always *now*. The Creation is ever now, not in the past.

Creation is eternal; it is not a historical event. Creation is a continuum. Where is it? You are in it as it is happening! How can I know this? By becoming one with the Source Itself, from which the All has gone forth!

In one of his poems, Wordsworth proclaims:

> 'Trailing clouds of glory do we come from God who is our home.'

He is right, as long as we don't project this unfolding splendour of consciousness into the past.

Now, can you understand why Jesus said, 'Before Abraham was, *I am*', and not '*I was*'? He could have said, 'Before creation was, *I am*.'

Let me turn to a few other sources, apart from Eckhart. I've copied these into my notebook. Give me a moment."

Fitz picked up a couple of notebooks and flicked through them until he was satisfied that he'd found the right pages.

"OK. This is from Jacob Boehme, a few centuries later than Eckhart:

> 'The treasure of treasures for the soul is to pass from the something into this Nothingness from which anything can be born.'

I'll come back to things being born from 'this Nothingness' in a moment.

And finally, from the Gospel of Thomas. The disciples asked Jesus what to tell people who asked them where they came from. He told them to say this:

> 'We come from the Light, the place where the Light comes into existence through Itself alone.'

We come from the Light, we *are* the Light, the one Light that shines in all things.

Are there any questions before I continue? ... Yes, Adam."

"You said you'd get back to what Boehme said about birth from Nothingness."

"Ah, yes; thanks for reminding me. Birth from Nothingness. The eternal, the divine, is often called *Nothingness* in mystical literature because it transcends thing-ness. The eternal is not an object; it has no location, being beyond space and time. Yet it is pure potential. And, for example, it is this pure potential that the great artists tap into.

The true artist participates in this creative process, as Shakespeare eloquently described in his play, *A Midsummer Night's Dream*, which I'm now quoting from memory, so you might want to check this out.

> *The poet's eye glances from heaven to earth, from earth to heaven,*
> *and as imagination bodies forth the forms of things unknown,*
> *the poet's pen turns them to shapes, and gives to airy nothing*
> *a local habitation and a name.*

The poet's eye – note the singular – is described in some mystical writings as the inner eye of the heart, or of the soul. It is said to look both ways: outward towards the fully manifest world of the senses, 'heaven to earth', and also inwards towards the riches of eternity, 'earth to heaven'. Shakespeare's poetic words reflect the understanding at the Elizabethan court that great poets were divinely inspired. They bring down their masterpieces from 'heaven', the eternal No-thingness!

Mozart, in a letter to his father, expressed a similar phenomenon: how he effortlessly saw the whole of a symphony in its unmanifest seed-form, and all he had to do was patiently transcribe the inspiration.

On the other side, as observers of a great work, we are given a kind of doorway back into the artist's original creative revelation. That's why such works stand the test of time – they never go out of date, because they connect with us at a deep level."

Fitz paused for a moment to drink some water.

"Let us see if we can bring all this into our own context, as members of the group, as individuals seeking to be in alignment with truth, goodness, and right action. I may be in danger of repeating myself, but I consider this aspect really important.

If, as Eckhart encouraged us, we could 'possess this eternal now', we would find that our whole life would become a work of art. We would be standing in the creative flow, which is ever now. The smallest actions would reflect the eternal intelligence – shopping, cooking, reading to a child, writing an email – these are just examples that come to mind.

The creation is now. Join with it. Then everything you do becomes an expression of the Light of oneness, filled with love, and transformative for all you meet, whether known or not."

Fitz stood and collected up his books, which indicated that his talk was over. We knew not to clap, something Fitz preferred not to happen. We all gradually made our way into the dining room for refreshments; we could thank him as we chatted over tea and biscuits.

After the break, we returned to our seats to complete the afternoon with a period of meditation. Of course, deepening in meditation means letting go of all our associations with name, status, possessions, age, and the like.

It means returning to *this* moment, the *now*, in alignment with the creative flow, the stream of pure potential.

Chapter 66

My beloved fiancée returned home late on Sunday afternoon, not as laden as I'd anticipated. After we'd kissed, embraced, and settled down with some tea, she laid out the contents of the one shopping bag, one item in a cardboard box!

"Your mum knows how to have a good time," she declared. "I thoroughly enjoyed myself, Zac, whilst also trying to keep her from dipping too often into her purse. She was keen to get me some new clothes for my wardrobe, but I insisted I had enough to last me a lifetime."

"Come on, Hina," I said. "Show me. What's in that box?"

"Patience, darling … hear me out. Becky seemed a little disappointed when I said that about my clothes; I knew she wanted to get me something special, even though she'd already spent a fortune on the hotel and delicious meals in really great places. I told her I'd be delighted with a little something for our home, and suggested maybe a fruit bowl for our dining area. We ended up in John Lewis, and this is what she got me."

I let Hina open the box. Out came the carefully wrapped present. Once the layers of tissue paper had been removed, a stunning crystal bowl was revealed, about 10 inches in diameter.

"It's a well-known make," Hina told me. "Waterford, an Irish brand according to the salesman. And now, it's our very own cut-glass fruit bowl. Your mum insisted on *only the best*! I didn't see the price; she masked it well. I think she's the kind of person who just loves giving. By the way, Zac, I think you take after her."

She wrapped her arms around me and sighed.

The following day, during the lunch break at school, I was given some great news from Jason. Anahita's husband, Daryush, had made his way to Pakistan to visit his cousin, a businessman, in Lahore. Jason hadn't realised until a few days ago that there were a significant number of Baha'is in Pakistan, and also that Anahita's husband was originally from Lahore, and still enjoyed Pakistani citizenship in that country. His cousin was contributing to the cost of the flight to the UK, which was "in the air at this moment!"

When I pressed Jason on what would happen to Daryush when he arrived at Heathrow airport, he was quite upbeat about it.

"I'm sure he'll be reunited with Anahita," Jason insisted. "First of all, Anahita is here legally; she has a job, and Zari is attending a local school. And now, thanks to you, Zac, they have secure accommodation. They'll be no burden to the taxpayer because Daryush is an experienced acupuncturist and Ayurvedic herbalist. He plans to set up practice here once he gains the same residency status as his wife."

As Jason and Anara were regularly in touch with Anahita, I asked Jason to keep me up to date with the progress of Daryush's application for residency, especially if any problem should occur. I also had a good idea about how I might be able to help Daryush get going with his plan to set up in practice.

When I got home, I found Hina with Fitz and Jasmine in the living room.

"This is a nice surprise," I said as I joined them. Hina immediately stood to give me a hug in her natural and unaffected way.

"So glad you're here now. We can bring you up to date," she said.

"Oh ... what have I missed?"

It was Fitz who chose to enlighten me.

"Jasmine and I have decided not to move to York just yet. With your wedding ceremony coming up next month, we wanted to stick around a little longer. In any case, the properties we've looked at so far are a little on the small side. We want a house with a decent-sized living room, so that we can easily host a study group. We plan to rent in the first instance, and then when the right property becomes available, we'll fork out from our hard-earned capital."

"That's good news for us," I said. "We'll miss you when you go."

"We're more likely to move around February, or even March, next year," Jasmine stated. "But that's not the only reason we're here," she added.

I looked from Jasmine to Fitz, and then to Hina, who was smiling.

Fitz took over from Jasmine:

"Zac, it's not just me, I assure you. We'd like you to become the main teacher, starting with the first group meeting in January. By 'we', I mean Jasmine, Hina, Karolina, Elizabeth, and myself. You are more than ready now, so there is no real need to delay. It'll be good to allow an overlap, a natural transition ... It's not easy to explain, but this feels the right way to go about it. *We'll just get you married off first!*"

It was serious stuff, but I nevertheless joined in the others' laughter.

"So, Zac, what does being a teacher mean to you?"

I allowed Fitz's question to sit for a while, and then, without any hesitation, following a clear inner resolve, I invited Fitz and the others to meditate with me before launching into an answer. No words were needed for me to sense that Fitz was happy that I'd taken this initiative.

I wished to speak on the subject from an impersonal, objective space; it meant dissolving that question into its source, the inner knowing at the core of our being. Hence, the need for a period of stillness first. It helped that I was in the company of those who knew and loved me.

As soon as I knew that I was ready, I began to answer the question. The words just flowed with ease as I addressed my dear companions.

"To be clear, by teacher we mean specifically a teacher of spiritual awakening, a teacher as understood concerning The Work. Such a teacher always sees the potential in his student, because every quality that is in the teacher is in the student!

The teacher is simply someone who has walked further along the path than the student. He metaphorically puts out a hand to help the other along. Such a teacher would be authentic, teaching as much by example as by word. He lives the teaching. This naturally inspires trust and right intention in the student.

No one teacher has access to every formulation of truth. Therefore, there is a need to maintain an open mind, ready to listen to different perspectives and understandings. The other side of this is encouraging students to be discerning, so they can walk intelligently along their own spiritual path, drawing on their own innate wisdom. In a way, there are as many paths as individuals, and what is right for one may be a disaster for another.

When the teacher sits in front of the group, he then holds to an inner stillness, and is a bit like an empty vessel. Then, when he is asked any question, he will be able to respond from the level of universal principles, the words being fresh and appropriate to the level of the questioner. He can do this because, through his stillness and fully open awareness, he has transcended the level of the separate sense of existence. When he responds in this way, he is able to bring the student towards his own level of realisation.

I just want to add this. Fitz. While I feel honoured that you've asked this of me, and I'll take on this role as a way of giving back what I have received, I will still regard you as *my* teacher, even if you were to sit as a student in front of me!"

"Bless you, Zac," said Jasmine, before Hina indicated that she would like to add something.

"I feel that we have something in our group that strongly resembles the *guru* and disciple relationship that has existed in India for thousands of years, particularly within the Vedanta tradition. The *guru*, to use the Indian term, is regarded as *Brahman*, the Absolute, manifesting in an individual human form to guide the seeker.

The Sanskrit word *guru* evolved from two root sounds, *ga* and *ra*. According to Sanskrit grammar, these two sounds combine to give the meaning of one who leads you from 'darkness', *gu*, to 'light', *ru*.

The *guru* is often revered as a means of divine grace, which inspires devotion. His very presence, quite apart from any teaching, is itself uplifting. The gift of a *guru's* presence is called *darshana*, which I was once told had the double meaning of 'seeing' and 'being seen', as if the *guru* mirrors the seeker's very essence. I believe this also happens in our group, although it's not in the Western mindset to acknowledge this. People may vary, but I always feel this whenever we meet, whoever is teaching."

"Hina, thank you for sharing that," I said. "You've hit on something which I now recognise. When I first met Fitz in the café – all those aeons ago – it wasn't just our conversation that drew me; it was a certain presence which, with hindsight, I now know was deeply felt. The teacher's stillness and centredness, in fact his Self-realisation, is very attractive to those who are ready to receive it."

"Well," said Fitz, getting up from the settee, "Jasmine and I have to be somewhere else shortly. This has been a very productive conversation. Hina, Zac, we look forward to seeing you again on Saturday."

Once Fitz and Jasmine had left, Hina and I sat down, and with an unspoken understanding, we shared a peaceful time of meditation before engaging in anything else.

Chapter 67

Fitz turned the next meeting into an open session.

"I am emptiness itself," he proclaimed jokingly. "I am dependent on you to raise the inner teacher from slumber with your superb questions. Then, let's see what chooses to emerge into the light. We'll meditate for a short while first, then see what questions naturally arise. Let's keep it all effortless."

When we came out of meditation, I found myself with a question for which I felt I had an answer, but I somehow trusted that it was right to put that question to Fitz; he might be able to offer a different angle to the one I held; therefore, I put the question:

"If we are *already* that universal Self, what need or purpose is there for any kind of practice?"

"Well, Zac, that is *definitely* stirring up the soil at the bottom of this emptiness. I am reminded of an analogy given to me by the Indian swami I met in the Far East, who went by the name *Sangala*.

He told me that, when it came to spiritual practice, there were three kinds of seekers. Using the metaphor of combustion, he compared them to either gunpowder, charcoal, or wet coal. He'd learnt this analogy from Ramana Maharshi, a truly great saint he'd encountered in India during his youth.

The *gunpowder* type of seeker only needs to hear the truth about his real Self, and his realisation is immediate. You could say that his being is ignited by a single spark.

You could also say that he was ripe, or already sufficiently pure. Jesus called it, 'having ears that hear'.

For the *charcoal* type, more heat is required for a short time, meaning that they need some practice such as Self-enquiry, to overcome the limitations of a perceived separate identity, and uncover the truth of who they are.

Then there is the *wet coal* type. The approach for them has to be more systematic, sometimes lasting many years, just like coal gradually getting dried out enough before it could catch fire.

Of course, you are that already complete, boundless consciousness, the one Self that lives in all; but at the level of the apparent individual self, if you are unaware of your true stature, what then? That's where practice is useful, to help us become aware of what we already are."

After a short pause, another question was put to Fitz, this time by Karolina.

"It's obvious that everyone wants to be happy," she began, "but so many people seem not to be. If you don't mind me saying, Fitz, you always seem so cheerful. In all the time I've known you, I've never seen you downcast, disgruntled, or even slightly put out by anything. What's your secret?"

"As it happens, I've investigated the question of happiness for many years, not by studying books or articles, but by being watchful; to see how various situations unfold when I am fully present. *And what have I discovered?*

First of all, that I do not need a reason to be happy; I just am! When I am present, in the *now*, nothing appears to be lacking. Happiness is present and always accessible.

Also, I do not need to be loved or accepted to be happy, although it is nice to be loved and accepted. I do not need to be at my best physically to be happy, although I certainly enjoy being physically well. I do not need to be clear about what I should or should not be doing to be happy, although any degree of clarity is very welcome.

In short, happiness is part of my essential nature, and when I am in touch with who I am, happiness just is, as natural as the air we breathe. In the *now*, isn't it a joy to be resting in the eternal in which all separation is impossible?

Another aspect of being able to enjoy the natural happiness is the extraordinary freedom it offers. It frees you from negative emotions such as envy, jealousy, and the need to compete. This means that I can enjoy *your* success, *your* achievements, *your* happiness – without any desperate need to emulate or outstrip you, nor the equivalent urge to denigrate or judge.

My happiness is not something that needs to be flaunted, although I may not be able to help that it shines from me for all to see" – laughter, especially from Karolina – "and what is more, *your* happiness adds to my happiness.

On the other hand, your sadness or pain draws upon my happiness, which expresses itself in the form of compassion. I don't cease to be happy because you are sorrowful. I respond to you without any guilt or sentimentality. In serving with compassion, I do not cease being my Self, whose nature is happiness.

Because you are in pain, I do not have to be less happy, less truthful, less at home in the present moment.

What then is the secret of happiness?

It is to courageously open unconditionally to the very core of your being – your true nature, which lies uncontaminated beneath all the habitual forms of discontent.

OK. One more question before we take a break."

It was Ralph who put the next question to Fitz.

"What must I do to reclaim my true Self, as you rightly suggest?"

"The answer can partly be found within your question," Fitz replied, "which, as I will demonstrate, arises from a few false conceptions.

You begin by asking, 'What must I do?'. The error begins there. All 'doing' must be given up. Then the realisation of your true Self will unfold as a matter of course.

Also, the true Self, which is eternal and undying, cannot be 'claimed', as you put it. You, the subject, can only claim some object, and that would be a finite object, however grand. Your true Self is neither a subject nor an object; it transcends all possibility of definition. Therefore, it cannot be attained. But it may be *known.* It is known by *being it.* For you are already that which you seek."

"I think I understand what you mean," Ralph said. "But how can I give up doing when clearly in this life, action is required?

"Giving up 'doing' is not the same as giving up action. You are right. No one can avoid action. What has to be relinquished is the sense that '*I-am-the-doer*'!

This means action without the attachment to results, meeting each moment without the burden of past associations, expectations, and the like.

When you are fully present, you are your Self, acting or not acting as your intelligence reveals, without fear or favour."

Ralph persisted with a follow-up question.

"But how does one act without attachment to results?"

"Ralph, your determination will get you everywhere," Fitz said approvingly. "Stay fully in the present moment. Take *this* moment, for example. Give your full attention to it, without thinking about it. If thoughts concerning what is happening right now arise, pay no attention to them. Keep your attention here and now ...

Then what is required of you will be obvious without any thought or consideration entering the equation. The deep Intelligence within you is the reflection of your true Self – it knows whether to act or not, and if action is needed, then it will flow from that Intelligence, using mind and body as instruments, and praise be, the action will be a work of art. It will leave no *karmic* imprint; it will not drain your emotional energy, and will be unencumbered by the past.

Gradually, your life will become more and more effortless, peaceful and fulfilling."

"Thank you," Ralph said quietly. It was a good few minutes before Fitz invited us to break for refreshments.

When we returned to our seats after the break, Fitz sat with his eyes closed for a few moments. He then opened them and looked at us one by one with a beautiful, open expression.

It was Jenny who broke the silence: "I can say confidently that I understand and trust the teaching you've been giving us, and I am committed to this way of spiritual work. However, understanding is one thing ... but the outcome often seems beyond me. I enjoy only fleeting moments of present-moment awareness; then, before I know it, I'm lost in thought and acting in the old habitual manner. What's the way out of this?"

"Be easy on yourself, Jenny," Fitz counselled. "Your situation is not unusual. It helps to cultivate an attitude of *acceptance*. You can't give up the habits of a lifetime overnight.

Rather, keep practising what I've taught you, and when you find that your attention has succumbed to the distractions of the mind, use that moment of awareness – see, you have *noticed* the distraction – use that moment to start again, giving your attention to what is fully here now.

You cannot give up these wayward habits of the mind; rather, as you faithfully practice what I have taught you, they will give *you* up! You will notice the change – the greater freedom you experience, the less you are thrown by unexpected changes in circumstances, and so on.

Do not waver in your approach to this work. Stand firm, and in time your true Self must reveal itself, most naturally."

There being no more questions, Fitz invited us to complete our time together with a walking meditation, which we could carry out in the garden. He told us that sometimes the instructions for this could be unnecessarily long-winded. He kept it down to three simple instructions:

> Walk slowly, anywhere you like, keeping your attention focused about two feet in front of each step.
> If you notice thoughts distracting you, stop for five seconds or thereabouts.
> Then continue with the practice.

"This is important: it doesn't matter how often you stop and start. Avoid judging yourself, keep the whole exercise light-hearted, and even allow yourself to enjoy your walk. You can regard this kind of active meditation as a useful simulation of actions that are free of desire for a result, or non-attached actions. You can apply the principles behind this practice to any future activity you engage in.

Right, out you go. Enjoy! I'll see you back here shortly."

I had taken part in a similar exercise a few years earlier at a Buddhist centre I had visited a few times. Then, I remember, there was a lot of tension and frustration at not being able to remain focused. Fitz's counsel to 'avoid judging yourself' was very apt. On this occasion, the whole period of walking turned out to be a different experience altogether. Yes, there was much stopping and restarting due to the intrusion of those persistent thoughts. But there was also an underlying attitude of *acceptance* that I knew had gradually taken root since I first started meeting with the group.

Also, at the back of my mind, was an awareness that, despite the inevitable circle of thought processes that seemed to have a will of their own, whenever I was called upon to serve in any way, such as in leading the school meditation class, the deeper intelligence had a way of overriding the habitual mental activity.

Chapter 68

After everyone had left, Hina suggested we go out for a coffee and have a "business meeting", her term for looking at where we had arrived regarding important future events or commitments.

Once we had settled with our drinks, Hina brought up the subject of our wedding ceremony, which was now less than a month away. She had been in touch with Steph during the week and had been assured that all the contributors for readings were in place. We went over what we knew of the ceremony and were satisfied that it would be a truly special occasion.

"In a few days I'm visiting mum to collect my wedding dress, "Hina added, "assuming it fits OK, which I'm sure it will. What about you, Zac? Do you have a suitable outfit you can wear? Or do you need to get one?"

"I've got a couple of suits at home; I'll show you when we get home."

"Well," Hina replied, with a smile, "I've seen something that would look good on you. If you don't come up trumps at home, I'm threatening to treat you … right?"

"If you say so." Hina thumped me playfully.

"OK. OK. I'm going to make sure I look amazing …"

"Good," Hina said triumphantly. "Anything you want to bring up now?"

"Yes, there is. When I start teaching the group in January, I'd like you to sit beside me. Your subtle energy is extraordinary; I acknowledge it freely. I will benefit;

those who are present will benefit. Also, I've been on the receiving end of your wisdom, enough to know that you are a natural, and there will be times when I'd hand over to you, especially when it comes to meditation and other spiritual practices. Please consider it; I'm being serious."

I could see that Hina was deeply moved by what I had just said to her, and it appeared at first that she'd been rendered speechless. She took my hand, steadied her breath, and held my gaze for a while.

"I haven't upset you, have I?" I asked, eventually.

"No, no. You haven't ... This is ... it's just so unexpected. But you've touched me so deeply, Zac ... as you often do. Believe me, I want to say yes to you. But another part of me is uncertain. Can you understand that?"

"Of course I do, Hina. I'm just sharing with you what has gradually surfaced in my awareness these last few days. I will respect whichever way you choose to respond. I'll accept and move forward with you either way."

"Zac, can we run this by Fitz? Not for him to make a decision. I promise *I* will decide, based on my own light on the matter. But Fitz may be able to tease out what principles are at work here. My heart is saying 'yes'. I'm thrilled, Zac ... to be by your side ..."

"Hina, I'm fine with that," I agreed, as Hina immediately took out her mobile phone and rang Fitz's number. Typical of Hina; never waste a second!

Later that week, we were sitting with Fitz at his house. We put him in the picture about my proposal, that I would like Hina to sit with me when I teach in the group. Hina asked if he could shed some light on it; she was very open about being inclined to support me. She only wanted a fuller understanding of how this would work energetically. She had an inner sense that she already knew, but wasn't sure how to express it – and could Fitz shed some light on the matter?

"Well, this is all rather wonderful," Fitz said. "Let's be clear from the start, I'm not going to tell either of you what to do. What I *can* do is explore with you the merits of this new approach you are considering.

You may remember how I recently told you a little about my time in Spain and the Kabbalah group I sometimes attended. Ruth was the main teacher, but her brother Simon usually sat beside her. And when he contributed, it was with an equal authority.

Coming back to this situation, Elizabeth told me that, on an evening when she was unwell, you sat together, sharing the teaching for the Philosophy class. How was that?"

"That was a special experience," Hina said. "That evening, I felt I was being energetically held by Zac. I felt immersed in his love and strength, and the teaching just flowed."

"There was an interchange of *Shakti,* was there not?" Fitz asked.

"*Shakti*?" I queried. "Could you explain?"

"I think Hina would do a good job of that," Fitz replied,

"Oh my God, why didn't I think of that?" Hina exclaimed. "The teaching on *Shakti* is right at the heart of the Vedanta tradition, and I was introduced to it by Radha Devi when I was in India.

Shakti is the very nature of the Absolute, the pure consciousness. Without *Shakti,* there is no manifestation; nothing happens! Even in manifestation, *Shakti* is never separate from its divine source, just as heat cannot be separated from fire or the rays of sunlight from the sun. *Shakti* is also the mirror or doorway through which one may come to know the divine consciousness. To be clear, *Shakti* also *is* that consciousness.

There is another approach to this, which brings us closer to why we are sitting here discussing this. The divine is *nirakara*, without form, but when taking form, it diversifies into the male and female principles, which are complementary."

Hina continued, but now she was speaking more directly to me.

"I'm certain what is happening, Zac, when we're working spiritually together, is that my presence magnifies your own *Shakti*, your inner power of consciousness. For I am outside you, as Hina your Beloved; but I am also inside you as your inherent power, or *Shakti*."

"You've described it so well as usual, Hina," Fitz commented. "Further to what you've said, *Shakti* has numerous qualities, but the proportion of those qualities will vary from person to person. Let two people sit together engaged in conscious work, then some of those qualities will be magnified, and some qualities may be transferred.

That is how you both benefit if you work together with the right intention. And, of course, another consequence of your special working partnership is that, through a kind of fine energetic osmosis, those you are serving will also benefit and be suitably uplifted.

Zac, no two teachers are alike. I know that through the pure intention of your heart, you will serve The Work in ways that are right and true. The same goes for you, Hina. I am confident that I will be equally happy with whatever you both decide."

The three of us hugged each other before Hina and I left for home. We spoke no further of the matter. I now knew that all of Hina's minor doubts had dissolved, and that our partnership had just evolved to another level.

Chapter 69

The next Saturday, Hina visited her parents on her own. She hoped her fitting for the wedding dress would be the final one, meaning she could return home with it and hide it away until it was needed. Hina returned home, a big smile on her face and a big bag carefully carried to her wardrobe, without me seeing an inch of what was inside.

About my own "outfit" for the wedding, my wardrobe was judged wanting by Hina, and I had to agree with her. I had a couple of suits which I'd hardly worn, and they had something of a dated look about them. A visit to a charity shop with both of those suits looked to be in order.

An aspect of my love for Hina was to take more care about my appearance for the sake of both of us. I could see that this was not an ego-led attitude; looking good was important, not just for a loved one, but also for those around you, who had no choice but to behold what was in front of them!

When it came to clothes, I had to admit that Hina had a good eye for what worked best. The next day, I was happy for her to take me to an established men's clothes shop in the high street. She suggested that for me, a suit should be smart and comfortable, but not conservative, one that would go well with a matching collarless Indian style shirt. We agreed that we should go for natural fibres as far as possible.

We were in and out of the shop within an enjoyable half an hour or so, with Hina treating me to the suit and the shirt. As if that wasn't enough, she also insisted on taking me to lunch afterwards.

On Monday, at the end of the school day, I asked Jason to meet me to discuss our flourishing meditation class. At the previous session, a week ago, a couple of new participants had turned up, and I could tell the size of the class had reached its limit. In addition, Conrad, who had been singing the praises of meditation to other members of his year group, told me that two or three of his "mates" were keen to "give it a go."

It occurred to me that Jason was sufficiently grounded in the practice to help me now. We agreed to create two classes from next term, one for under-15s, which he would lead, and one for over-15s, which I would look after. Jason suggested that Anara might help him with the younger group, and I was more than happy with that, knowing her Sufi background and the wisdom she had access to.

Further down the road, there was the possibility of a class for parents. Conrad's parents had been delighted by the changes in Conrad's attitude to life and had indicated that they would be the first to sign up. Jason and I decided to shelve this development for the time being, get the two classes going next term, and then see about setting up an adult class during the term after that, trusting that the leadership it required would become evident nearer the time.

Once we had finished discussing the future of meditation teaching at the school, Jason brought me up to date with Anahita's situation. She and Zari had now been reunited with Daryush. Jason told me he hadn't realised that, although Daryush had been living in Iran, his Pakistani citizenship had made a big difference. He hadn't arrived in the UK as a refugee fleeing persecution, and therefore going down the asylum route; he was here as a Commonwealth citizen seeking residency. His case was strengthened by the fact that he spoke excellent English, already had family in the UK, and could show that he was a well-qualified professional acupuncturist.

I was delighted, of course, and resolved to visit Anahita, Daryush and Zari at the first opportunity. When I mentioned this to Hina later in the evening, she whooped joyfully and said she'd like to come with me. Because the Philosophy class was held on Wednesdays, we agreed to call on the family the next evening. I rang Anahita to check if it would be convenient for us to visit, and she said she'd look forward to seeing us and being able to introduce us to Daryush.

As Hina and I approached the house, I reminded myself to ring the bell and not use my front-door key. Even though I owned the place, I was turning up as a visitor, and the family who were tenants, although not yet paying any rent, were deserving of their privacy. In my mind, there was a clear etiquette to being a landlord, and although I didn't think there was a guidebook called *The Ethics of Landlordism*, or *Landlordism for Dummies*, I inwardly knew what was respectful and what wasn't.

It was Zari who opened the door and immediately hugged us both. Once we'd settled down with home-made scones and hot drinks of our choice, we enjoyed this opportunity to get to know Daryush. He didn't appear much older than me; he was slimly built, neatly bearded, with a boyish face and shoulder-length dark hair. It was clear how much Zari adored her father, as she sat next to him and held onto his hand.

"It's a miracle," Anahita said at one point. "The three of us together again. We have lots of plans. Being together is first; everything else comes second."

"We're so thankful to you," Daryush said, addressing Hina and me, "for providing this lovely house for us to live in. Now we can move forward as a family, especially when I can start giving acupuncture to clients."

Hina took the words out of my mouth when she responded to Daryush:

"Well, it's possible I can put in a word for you, although I can't guarantee the outcome. I work at a clinic which specialises in natural therapies, and currently we don't have an acupuncturist in practice there. I'll have a word with Elizabeth, the owner; she may be able to offer you an opening."

"Thank you," Daryush replied. "I am well qualified and experienced, but I understand I will need to prove that, and then join a professional body of some sort."

Our conversation turned to other matters, during which our forthcoming wedding featured.

"I've never been to a wedding," Zari announced, apparently all innocence.

"Well, you could come to ours," Hina said, obviously happy to be led by the young lady. "Would you like that?"

"Zari!" her father exclaimed, before his daughter could speak again. "You can't just wriggle your way into getting an invitation like that!"

"It's OK," I said, looking at Hina expectantly, "I'm sure we can find her a role during the ceremony. What do you think?"

"You know what," Hina said, taking command of the situation, "I think I know just the thing. I believe it's a very ancient custom. A young girl leads the bride and groom as they make their way towards the altar, throwing down flower petals as she walks. I think I'd like violet, symbolising majesty and the crown *chakra,* which is the gateway to higher consciousness and wisdom. Please! I'd love Zari to do this for us! Of course," she added, turning to Anahita and Daryush, "you are also invited."

Zari was very excited by the prospect, and her parents were happy too, offering to obtain the flower petals for the occasion.

Chapter 70

It was the final meeting of the year, and Fitz had decided it was time for him to inform everyone about the changes ahead. After an opening period of meditation, he made the announcement in his usual direct manner:

"In the new year, there are going to be some changes. Some of you already know that Jasmine and I will be moving to York in a few months. However, you will all be in very good hands. I've asked Zac to take the lead teaching role from January. You might well be surprised by this, since Zac has only been with us for a few months. But don't be misled by the time frame; depth of spirituality cannot be determined simply by linear measurements.

I saw Zac's potential when I first met him; he only needed the right conditions for his various strengths to be brought to the fore, and, my word, they have been. To use a modern phrase, he's been truly fast-tracked. The proof of the pudding is in the eating, is it not? So, I do not need to say much more. Give him all the respect that you've always given to me and Susan.

Zac will be ably supported by Hina, who will teach beside him in a way that has a precedence in some ancient streams of spiritual philosophy. In addition, there'll also be times when Karolina will take on the same role, as and when Zac calls for her special qualities.

Any questions?"

Gordon stood up to speak.

"Not a question," he said. "I want to thank you from the bottom of my heart for your priceless service and dedication to all of us here. Not just for your teaching, which is such an incredible gift. But, in addition, your kindness, your love, your attention to all the little things that we've needed, that have nurtured our inner growth."

While Gordon was speaking, others began to stand, Hina and I joining them. I even found tears in my eyes as I spoke next, the words tumbling out of me:

"I, too, want to thank you, Fitz. You found me, didn't you? You've been the catalyst for my continuing awakening, and through you, my confidence has grown a hundredfold. And … here I am, standing next to Hina, the love of my life, the one you assigned to be my meditation *guru*. Look what happened after that! You are my friend and mentor forever.

May you and Jasmine thrive in your new home, and in whatever is calling you there …"

A wave of clapping broke out, and as I looked at Fitz, I could see that his expression was also tearful, something I hadn't witnessed before. *He's human, after all, but I knew that!*

If Fitz was intending to give some teaching at this point, the spontaneous outbreak of affection from everyone put paid to that. We began splitting naturally into informal groups so as not to mob Fitz, and he was able to move amongst us easily.

In that way, we all got a chance to share with him individually, sometimes without words, a hug or gentle kiss being enough. As a result, the refreshment break came a little earlier than usual.

When we'd all returned to the main room, Fitz invited us to share a period of meditation before addressing us for the last time as our teacher.

"I do so appreciate the warmth of your friendship and love," he began. "Being your teacher hasn't stopped us all from being close friends. That won't change when I'm up north. And when I get the opportunity, I'll be visiting and sitting with you, drinking in the wisdom of whoever's sitting in this chair – or chairs!

What I'd like to do now is reflect with you on the nature of this group, which is more than a group. The Work we are engaged in has given rise to some developments which are clearly seen and others, no less important, which are unseen.

The School of Philosophy, led by Hina and Elizabeth, is reaching the end of its first term. The feedback from the first crop of students has been very positive, and I believe that many are planning to continue next term. The meditation teaching at Zac's school is creating enough interest to warrant the start of an additional class next month. We also have two study groups, which are well supported. All this we can see for ourselves.

But let us not forget the impact of living consciously in the *marketplace* of life. In this, we all play a part. Within the family life, in the office, the factory, on the buses and trains, in the shops, with your clients, and in all the other ways through which we act and react with the world around us. This is what is meant by 'let your light shine'; it's the light of consciousness which, permeating our active lives, quietly works away as a 'leaven' to raise consciousness generally.

You are sowing seeds, although you may not always see the developing shoots.

As we are approaching the Christmas period, I'd like to end on a seasonal note. Let me share some thoughts with you about the inner meaning of Christmas.

In one of his letters, St. Paul spoke of a mystery that had been kept hidden for ages. That mystery, he claimed, was 'Christ in you, the promise of glory.' In another letter, he described himself as a kind of spiritual midwife, helping to bring forth that divine birth in those who were ready. A birth that would bring them to 'the measure of the fullness of the stature of Christ, which is human perfection.' Is that not the aim of our Work, although, in this instance, borrowing Christian terminology?

That is the essence of Christmas – not a baby in a manger two thousand years ago, nor all the presents under the tree. Christmas is about the birth of Christ in *you*. You are born to be Christ in the world – your birth was the birth of the daughter or the son of God.

Your physical birth means that God is now with us. Once we understand that the Christmas story is about our spiritual birth, that of Christ being born in us, we can also understand that it refers also to *every human being on the earth*.

Christ is everyone. If I was speaking in Thailand, I might say, 'Look within, you are Buddha!' Same reality – only the name is different. It's the substance that matters, irrespective of language, culture, or religion.

Experience the birth of Christ within your heart, perhaps this Christmas, for the very first time.

Experience the sacred nature of every individual human being around you.

May every one of you have a very happy *Christ-in-you-mas.*"

With that final greeting, Fitz stood and quietly left the room.

Chapter 71

Monday, after the school day had finished. It was the last meditation class of the term. I had invited Jason to lead it since he'd be teaching the younger class starting in January. *Why not get him on track straight away?*

Jason had a laid-back, easy-going way with children and was well-liked. I myself enjoyed being his student for this occasion, and I let him know that before we left for home. He brought his storytelling skills into the teaching, and I made a mental note that this was a very natural way of reaching young people. He began the evening session with a story I was familiar with from my small collection of books on Buddhism.

"Let's start with a story," Jason said. "It's one of my favourites from a book on Zen that I have at home. Zen is a particular school of Buddhism that's popular in Japan:

> A young Zen student was walking through a busy marketplace when he overheard part of a conversation between a butcher and one of his customers.
>
> 'I'd like to buy the best piece of meat in your shop,' the customer said.
>
> '*All* the meat in this shop is the best,' insisted the butcher. 'You won't find any meat here that isn't the best.'
>
> As soon as he heard these words, the young man was immediately enlightened."

After a short pause, Jason asked if anyone wanted to comment on this story. Conrad's hand shot up.

"It means that whatever you're doing, you should give it all you've got, one hundred per cent," he said. "If you're doing something really big like running hundreds of superstores, or something really small like, I don't know, say, quickly removing litter from a seat someone's about to sit on, they're equally as important."

"That's a terrific explanation," Jason replied. "And how might that attitude relate to the practice of meditation? Anyone."

Brenda, a sixteen-year-old girl and newcomer to the class, took up the challenge.

"Because meditation helps us become less selfish and helps us to be ready for anything ... before the old 'I can't be bothered' stuff takes over, which makes us not care or give things our proper attention."

"Another great answer," Jason said, beaming. "Well then, let's meditate."

Jason guided us skilfully into meditation, although I thought he overdid the amount of instruction needed. However, I thought back to when I first started to teach meditation, and I could see that I gradually noticed, with experience, that fewer words were needed. I decided to let well be, and let Jason's style of teaching take care of itself.

Two days later, it was the tenth and last session of the School of Philosophy's introductory course. Elizabeth arrived early at Unity House, which allowed Hina and me to discuss with her the situation regarding Daryush's future acupuncture practice.

"First, he'll have to satisfy one of the UK's professional acupuncture bodies," she said. "His qualifications will need to be in line with those accepted in this country. Then he'll probably be asked to take a Point Location exam. If he gets through all that, I'd be happy to meet him.

I usually ask prospective therapists to give me a treatment; it helps me assess their level of competence and how they approach a client. I like therapists working at my clinic to be competent, professional, *and* personable.

By all means, give him my contact details. I'd be delighted to meet him once he's progressed to being accepted as a UK practitioner."

I thanked Elizabeth and said I'd convey all that to Daryush.

The three of us had an early meal together before Hina and Elizabeth went to prepare for the evening's teaching. When Hina returned to join me once the class was finished, she threw her arms around me.

"Guess what, Zac!" she exclaimed, whirling me around.

"Tell me," I gasped, entering into her excitement.

"Every single person on the course enrolled for next term!"

"That's fantastic, Hina! It speaks volumes about the quality of the teaching you and Elizabeth have delivered every week."

"Thank you. Elizabeth and I have decided to complete three terms with this class. Then next year, we may be ready to start a new introductory class. If that happens, Elizabeth will continue with the current group, and I will start up a new introductory course on a different evening. By then, we should be able to draw on two more tutors to assist us, one for each of the courses."

"You can put me on standby, if necessary," I offered.

"You'd be great, Zac. But let's see. You are, first of all, responsible for the Saturday group. There could be one or two of our lovely members ready to step up in the months ahead. You can help me discern who they might be. But terrific to know that Elizabeth and I could call on you if need be."

Now that my school meditation class and Hina's Philosophy class were 'done' for this current term, we had about ten days to sew up any last-minute arrangements for our marriage ceremony. That would be our main focus now.

I still had my school teaching to attend to, the term ending on Thursday, 19th December, two days before our marriage ceremony. Hina decided to take the week beginning Monday, 16th December, as a holiday, which gave her some extra breathing space to carry out any further preparations that might be needed.

Chapter 72

On the Saturday before our big day, Fitz rang and suggested that Hina and I meet him for lunch somewhere. Having no fixed agenda for the day, we readily agreed. We chose *The Urban Lounge*, and said we'd be there at 1.00 pm. Before we left the house, Hina remembered that we'd put aside the wedding rings, which were still in their little presentation boxes. She suggested we give them to Fitz for safekeeping, and he could then hand them to Steph at the appropriate time during the ceremony. I was happy to go along with Hina's suggestion; she put the rings in her handbag before we set off for the restaurant.

Not long after we'd found a table, Fitz arrived to join us. Once greetings were over, Hina asked Fitz if he would look after the rings and produce them during the ceremony when they were required. Fitz said he'd be happy to provide that "small service", and duly pocketed the presentation boxes containing the rings.

"This is a nice surprise," I said. "To what do we owe the honour?"

"Well, one never needs a reason when meeting with friends. For me, it's a joy, so this meal's on me. Nevertheless, there are a few things I want to speak to you both about.

It would please me greatly if you would truly *own* your vocation as teachers supporting inner awakening. I don't mind at all being asked questions about decisions you might be facing. But that's not the point. The point is: I believe you don't *need* to.

Trust your innate authority. I'm speaking to both of you. I hope this dispels any lingering doubt that you might not be up to the job! I can sense the strength, the knowledge, the capacity for empathy, and many other key qualities in both of you. You both possess the natural gifts needed for those whom you will serve. You get the substance of what I'm trying to say, don't you?"

Hina sat quietly, clearly moved by Fitz's generous endorsement of our abilities, so I took it upon myself to respond.

"Fitz, you are the most remarkable man I've ever met. You were born to encourage others and empower them, without being attached to any position you might hold. You transcend any role you are in. I only hope I can embody a fraction of what I see in you."

Hina reached for Fitz's hand before speaking.

"Fitz, I see you in the same light as Zac does. When I am with you, I always feel seen. Your encouragement, ever since I first met you ... it's impossible to express how much it's meant to me, and helped me."

Then turning to me: "But Zac, please don't you be *too* humble. I see in you what Fitz does, so you are outvoted!" The three of us laughed, and now all our hands were joined.

"Let me be open with you," Fitz said gently, speaking specifically to me. "I wouldn't have planned the move to York if I'd been the least bit unsure whether the group would continue to be in good hands. As I said before, Zac, I'm not alone in assessing its well-being with you as the leading teacher."

Fitz then turned towards Hina.

"Hina, over the last few years, I've been aware that you're extremely conversant with the Vedanta teachings. I hope you will continue to draw on that wisdom. Whenever

I've heard you speak from that great treasure house of knowledge, you have been inspiring.

Of course, I know that you will freely draw on any other sources of knowledge that work for you, including your own innate wisdom."

After the meal, Hina and I returned home, speaking very little on the way. What was there to say? Apart from the good meal, we were full up with the simple *joy of being*.

Midway through the next morning, I received a phone call from Steph, and Hina came over to join me. Some arrangements still needed to be finalised. The idea of having the ceremony in the garden had already been dropped. There had been a lot of wet and windy weather recently, and apart from that, it was a cold time of year.

We agreed on a time for her to visit Unity House on Friday so that she could set up the room being used for the ceremony and then take us through a short rehearsal. She also wanted to "leave some stuff" for the day following. She'd already spoken to Fitz, and he had agreed to join us then. We mentioned the inclusion of Zari with her petal throwing, and Steph said that was very welcome; it fitted neatly into what she had already organised.

"There's something else, though," she said. "What word would you prefer me to use when the divine reality is mentioned, especially during the various blessings – God, Beloved, Lord, Father, or some other name? It's all the same to me ..."

"Eternal One," Hina said suddenly, interrupting Steph's flow.

"Settled," I added, knowing full well that we had to use a name, but no name alone could ever describe what is ineffable.

"Great, see you on Friday," Steph said, before ending her call.

"Sorry, Zac. I know, I didn't consult you," Hina said, pulling me close. "The phrase, 'Eternal One', just came from nowhere, and I said it before I knew what I was doing!"

"Hey. It's perfect," I reassured her. "You acted spontaneously, and remember – we are also one. You were speaking for me, darling. And after all, the divine *is* eternal. And is also, the One – all that is!"

"Yes. In Vedanta, it's common to say, '*Brahman* is One without a second'. Zac, you're so understanding – I think I could marry you!"

Chapter 73

Along came the last week of the Autumn term. There seemed to be no end of things needing our attention. Apart from the working days, there were many phone calls and arrangements to be made for our special ceremony. I was reminded of Conrad's wise words at the last meditation class: *Whether you're doing something really big, or something really small ... they're equally important.* Thank you, Conrad.

We settled on which bedrooms to make available for my parents and for Mahendra and Fiona. We had not paid much attention to the rooms we weren't using since our move; now it became necessary to make them presentable for our guests. There were phone calls, such as the one with Jason and Anara, who would be our witnesses at the registry office; a visit to Zari, who wanted to show us the petals Anahita had managed to obtain, together with the small basket which would contain them. And many other matters, which included a private call between Hina and her mum. *What were they secretly hatching up?*

On Thursday, Mahendra and Fiona arrived while I was still at the school, but Hina was at the house to welcome them. They planned on staying till after Christmas. I arrived later that afternoon to meet them for the first time. Mahendra was the perfect representative of "tall, dark and handsome"; Fiona was very pretty, very fair, with natural blonde hair reaching her shoulders.

Just as we were settling down to share our news, my parents turned up, cheerful though somewhat weary due to their lengthy journey from Dorset. Dad looked a lot better than when I'd last seen him, and it was good to see him enter without any walking aid, and only a slightly discernible limp; only noticeable because I knew about his accident. After I'd taken charge of their luggage and shown them to the room that would be theirs for the next few days, they spent a while getting refreshed before rejoining the rest of us.

Whilst taking part in the now augmented conversation, I was aware of also inwardly sitting back and enjoying the experience of our two families beginning to draw closer. They will be even closer, I thought, when Hina's parents turn up on Saturday.

Then it was the day before the day. Hina and I arose early. There were preparations to be made, and we wanted to be ready. The caterers we'd hired would be in to stock up the fridge and cupboards, as well as bringing crates of drink, and extra cutlery and crockery. By now, Hina had revealed to me part of her discussion with her mother: her parents had offered to meet the cost of the post-ceremony buffet, and insisted on the invoice being forwarded to them.

On the dot of 10.00 am, Steph and Fitz arrived to organise the main room before inviting us in for a rehearsal. Steph came in wheeling a large suitcase behind her, which I suspected had items needed for the ceremony. Fitz carried in a Sony hi-fi music system and told us that Steph had put him in charge of the music that would begin and end the service. Hina and I were told to stay away until called, but Mahendra and Fiona were keen on helping them, and Steph was fine with that. Steph asked for a list of guests to help her arrange the right number of chairs; any spare chairs were to be placed out of sight somewhere else!

While Steph and her helpers were busy in the main room, I opened the door to a delivery man, who handed over a heavy box I had to sign for. Hina and I opened it in the kitchen and discovered the collection of books that dad had promised. We only allowed ourselves to take out one book each for a quick inspection. Mine was *The Invisible Man* by H. G. Wells. Hina's was *Tales of Mystery and Imagination* by Edgar Allan Poe. They were beautifully produced, with gilt edging. We put the books back into the box and decided to leave going through wedding presents until Sunday.

Eventually, Hina and I were invited into the main room. The chairs had been carefully arranged into two horseshoe shapes, one row behind the other, and not the theatre style I was expecting. There was a space going through the two rows so that Hina and I would be able to process in at the start of the ceremony and leave the same way at the end.

Facing the two rows were three chairs. The central chair was for Steph to sit on when other contributions to the ceremony were being made. The two chairs to the right shared the same purpose for us. To the left was a table covered with a purple and golden cloth. On it were various artifacts representing different religious and spiritual traditions, and a large central squat candle resting on a shiny silver tray.

On each of the chairs was a folded *Order of Service*. Steph explained that it did not contain everything since her address and our vows would be "off the cuff!" Steph said she would arrive at least an hour before the ceremony to ensure everything needed was in place. She wanted to speak with all the contributors. Because of the limited space, she would ask that each reader, "or chanter" in Mahendra's case, stand by their chair when making their offering. She also wanted to check in with Zari, who was not here for the rehearsal.

The rehearsal took up very little time, but Steph was extremely thorough, making clear when we were to sit or stand, and where, and how we should face each other when making our vows. She also emphasised that, despite how it was generally described, she was not marrying us. *We were marrying each other*; she was the facilitator, simply holding the ceremony together. And unlike in some conventional weddings, when Hina and I have been proclaimed "husband and wife", she would not be saying to me, "You may now kiss the bride!" Whether we kissed or not was purely a matter for us.

Before Steph left with Fitz, the two of them joined us, together with our guests, for a well-deserved midday snack.

Once we had cleared up in the kitchen, mum wanted a "peek" at the room where the ceremony was to be held. She liked what she saw and was pleased that she and dad had been allocated seats at the front near Hina's parents. But after surveying the entire setup, she looked slightly puzzled.

"Something is missing," she said. "There's no Gift Table!"

With the number of guests we were expecting, and the room already beautifully arranged, with very little space to spare, I didn't want to disturb Steph's carefully organised room plan.

After a short discussion, we agreed to place a table to the right of the entrance to the room, which we covered with a suitable tablecloth. Mum suggested we put the box of classic books on it so that when guests arrived, it would be obvious where to put their wedding presents and cards.

When Mahendra saw the table, he immediately said he'd create a "Cards and Gifts" sign for it, waiving away his usual professional fees! Fiona went off to collect the present they'd brought down from Edinburgh. Their gift turned out to be a colourful Moorcroft vase which depicted a bow and a quiver of arrows. The gift box displayed the title, *Cupid's Arrow*.

Our evening was spent getting to know each other. The conversation was light-hearted throughout and included amusing anecdotes based on our varied experiences. Dad asked Mahendra how he and Fiona had met.

"We met at university in Edinburgh," he replied. "Fiona was a fellow student, and from day one I wanted to get to know her; she was – *is* – lovely in so many ways. Being uncertain how to approach her, I mentioned this to a friend, who said bluntly, 'Just get on with it, mate; then you won't be plagued by *what-ifs* if someone beats you to it.'

Having been so strongly encouraged, I caught up with her the following day as she was leaving the college building. I asked her whether she was doing anything that evening. She said she'd be out at the cinema with her mum. OK, I thought – better try again. I asked her, 'What about tomorrow?' She said she had an evening class in dressmaking.

Steeling myself, thinking *now or never*, I tried one more time. 'What about the day after that?'"

Fiona then chipped in: "And I said to Mahendra, 'You're going to take me out somewhere nice on a date!' Then, when I got home, I said to mum, 'Let's go and see a film tonight.' I insisted, and we did; I wanted what I'd said to my future boyfriend to be truthful!"

"How lovely," my dad said.

"OK. What about you, then?" Mahendra asked, addressing my dad in an attempt to turn the tables.

"We met at a local youth club and became friends," he replied. *Short and sweet.*

"Then we became *more* than friends," mum added.

"And then we became *more* than more than friends," dad proclaimed with a mischievous grin.

"We get the gist, dad," I said before this could go any further.

Not to be left out, Fiona asked Hina how she had met me.

Hina wasted no time in talking about my first visit to her group; how she was asked to mentor me, especially in meditation; how we'd gone to the park; and how I'd overcome a couple of bullies, before seeing her home.

"Wow," Mahendra exclaimed. "An English *kshatriya*. I knew they existed!"

From how we'd met, the sharing went on to other disclosures about each of us, until my practical mum pointed out that an early start was needed the next day. Hina and I needed no further encouragement and led the way in retiring for the night.

Chapter 74

A good night's sleep appeared to have been had by all, and as a result, we all managed to arrive together for breakfast. Not long after that, Jason and Anara stopped by to collect Hina and me for the registry office service. They were our "minimum witnesses". With no religious or spiritual content being allowed, we preferred this event to be low-key, considering the afternoon ceremony to be the true declaration of our union – body, soul, and spirit. We went out to Jason's car dressed casually, saving our wedding attire to be donned later, shortly before the afternoon ceremony.

The service took less than 15 minutes, during which I took Hina "to be my wedded wife", and she took me "to be her wedded husband." Once all was complete, we signed the register, followed by our witnesses. Hina then took charge of our copy of the marriage certificate, which she placed in her bag.

We arrived back at Unity House to find Hina's parents present. We welcomed them with hugs and kisses. Knowing what was happening shortly, neither Hina nor I were hungry, but Mahendra and Fiona insisted we should have something, and they rustled up some soup and crusty rolls for us.

Soon, the rest of our guests started to arrive. They included all the members of the group, Steph, Anahita, Daryush, and an excited Zari. Jason and Anara were already present. Steph suggested that we go and get changed for the ceremony, and she would send someone to get us about 10 minutes before the ceremony was due to start. Meanwhile, she would make any final preparations or adjustments, which would include giving some simple instructions to Zari.

For this special occasion, Hina and I had agreed to change into our wedding outfits in different rooms. Therefore, when we met on the landing before being called downstairs, I was seeing Hina in her new dress for the first time. Her mother had done her proud. Hina looked stunning in a beautiful light green dress, representing the heart chakra, she told me later. It was a mixture of Western and Asian styles, full-length with short sleeves. The bodice and sleeves were embellished with small beads and gems in an attractive pattern.

Fiona was sent to collect us, and when we came near the door to the main room, we found Anahita waiting with Zari, complete with the basket of petals, looking lovely in her violet dress. Anahita then left her daughter with us and went in to sit with her husband. Zari told us that the "nice lady" had shown her where she was to walk, and what to do when her "special role" was over. We told her she would be brilliant.

Zari had been told that as soon as she heard the Indian music begin, she was to start leading us towards Steph, walking as slowly as she could. Hina and I shared a short, sweet kiss, and then, just as we began to hold hands, the music started, and Zari led the way into the room, immediately throwing down the petals as she went.

Chapter 75

Later that day, I discovered that my brother-in-law had taken the initiative and recorded the ceremony on his mobile phone. I asked him to make a copy of it for me, and he happily obliged. I'd already asked Steph if she wouldn't mind emailing me a copy of the script she'd used, and she wasted no time letting me have her "schema" that same evening.

What follows is Steph's "schema" interposed by my notes, written later in italics, to complete what Steph had deliberately left blank, since the vows could not be written down beforehand! Mahendra's recording was a great help.

The full marriage ceremony, together with my notes, now looked like this:

MARRIAGE CEREMONY
HINA JAISWAL and ZAC MARSHAL

Saturday 21st December 2024
2.00 pm, Unity House

Celebrant: Rev. Stephanie Bamford

Entrance:

Zac and Hina enter to classical Indian music. They are led in by Zari, a young girl throwing violet flower petals before them as they move forward to stand before the celebrant. Zac and Hina are invited to sit, and Zari goes to join her parents.

NOTE: Zari looked very pretty in her dress, which matched the colour of the petals she was distributing. I have the distinct feeling that she and her parents were now part of our extended family.

Opening words – Elizabeth West

From every human being there rises a light that reaches straight to heaven. And when two souls are destined to find one another, their two streams of light flow together and a single brighter light goes forth from their united being.
(Baal Shem Tov, 18th century Jewish mystic)

The Celebrant:

We are gathered here, held in Divine Presence, to unite Zac and Hina in marriage, and to share in their joy. This celebration is an outward sign of their inward union of mind, heart and spirit; it is a celebration of two souls already attuned to each other.
When such a true bond exists between a man and a woman, it is only natural that an outer acknowledgement be made; so here we are!
Therefore, on this day, we pray with them that, being always open to divine guidance, they may fulfil the purpose which brought them together.
Zac and Hina, we are here to support your commitment to love, understanding, and inner transformation, which reaches out and touches everyone around you. Our lives are changed as we share a part of your love.

Like a stone dropped in a still pond, the ripples of the love from this celebration extend out and change the world we live in.

Reading – Rebecca Marshal, mother of Zac:

Marriage is not a promise to be together through all eternity, for no one can promise that. It is a promise to be present *now*. It is a vow that must be renewed in each moment if it is to have meaning.
In truth, you can be married in one moment and not in the next. Marriage is a process, a journey of becoming fully present to yourself and your partner. (Paul Ferrini, *Reflections on the Christ Mind*)

The Address Given by The Celebrant

NOTE: *Rev. Stephanie Bamford spoke about the spiritual purpose of marriage as a pathway to enlightenment in itself. Her words were spoken from the heart without notes. Spontaneous clapping erupted once she had finished. Not in the script, she confided with me later!*

The Vows

NOTE: *The vows were made spontaneously and are transcribed here based on Mahendra's recording.*

The Celebrant:

Zac and Hina, please stand, face each other, and join hands.

Zac, as you take Hina to be your wife, let your heart freely speak to her whilst in the presence of your family and friends.

Zac: *Hina, you must be an angel.*
Your presence lifts my spirit.
Your beauty and wisdom have enriched my life.
I promise to keep myself open to you.
I will love and cherish you
Whatever our circumstances,
Through all the highs and lows,
That we might share.
All that I am, and all that I have,
I give to you, now and always.

The Celebrant:

Hina, as you take Zac to be your husband, let your heart freely speak to him whilst in the presence of your family and friends.

Hina: *Zac, you are my best friend and my one true love.*
I love the way you love and care for me.
I love the way you trust and believe in me.
When I am with you, I can be who I am, and I cannot imagine my life without you.
You make me smile, and you are always interested in what I have to say and do.
Today, I want to promise in front of my family and friends, to love, honour, and respect you always, and always.

Blessing of the Rings

The Celebrant receives the rings from Fitz and allows time for Zac and Hina to help each other slip them onto their ring fingers. They hold out their left hands to receive the blessing of the rings.

The Celebrant:

Eternal One,
we call upon your blessing; may these rings be a symbol of unending love and truthfulness, a reminder of the vows made this day and your undivided presence in our hearts. Amen.

Reading – Fitz Temple

A wife loves her husband not for his own sake, dear one, but because the Divine Beloved lives in him.
A husband loves his wife not for her own sake, dear one, but because the Divine Beloved lives in her …
As long as there is the sense of separateness, one sees another as separate from oneself …
But when the Divine Beloved is realised as the indivisible unity of life, who can be seen by whom?
(Upanishads)

NOTE: *I must check out the exact source of this beautiful passage.*

Blessing of the Couple

The Celebrant:

Eternal One, whose sacred Life
dwells in the heart of all beings,
bless, preserve, and keep you,
and adorn you with grace,
that in body and soul you may be
channels of peace and light,
and living together in truth and love,
may enjoy the blessings of eternal life.
Amen

Proclamation

The Celebrant:

In the presence of the Eternal One, Zac and Hina have expressed their love and commitment to each other. They have declared their marriage by the vows spoken to each other, magnified further by the exchange of rings.
I therefore proclaim that they are husband and wife.

NOTE: *Hina and I shared a loving kiss; no prompting required!*

Chant: Gayatri Mantra – Mahendra Jaiswal, brother of Hina

NOTE: *Fiona stood with Mahendra while he chanted, and then read out a short translation of the mantra:*

May we all attain to that adorable splendour
of the divine reality, Savitri.
May she enlighten our hearts
and direct our intelligence.

The General Blessing

Celebrant:

Go in peace and love.
Let your light shine for all to see.
Serve one another with joy.
And may all the blessings of Eternity
be with you, and sustain you.
May all that is noble and true in the universe
inspire your lives.
May peace find its place in the heart
of every sentient being. Amen.

Zac and Hina bring the ceremony to a close with words of blessing for everyone present:

NOTE: *Hina and I had prepared this final blessing together prior to the ceremony, and read from the text which Steph had just passed to us. It was partly inspired by the words of a Buddhist prayer mantra.*

Hina: *May the blessings and the joy of this occasion*
Enrich us all inwardly and outwardly;
Zac: *May all beings be free from suffering;*
Hina: *May all beings be healed;*
Zac: *May all beings know their wholeness;*
Hina: *May all beings be happy and at peace.*

Both: *OM. Shantih, Shantih, Shantih.*

Exit:

Zac and Hina, now husband and wife, leave the main room to music from Mozart's *Clarinet Quintet*.

Chapter 76

Once we'd left the main room, our family and friends soon followed. But I determinedly held Hina in a long embrace before engaging with anyone else. Hugs and kisses abounded before Hina and I made a beeline for Steph.

"Thank you, Steph," I said, after I'd embraced her wholeheartedly, "that was such a lovely ceremony; wow, we're very grateful."

"Don't you forget," she replied, "we created it together, with such great contributions from your friends and family."

Hina joined in: "You deserve all the praise you get, from us and everyone else. Now you can come and help us eat the ton of food we've got next door."

Three caterers were serving drinks, both hot and cold; otherwise, it was "take a plate and help yourself" from the array of food that seemed to fill every available surface. The atmosphere was delightfully convivial, with conversations spilling out into different parts of the house. I noticed Daryush deep in conversation with Elizabeth, no doubt discussing his potential practice at her clinic, while Anahita and Zari had settled in a corner with Jason and Anara. Our two sets of parents seemed to be enjoying a joke.

Hina and I separated for a while so that we could speak with as many different people as possible. After about 20 minutes, there was some gentle tapping of a spoon on glass, which eventually succeeded in eliciting the required silence. It was Hina's dad, standing beside his wife, with my parents close by.

"Forgive me for claiming your attention this way," he said. "I just want to thank you all for coming and making this such a special gathering. Occasions like this don't happen without a lot of hard work going into them. I'm pretty sure that Hina and Zac will endorse what I want to express right now.

Firstly, a big thank you to our lovely celebrant, the Reverend Stephanie, who gave us the most fantastic wedding service I've ever attended!" Cheers and clapping.

"To our brilliant caterers, what a spread! And you can't put a price on service given so graciously." Cheers and clapping.

"Not forgetting Zari, flower girl supreme, who led in Hina and Zac so beautifully!" Cheers and clapping, and Zari blushing.

"And speaking as a father: I've never seen my daughter look so happy – thank you, Zac; that your *karmic* adventure led you to Hina, and that our two families have become one!"

Hina immediately made her way over to her parents.

"And I want to thank whatever *karmic* credit balance got me such amazing parents. You've always supported me, even when you weren't sure I was making the right choices. You've been my first teachers – deeply spiritual, guiding, but never forcing; strong in your convictions, but never dogmatic. You were always there for me, protective, but without taking away my freedom. Thank you, thank you both."

By the time Hina had finished speaking, I had returned to her side.

"The gods have blessed me too," I began, not knowing where I was going with this. "My dad is seriously easy-going, and my dear mum unstoppable! Apart from that, I've benefited from their unconditional love. Who knows?

Maybe some of their characteristics have rubbed off on me. I hope so. Enough from me, though. Only to admit that" – putting my arms around Hina – "I'm the happiest of men ..."

I quickly added: "Does anyone else want to share something?"

"Yes, I would like to." It was Steph. "Firstly, thank you for the appreciation you awarded me earlier. But this was the easiest marriage ceremony I've ever done. Two mature adults. Their love so strong and assured, they didn't need coaching for their vows. They spoke their love to each other in the sacred now. They also created their own blessing to offer you, by way of closing the ceremony. Hina and Zac, you are the ones I want to thank for letting me in on this."

This was followed by more gentle cheers and clapping, but as no one else volunteered to speak, there was a gradual return to food, drink and conversation. At some point, Hina and I glanced at the Gift Table, now piled high with wrapped presents and cards, some larger items placed on the floor nearby. But we knew that this was not the time to investigate further. We wanted to give our all to our lovely guests while we had the opportunity.

After about an hour, the first of our guests started to leave. By the early evening, only Hina and I, our parents, and Mahendra and Fiona were left. Before they departed, Fitz and Jasmine invited Hina and me over to see the new year in with them.

Once the caterers had cleared up the buffet, collected all the crockery and other items they'd brought with them, and left taking our hearty thanks with them, we were left with a profound sense of peace, in which I realised that Hina and I possessed friendships which were not at all superficial; in fact, the opposite: they were deep and generous.

Our parents took the opportunity to go out for a short walk together before Raj and Sushma took their leave. They insisted that we visit them again early in the new year. My parents retired for the night not long afterwards. There was no need for an evening meal; we'd all eaten enough for several meals!

It created an opportunity for Hina and me to spend some time alone with Mahendra and Fiona for the first time. We found that we had a lot in common. Their love for each other, like ours, included a love of the spiritual life, although they were more engaged with its Buddhist expression. After a while, we decided to share a short meditation before calling it quits for the day.

We opted for a practice called *tratak*, meaning "steady gazing", suggested and guided by Fiona, which began with giving attention for about a minute to a candle flame, before closing our eyes and focusing on the afterimage. If the afterimage faded, we were to keep our attention at the point where the image disappeared. We were to be unconcerned whether the image changed shape or colour. We were simply to keep to the "steady gazing."

I found the practice very restful and refreshing. Mahendra said afterwards that the practice helped to cleanse the *ajna chakra*, the subtle centre located between and behind the eyes.

Chapter 77

In the days that followed, we spent many quality hours with my parents, Mahendra and Fiona. Every day felt so much like a new birth that we barely noticed the passing of Christmas Day. My parents finally departed on the day after Boxing Day; Mahendra and Fiona stayed for one further day.

Hina and I only went through our wedding gifts when we were on our own. We found it to be an interesting experience. Two gifts had been left anonymously: an anthology of mystical poetry and an original framed painting of a female Indian *guru* surrounded by her disciples. Hina said it reminded her of her time in India with Radha Devi.

There was a generous voucher for the John Lewis Department Store. Hina told me that it was from her parents. The second part of her quiet conversation with her mother related to this. Sushma wanted to know which store contained the items we were most likely to need for our home so that we could get what we needed, "avoiding the danger," we were told later, of being "lumbered with something not to our taste."

There was not a single present that didn't seem relevant to the life that Hina and I were sharing. There were quality spiritual books, a beautifully coloured table lamp, crockery and cutlery sets, a statue of St. Francis with a bird in one hand and another on his shoulder, and much more.

We agreed to send out thank-you cards in the early part of the new year.

On the last day of the year, we visited Fitz's house, as invited. Jasmine was also there, as well as Elizabeth, Daniel, Tamara and David. We sat and enjoyed drinks and nibbles together, but rather than engage in small talk, we chose to share our love of poetry. Fitz had left out a good supply of his favourite books, and we took turns choosing something to read. Rumi, Blake, Tagore, Traherne, and Hafiz. They all got a look in.

I went for a collection of Wordsworth's poetry, remembering how I'd briefly referred to *Intimations of Immortality* during that first meeting with Fitz in the café. I found the poem in question and read the part which included the reference to the soul coming from afar, "trailing clouds of glory ... from God, who is our home." I stopped at that point, and Fitz then made an interesting comment on Wordsworth's verse:

"We all signed up for this divine adventure before we entered our mother's womb."

There was a hush before Daniel asked Fitz to repeat that statement; he also asked if we could all have a few moments to reflect on it quietly together. Fitz readily repeated his statement, following which there was a good period of silence.

David said quietly: "Maybe that's what some people mean when they say that we *choose our parents*."

"Indeed," Fitz agreed, "We are energetically drawn to the vibrations best suited for our continuing journey towards wholeness. It's therefore important to make the best use of the opportunity that comes with a human birth. We are therefore masters of our own destiny. And that is the power of destiny, enabling us to realise our full potential.

This happens over lifetimes. *Karma* is our reaping of what we've sown across lifetimes, as well as within one particular embodiment. It is a law which is full of grace, because whatever we are reaping also contains the seeds for our liberation."

"So, whatever you are facing in this moment," Jasmine added, "meet it fully, with all your intelligence and love."

"Let's take that into the new year," Hina suggested. "All our love, intelligence, goodness, and strength … in fact, all that we are."

That seemed a good note on which to end the evening.

Hina's working life recommenced on the first Thursday of January, and the spring term for my school took off on the Monday following. Before my return to school duties, however, there was the simple matter of leading the group on the first Saturday of 2025.

Chapter 78

I entered the meeting room with Hina, and we took our seats at the front, side by side, facing everyone. Looking around, I saw all my beloved friends, each one a teacher in their own right, whether by word or deed.

I remembered Susan's statement that the teacher reflects back to the student the knowledge that is already within them; it is there, merely dormant, waiting to be brought out of cold storage!

My students, this day and any day, were also *my* teachers. Therefore, I resolved to be in tune with them right now, in this sacred present, knowing that whatever teaching chose to be delivered would assuredly be perfect for the situation, meeting the needs of everyone present.

After making individual eye contact with each one in turn, I began the afternoon's teaching.